When Love Comes Around

Acclaim for Radclyffe's Fiction

Finders Keepers "is a delightful slow-burn, enemies-to-lovers romance…It also has puppies—six adorable, bright eyed, floppy eared, soft and cuddly puppies. I admit it. I'm an absolute sucker for sweet, furry baby animals. Add them to a romantic couple in a story, and I'm hooked."—*Rainbow Reflections*

Only This Summer "is an absolute must-read for anyone who enjoys a well-written lesbian romance novel…A law enforcement officer with a penchant for trouble meets a doctor who is desperate to get away and find some modicum of peace…What I've found is typical in Radclyffe's storytelling is the depth and complexity of the characters. They are richly drawn and fully realized, making it easy to invest in their journeys and root for their happy endings." —*station12reads*

"Radclyffe writes fantastic books. They are easy to read, well-paced, with relatable and realistic characters. I find [the ***PMC Hospital Romance***] series particularly fun to read because Radclyffe was a practicing surgeon before turning full time to writing, so the medical storyline reads so well. Her stories tend to be a slow burn with lots of flirting and tension building and a spicy, well-written, realistic payoff at the end…I really enjoyed that the 'rivalry' [in ***Perfect Rivalry***] was more of an ambitious respect for another—so, not enemies to lovers but more cranky to inseparable."—*rubiareads*

"After seven books [in the ***Rivers Community Romance*** series] about the lives and loves in this small town, I do admit that I am starting to wonder if there may be some pheromone that lures unsuspecting, brilliant, handsome/gorgeous, brooding/plucky lesbians into town where they get sucked into the Rivers hospital community…All that [in ***Pathway to Love***] with smoldering chemistry between the mains as well as lots of action in the ER/OR and the bedroom. But, hey… these are Radclyffe novels. And I get sucked into each and every one of them."—*MEC for TBR Reviews*

"Medical drama, gossipy lesbian romance, and angsty backstory all get equal time in [***Unrivaled***], Radclyffe's fifth PMC Hospital Romance…[F]ans of small community dynamics and workplace romance without ethical complications will find this hits the spot." —*Publishers Weekly*

Praise for Ronica Black

Hearts Aflame

"Sleek storytelling and terrific characters are the backbone of Ronica Black's third and best novel, *Hearts Aflame*. Prepare to hop on for an emotional ride with this thrilling story of love in the outback…Along with the romance of Krista and Rae, the secondary storylines such as Krista's fear of horses and an uncle suffering from Alzheimer's are told with depth and warmth. Black also draws in the reader by utilizing the weather as a metaphor for the sexual and emotional tension in all the storylines. Wonderful storytelling and rich characterization make this a high recommendation."—*Lambda Literary Review*

Lambda Literary Award Finalist *Wild Abandon*

"Black is a master at teasing the reader with her use of domination and desire. Black's first novel, *In Too Deep*, was a finalist for a 2005 Lammy…With *Wild Abandon*, the author continues her winning ways, writing like a seasoned pro. This is one romance I will not soon forget."—*Books to Watch Out For*

"This sequel to Ronica Black's debut novel, *In Too Deep*, is an electrifying thriller. The author's development as a fine storyteller shines with this tightly written story…[The mystery] keeps the story charged—never unraveling or leading us to a predictable conclusion. More than once I gasped in surprise at the dark and twisted paths this book took."—*Curve*

Lambda Literary Award Finalist *In Too Deep*

"Ronica Black's debut novel *In Too Deep* has everything from nonstop action and intriguing well developed characters to steamy erotic love scenes. From the opening scenes where Black plunges the reader headfirst into the story to the explosive unexpected ending, *In Too Deep* has what it takes to rise to the top. Black has a winner with *In Too Deep*, one that will keep the reader turning the pages until the very last one."—*Independent Gay Writer*

By Radclyffe

Innocent Hearts

Promising Hearts

Love's Melody Lost

Love's Tender Warriors

Tomorrow's Promise

Love's Masquerade

shadowland

Turn Back Time

When Dreams Tremble

The Lonely Hearts Club

Secrets in the Stone

Desire by Starlight

Homestead

The Color of Love

Secret Hearts

Only This Summer

Fire in the Sky

Wild Fire

First Responders Novels

The Honor Series

The Justice Series

Midnight Hunters (writing as L.L. Raand)

PMC Hospitals Romances

Provincetown Tales

Rivers Community Romances

By Ronica Black

In Too Deep

Deeper

Wild Abandon

Hearts Aflame

Flesh and Bone

The Seeker

Chasing Love

Conquest

Wholehearted

The Midnight Room

Snow Angel

The Practitioner

Freedom to Love

Under Her Wing

Private Passion

Dark Euphoria

The Last Seduction

Olivia's Awakening

A Love That Leads to Home

Passion's Sweet Surrender

A Turn of Fate

Watching Over Her

The Business of Pleasure

Something to Talk About

Decadence
"Passionate Pursuance"

The Murders
at Sugar Mill Farm

The Curse
(writing as Alexandra Riley)

The Breakdown

Stranded

Behold My Heart

The Fame Game

Visit us at www.boldstrokesbooks.com

When Love Comes Around

by

RADCLYfFE AND
RONICA BLACK

2025

WHEN LOVE COMES AROUND

© 2025 By Radclyffe and Ronica Black. All Rights Reserved.

ISBN 13: 978-1-63679-930-8

This Trade Paperback Original Is Published By
Bold Strokes Books, Inc.
P.O. Box 249
Valley Falls, NY 12185

First Edition: October 2025

THIS IS A WORK OF FICTION. NAMES, CHARACTERS, PLACES, AND INCIDENTS ARE THE PRODUCT OF THE AUTHOR'S IMAGINATION OR ARE USED FICTITIOUSLY. ANY RESEMBLANCE TO ACTUAL PERSONS, LIVING OR DEAD, BUSINESS ESTABLISHMENTS, EVENTS, OR LOCALES IS ENTIRELY COINCIDENTAL.

THIS BOOK, OR PARTS THEREOF, MAY NOT BE REPRODUCED IN ANY FORM WITHOUT PERMISSION.

Credits
Editor: Stacia Seaman
Production Design: Stacia Seaman
Cover Design by Inkspiral Design

Acknowledgments

With thanks to Ronica Black for the excellent collaboration; to Stacia Seaman, for insightful comments and astute edits; and to Sandy Lowe for brainstorming and a legion of other reasons.

—Radclyffe

My deepest gratitude to Radclyffe for asking me to join her on this co-writing venture. It was such a privilege and so much fun. I couldn't ask for a better publisher or a finer mentor.

I'd also like to thank my dear friends and family for their unwavering support of my writing. You all mean the world to me, and I love you!

And to the readers…thank you…your continued support keeps me writing.

—Ronica Black

Dedication

To Lee, for eternal patience (I can hear you laughing)
—Radclyffe

PROLOGUE

December

Maya Sanchez hesitated just inside the double doors of the middle school auditorium, wiping wet snow from the toes of her flats. The blast of heat hit her first, then the faint smell of cookies left over from the fifth-grade bake sale that still hung in the air like a hug that hadn't let go. Parents and kids streamed past her toward the ticket table at the far end of the foyer. The air of rushed expectation was contagious, and Maya glanced at her watch, worried she was running late.

Shit.

She didn't have much time. Digging blindly in her shoulder bag for her ticket, she edged her way through the mass of people. Fortunately, the line moved quickly, and a minute later she made it to the front, still riffling through her bag, hoping to find the rectangular bit of paper by feel.

"Sorry," she muttered to the smiling blond teen wearing a plain gray T-shirt that simply said *overstimulated.*

She could relate. At some point while getting Emmie dressed for preschool that morning, reminding Dantas of the show time, and trying to eat a piece of toast in between blessed gulps of coffee, she'd put both her ticket and Dantas's in their respective bags. She'd learned that if she didn't, one of them would forget. Keeping the household organized had somehow become her job, not that she minded. Taking care of her family wasn't work.

"I know I've got it here somewhere."

"You can buy one if you need to," the teen said helpfully. "They're only seven dollars. And all proceeds go to the dance club."

The girl smiled as if having to purchase another ticket was the honorable and maybe even the preferred thing to do.

"Just one sec…I put it in here this morning." Maya ignored the slight bump on the shoulder as a burly guy reached around her to drop his ticket on the table. She shoved aside first her wallet and cell phone, then a sizable plastic container of wintergreen gum.

"Aha!" She plucked the bent ticket out and handed it to the volunteer, who once again smiled, though this time with a hint of disappointment.

"Enjoy the show," the girl said. "And happy holidays."

"You too," Maya said and rushed into the gym.

Seats were filling fast.

Maya threaded her way around clumps of milling parents eager to see their little ones dance to a selection of holiday hits and grabbed a chair near the front of the stage. Probably more anxious than Emmie, Maya set her purse in the next seat to save it for Dantas, who should arrive any minute. But it was hard telling with Dantas. She worked crazy shifts in the local ER and often stayed beyond her assigned hours tending to patients in need. Tonight, however, she had planned to leave right at six so she could make the recital starting at seven.

Ten to seven. Maya scanned the few remaining people who hadn't found seats, hoping to see Dantas scrambling her way down the aisle with her beautiful face tinged pink from the cold. Squelching the surge of disappointment, she focused on the little ones in tutus or velvet pants with glitter-sprinkled vests and ruffled white shirts who hopped up and down at the edge of the stage.

She couldn't find Emmie in the swirls of ruffles and color. Her heart swelled, imagining Emmie bouncing next to her friends, excited to go onstage. She *wished* that was the way it was going for her but suspected Emmie's feelings were probably far different. Emmie loved to dance, but she was shy about performing. At almost four, that was understandable.

Maya relaxed, knowing Emmie's teacher would give her extra encouragement if she needed it. Mrs. Robbie had even brought the little ones to practice in the empty gym a few days earlier so they'd be used to the much bigger space than their small preschool.

And if Emmie fled the stage like she'd done once before, who cared? She had plenty of time to gain confidence. After all, *she* wasn't all that big on interacting with strangers. Maya smiled to herself. Dantas, who loved interacting with dozens of people all day long in the ER, called her a hopeless homebody. With love in her voice, of course. And Maya always reminded her that parenting was a real job, too. Which generally earned her a kiss. Or more.

Speaking of…where the heck was Emmie's other parent? The lights dimmed to signal showtime was nearing. Maya checked her watch again. Nearly seven. Where was Dantas?

She pulled out her phone and checked the screen for messages. None. She dialed Dantas, pressing the phone to her ear to muffle the sound.

It rang and rang. Then went to voicemail.

"Damn it," she whispered. "Where are you?"

She checked the entrance to the gym once more, envious as the last of the parents filed in. They'd made it in time and could settle in and enjoy the show. Dantas was going to be late and would have to sneak in in the dark. She'd give Maya a cold kiss on the cheek and ask what all she'd missed. Maya would help her shake out of her coat, and they'd sit and look on, anxiously awaiting Emmie's performance. *If* Dantas hadn't already missed it.

The lights dimmed, and the gym fell silent. The music came up, and a dozen children in bright costumes tiptoed out onstage. Emmie wasn't in this group, but she'd be out soon for her short role. Maya's heart raced. Would Emmie come out? Would she be okay or would she panic and run for stage right, never to come out to dance again?

Maya needed Dantas next to her to cling to when Emmie's turn finally came. Where was she?

She grabbed her bag and, muttering, "Excuse me, excuse me, so sorry," snuck out of the row and hurried to the back of the darkened gym.

She dialed again, and after several rings, someone who wasn't Dantas answered.

"Hello?" a male voice said.

Maya blinked and checked her screen to make sure she'd correctly dialed her wife. She had. She put the phone back to her ear.

"Um, who's this?"

"This is Deputy Mike Billings. Do you know the owner of this phone?"

Maya's throat constricted, and her heart nearly stopped in her chest. *Of course.* Dantas had lost her bag somewhere. She was always putting something down and then walking off without it. She was probably still searching for it—with the ticket to the show inside. "It belongs to my wife, Dantas. I'm sorry, who are you again? And where did she leave her phone this time?"

Silence.

"You're her wife?" he finally said.

"Yes."

More silence.

"Hello?" Maya pushed through the double doors into the foyer. Once she got out of the hot, dark room, everything would become clear. Everything would be okay.

"I'm sorry, ma'am, but there's been an accident."

"I'm sorry, what? Is Dantas there? Let me speak to her."

She must have raised her voice. One of the teens at the table was staring at her now.

"Ma'am?" the deputy said. "We'll need you to come to the ER at City General as soon as you can."

Maya closed her eyes, swaying as her head swirled. She braced herself against one of the double doors. Emmie. She couldn't leave her behind. "I have to get my daughter. I'll…I'll be there in just a few minutes."

"Where are you, ma'am? We'll send a patrol car to escort you."

Maya told him, her mind numb. Once she saw Dantas, everything would be fine. Whatever was wrong, they would fix it. Together, just like always.

Chapter One

March, fifteen months later

"Will we be there soon, Mommy?" Emmie asked from the back seat.

"Very soon now, baby." Maya smiled at Emmie in the rearview mirror as she kicked her feet. They'd been driving for hours. All day, and the day before that. Emmie had been a real trouper, but she had to be aching to get out of the car by now. Maya was aching, too, her back sore and her mind stretched thin. Thankfully, their long trek was almost over.

The memory ambushed her again, of Emmie in her tutu, the darkened gymnasium, and the deputy's voice on Dantas's phone. Maya gripped the steering wheel tighter, forcing herself back to the present.

"What do you think about all these bumps?" She maneuvered the hulking U-Haul trailer down an isolated dirt road that carved through a dense forest of Ponderosa pines. Her GPS had promised a shortcut. Hopefully that would be true. "Kind of like that roller coaster ride we took at the fair one summer, remember?"

"I do." Emmie squealed and raised her arms as the car hit another pothole.

Maya's heart twisted at the first real sound of joy she'd heard from her in days. Emmie's laughter was the only true barometer of her happiness, and her joy had been heartbreakingly absent for much of the last year. Losing Dantas so suddenly had cracked their world wide open, and for a while, Maya hadn't been sure they'd come through it at all. They'd both sunk into a kind of endless quiet until Emmie had gone entirely silent. No words, no songs, not even humming. Just stillness.

The silence had been a physical pain that lived in Maya's chest, stealing her breath when she'd lie awake at night listening for any sound from her daughter's room. Even now, months later, the memory of it burned.

Seeing her baby suffer had mobilized Maya to drag herself beyond her own despair. She'd gotten up each day and wrapped Emmie in every ounce of love she could manage, even when she'd felt empty inside, as if love was a distant memory. With time, and the help of a wonderful child therapist, Emmie had begun to return to herself. She'd started talking again. Asking questions. Wanting to know where Mommy D was and why she wasn't coming back.

Maya always answered as honestly as she could, but Emmie still struggled with their new reality.

Maya did, too.

Sleepless nights, a chasm of longing for what she had lost. Tears shed in private. The grief lived in her body now—in her shoulders that never quite relaxed, in the hollow beneath her ribs that never quite filled.

She shook away the dark thoughts once more. They were headed for a new start, if only for Emmie. She would create a happy life for her. She leaned forward slightly and squinted at the dusty road signs that hinted at their destination. There. Sycamore Drive.

"Here's our street, sweetie! We're almost there."

She turned onto a quiet street lined with small, one- and two-story houses on big grassy yards, searching for 4117. A faded black mailbox displayed the numbers in peeling white paint, and she turned into the gravel drive beside it. She braked for her first view of their new house.

The green bungalow stood at the end of the lane, quiet and pale and waiting. Beyond the house, tall evergreens formed a protective circle. She'd purchased it from afar after a handful of video walk-throughs and a whole lot of second-guessing. If it hadn't been for Izzy walking through it in person, FaceTiming her from every creaky corner, she wasn't sure she'd have had the nerve to follow through. But when she'd finally decided that Emmie—and her too—needed to start a new life somewhere that wasn't filled with reminders of all they'd lost, she hadn't wanted to wait. She wanted to go home. She wanted, needed, family—even if it meant making the most nerve-wracking purchase of her life.

She exhaled, long and slow, and eased the old Toyota Land Cruiser up the drive. She glanced back at Emmie, now quiet in her booster seat, her big hazel eyes fixed on the house. A tendril of dark curl stuck to her cheek.

"We're here, sweetie. We're at our new house." Maya unbuckled and almost had to crawl out, every stiff muscle screaming, but she put on a smile as she opened Emmie's door. "Wanna go see?"

"It's green," Emmie said.

"It is." Maya's heart thudded. Would Emmie hate it? Would she? Maybe this whole move was a mistake. She pushed down the rising panic and took Emmie's hand, helping her down. "Let's go explore."

"Our other house was yellow."

"Uh-huh. Do you like the green?" The question felt unbearably important.

Emmie scuffed at the gravel with every step, her small face serious. "No. I like white."

Maya's chest tightened. This was the first opinion Emmie had expressed in so long. Her therapist had said to encourage even the smallest choices. "White? Okay. We'll paint it white, then."

Emmie beamed up at her. "Really? Like my unicorn?"

"Sure. White it is."

"Yay." Emmie bounced on her toes, her little pink-and-white high-tops lighting up at the soles. A comfort she'd insisted on, even though it wasn't dark.

Maya laughed and pulled her close, wrapping an arm around her as they studied the bungalow. The faded light green paint was peeling in places. The porch sagged a little at one end. But still, it had charm. Izzy had said it had good bones, and Maya believed her.

She'd fallen in love with it on her screen, imagining lazy mornings on the porch with Emmie, coffee in hand, the woods curving protectively around them. Acres of trees, quiet trails, new adventures.

But in her mind, Dantas would be there, too. This should've been something they'd done together. A house they'd picked together. Dreamed about together.

She blinked back tears before they could fall and breathed deep. Not today. Not at the start of something new. There'd be time enough when she was alone.

Cold, woodsy air filled her lungs. Bracing and clean.

Early spring in Arrowvale, some fifty miles north of Prescott, still held the chill of winter, but soon the warmer weather would arrive. She'd have five solid months to work on the house before Emmie started kindergarten. Inside first. Emmie needed comfort and stability. A little softness after the hard last year. The outside could wait.

The inspector's report had indicated a few things would need attention sooner rather than later, but for now, she wasn't going to worry.

She couldn't. Not yet.

Emmie jumped on each of the front steps as they climbed to the board porch that spanned the front of the house. Plenty of room for rockers, a table, maybe a porch swing. Dantas could hang it—

No, now all the chores, all the decisions, everything was up to her. A plank dipped and creaked beneath her feet, and she grabbed Emmie, suddenly afraid of losing her. "Careful."

"The porch is talking." Emmie giggled.

Maya laughed, lightness replacing the encroaching despair. Emmie always brought the sunshine. "It sure is."

She unlocked the door and stepped inside, the familiar scent of dust and time settling around her like a forgotten sweater. The old wood floor popped beneath their feet.

"The whole house talks," Maya said with a laugh.

Emmie crinkled her nose. "It smells funny in here."

"It's musty. The house has been closed up for a while." Maya smiled despite the odor. That was something they could clean. Something they could change.

Standing just inside the front door, Maya took in the small living room to her right with an old stone fireplace centered on the far wall and the dining room with adjacent kitchen to the left. The layout was spacious but manageable.

"Where is my room?" Emmie tugged Maya down the surprisingly wide hallway.

"Let's find out."

They checked the two bedrooms, the larger hers with an en suite bath and a smaller one across the way for Emmie's someday-room. Down the hall from there, a small den and tidy bath. All livable. Tired and a bit worn, but standing. The second bedroom clearly needed work. Peeling paint, stained carpet, and a closet door that hung at a tilt. Plenty of windows, though, to fill Emmie's room with sunshine and fresh air.

"What do you think?" Maya asked when they entered the room to be Emmie's.

Emmie cocked her head. "Can we paint it blue?"

"We sure can." Maya hugged her. "How would you like to sleep with Mommy in my room until we fix this one up for you?"

"You mean like we did at the other house?"

"Yep. Just like that." Maya took her hand again. "Come on. Let's see the kitchen."

Clearly the blemishes had not shown up on the videos she'd seen on Izzy's walk-through. The white enamel sink carried stains and scars, the faucets displaying a patina of tarnish. To her relief, the water flowed clear when she turned it on.

She lifted Emmie onto the countertop to keep her close while she checked the cabinets.

"Look, Mommy. Freckles," Emmie said, pointing to the speckled gray laminate.

The counter was worn, a chunk missing along one edge where the particle board showed beneath. Functional but barely. The white cabinets showed cracks at the seams, and the wallpaper—pale yellow with faded flowers—curled at the corners. The linoleum floor was scuffed and bubbled in places.

Still, they had water. And walls. And each other. She could work with that.

A knock echoed from the front of the house.

"Hello, hello! Anyone home?" Izzy's voice rang out, bright and familiar.

Maya smiled. "It's your Aunt Izzy."

Emmie squealed, and Maya barely managed to catch her as she scrambled down. Then she was off running. Maya made it into the hall just in time to see Emmie leap into Izzy's arms.

"Heya, kiddo! How's my little squirrel?" Izzy swung her around. "You're twice as tall as the last time I saw you."

"I'm growing," Emmie declared.

"You are, so fast." Izzy tickled Emmie's sides until she shrieked with laughter, her gaze meeting Maya's above Emmie's head. "And how's my little sister?"

"Surviving." Maya raised her hands, warding off tickles.

Izzy laughed and hugged her. "It's good to see you."

"You too, Iz." When they were younger, they'd been taken for twins—the same dark curls and hazel eyes, but Izzy's current close-cropped do and wire-rim glasses made them easy to tell apart. They'd been as close as twins, too. Still were. Izzy had been her rock after the accident.

"Why didn't you call when you got in?" Izzy set Emmie down and lifted two bags of groceries.

"I got caught up trying to find the place. GPS went full cryptic forest fairy on me."

"Well, I figured you'd be here by now, so I came to check in." Izzy tilted her chin toward the bags. "And to feed you."

"Good. We're starved, right, Em?"

Emmie's brow furrowed. "Where are we gonna eat? We don't have a table."

"On the porch," Izzy said. "We'll have a picnic."

Emmie's eyes lit up, and she scurried outside and plopped down on the top step.

From the doorway, Izzy murmured, "She seems happy."

"She's doing a lot better…most days." Maya smiled as Emmie kicked her feet in her glowing sneakers. She was so small, but so resilient.

"And you?"

"I'm…" Maya exhaled. "Okay. Just antsy over the move."

Izzy nodded. "What do you think of the place?"

"I love it. But you were right. It needs work. More than I appreciated. The ceilings, the drywall…" She pressed her foot into a creaking floorboard. "The flooring."

Izzy slung an arm around her shoulder. "Bathrooms, too. But it'll get done."

"I wish I'd had time to do it before we got here. But Emmie needed the change. And I…I did, too." She glanced at Emmie and murmured, "I kept running into him in town."

"*Him* him?"

Maya nodded. "He'd just look at me like he wanted to say something. Then he'd walk away."

"Coward," Izzy said. "I still can't believe he got off with so little jail time."

Maya held up a hand. “Don’t. Please. He took a plea. There’s nothing I can do.”

“You’re right.” Izzy squeezed her shoulders. “You’re here now. You don’t have to see him again.”

“Yeah.”

They joined Emmie on the steps, and Maya handed out the sandwiches and drinks. Izzy had wisely thought to pack plates, napkins, and even forks for the potato salad.

“When do the movers arrive?” Izzy asked around a bite of Reuben.

“Should be within the hour. They weren’t far behind us.”

“Good. Dad was worried we’d have to wait forever.”

Maya wiped her hands. “Where are he and Mom today?”

“The Grand Tetons. They want you to call once you’re settled.”

“Settled,” Maya snorted. “Sure.”

“You know what I mean.”

Maya handed Emmie a juice box and smoothed her curls. “Good, Em?”

“Uh-huh.” She nodded, chewing.

Maya stared out at the yard. The grass was mostly yellowed from winter. Three trees in need of trimming. No landscaping to speak of.

Izzy followed her gaze. “Just think what you can do with it.”

“I was,” Maya said softly. “I was imagining it.”

“The yard is going to be beautiful. The house, too. With your vision and a decent contractor?”

“I was hoping to do a lot of it myself.”

Izzy frowned. “I thought the settlement—”

“It’s not about the money,” Maya said more sharply than she’d intended. She flushed when Izzy’s brows rose. “Sorry. I just meant I want…I need to be busy.”

“Well, then,” Izzy said gently, “your wish has come true. You can make this place into whatever you need.”

“The sky’s the limit,” Maya murmured. Dantas used to say that. She could almost hear her voice.

She blinked up at the clouds as the moment passed, quiet and bittersweet.

“Yeah, Iz. You’re right. The sky’s the limit.”

Chapter Two

Nolan Wright sighed with relief as the music in the overcrowded bar died down. Between the blaring bass beat and the shouts of the after-work crowd trying to be heard above the din, she'd grown a killer headache.

"What's wrong with you?" asked Gruff, one of her longtime subcontractors and close friends. "You look like you're either gonna keel over or punch someone out."

"My damn head hurts." She rubbed her temple, which helped not at all.

"That mean you're gonna bail on me?" He slurped from his glass of Miller Lite. The foamy head stuck to his mustache, and it took him a moment to notice. He swiped it off with a brush of his hand rather than licking it. "Because you bailed early last week, too. And the week before that. What gives?"

Nolan considered explaining, but the words dried up before they formed. She'd started hitting the Roadrunner with the rest of the crew to blow off steam after a long, hard day. Now she said yes more out of habit, just to make everyone else happy. It wasn't their fault she was often uncomfortable. After all, they weren't the recovering alcoholics—she was. And if she didn't want to go, she should've just said so. Only saying no still made her feel like the broken one.

Gruff studied her closely and glanced down at his now half-empty glass. "Is it the beer? Because I can drink it at the bar."

Nolan followed his line of sight. The bar as well as the billiard room and dining booths was full. The Roadrunner was the place to go, and everyone in town seemed to know it. With its dark walnut interior and live sports on huge flat screens, it had become the main draw for people looking to unwind before heading home. Cheap drinks and greasy food didn't hurt the appeal either. Not with this bunch.

"You don't have to do that, Gruff. Not on my account. I'm just not a hundred percent tonight. No big thing."

That was the truth. Most nights, she could fake it. Tonight, she just didn't have it in her.

His usual jovial face fell, and he slumped in his seat, stroking his long beard. Music from the old-fashioned jukebox played Journey's "Don't Stop Believin'" through the overhead speakers—a song that used to make her smile. Now it just made her jaw tighten.

Nolan winced as the pain drilled into her skull.

"I just wish you could relax and enjoy yourself," Gruff muttered. "You're not the same as you were before."

"That's because I was a drunk, Gruff."

"Not all the time."

"A lot of the time."

"Yeah, but you smiled. You laughed. Times seemed…better."

"They weren't better for me." Nolan kept her tone mild. Gruff meant well, even though her hackles rose at his remarks. As if appearances indicated what she'd felt back then, before she got sober, when nothing had been fun or easy. Most of the crew likely felt the same way Gruff did. Alcohol was part of their culture, an accompaniment to every celebration, including after a long day's work. So…she tried not to get defensive, and she tried even harder to remember exactly *why* she had to keep saying no to the next drink. Every day.

Memories of flashing blue and red lights surfaced, along with the hard pinch of tightening cuffs and the way her mouth had gone dry as she tried to remember what she'd done. She forced the thoughts away, but the nausea came anyway, sharp and cold. Remembering the aftermath of episodes like that, the self-loathing, remorse, and the fear of turning out just like her father, kept her sober. Tim—her longtime sponsor—and the meetings kept her on the right path.

"I guess not." Gruff cupped his glass and stared into his beer.

"Hey." Nolan cuffed his shoulder lightly. "I'm okay. Really. All this," she waved her hand, "is sometimes a lot for me to handle."

Sometimes she wasn't sure why she still came. She didn't even like the Roadrunner anymore, but there was something about showing up, about trying, that made her feel less alone. She wanted to be with her crew, but it was hard to sit and watch them drink and shoot the shit when she couldn't.

"I get it," Gruff said. "So if you want to leave, I'm good."

"You sure?" She wanted to stay a bit longer to prove she still belonged, but mostly to put him at ease and erase his faint flush of guilt. But that was part of the problem, wasn't it? Her worrying about him, while her head split open, and she'd *really* like a beer.

Gruff frowned, looking like he'd just lost his best dog. "Yeah."

"I'll see you tomorrow, then?"

He nodded. "I'll just go hang with the rest of our guys."

"Thanks." She slid from the booth and tossed some cash down on the table for her two Cokes and another round for Gruff. "Next one's on me."

She said goodbye to a few people as she wove through the crowd and pushed out into the crisp night air. The pain in her head instantly receded to a distant pounding.

"Thank you, Jesus," she muttered as she climbed into her Silverado. Leaning back, she sighed. That had not been fun. She needed a good night's sleep to purge the rest of the headache, but her nerves jangled in a way that signaled she'd be lying awake staring at the ceiling if she went home now.

She needed a meeting.

She checked the dash clock as she started the truck. If she didn't hit much traffic, she could still make the late evening meeting at the Lutheran church in time for the shares. A few minutes later, she hurried down to the meeting room in the lower level and quietly eased inside. The faint scent of mold and baked goods in the dimly lit, hushed space was exactly what she needed—the familiar. Comforting and safe for the moment. The kind of stillness that calmed something deep inside her.

She poured a cup of strong-smelling coffee and found a seat near the back, nodding to a guy named Billy.

She knew most of the others in attendance, a few since childhood. Growing up in a pretty small town left little room for privacy—although probably plenty of secrets. She sensed a kinship even with the strangers in the room, though. They all suffered, and with them, she didn't need to explain. She didn't have to justify or pretend.

Here, she just had to show up to feel she belonged.

And that was enough.

She sipped her coffee, listening to the quiet words of the speaker, and truly relaxed for the first time that day. So much better than the Roadrunner. She closed her eyes and listened to the person sharing. Their soft voice, like a metronome, eased her further.

She'd heard the story before. It was her story. His story. Everyone's story.

They all could relate.

Her friends would say they understood—but they didn't. Not really.

Why should she have to avoid going out with Gruff? With any of her friends? The distance stung—a constant reminder of what she'd lost.

Maybe if she kept coming here, she could rebuild her life without the craving chewing at the edges. Maybe someday not drinking with them wouldn't bother her. Wouldn't make her feel so apart. So…alone.

If she kept working the program, kept showing up, maybe it would get easier. She had to believe that. That's why she'd come.

The speaker finished, and everyone softly applauded. The leader, a longtimer named Jo Beth, came to the podium and asked if anyone else wanted to share. No one raised a hand.

She asked again.

Nolan cleared her throat and stood. "I do."

Jo Beth brightened. "Nolan, come on up."

Nolan set her coffee next to her chair, walked to the podium, and gripped it with both hands. She probably looked much like the faces turned to her—tired and solemn, but eager to listen.

"I'm Nolan, and I'm an alcoholic."

"Hi, Nolan," the group said in unison.

"I hadn't planned on sharing tonight, but something inside told me I needed to."

A few people nodded.

"I was out with friends, and they were drinking. Everybody seemed to be having so much fun. Laughing, cutting up, winding down from a long day at work." She lifted her hands. "Well, I worked hard, too. I broke a hard sweat for a solid twelve hours. Shouldn't I be able to do the same as all of them?"

Murmurs of agreement.

She shook her head. "I didn't drink. You know why? Because I can't drink to just unwind. To just shoot the shit and kick back. When I drink, it all goes to hell. I end up doing things I don't remember. Winding up in places I don't recognize or don't want to be."

The flickering of flashing lights in her mind caught her off guard, but she sucked in a breath and kept going.

"Drinking isn't fun for me. It's dangerous. It beats me down and ruins my life. So why would I want that?" She drew a breath. "Why *do* we want that?" She tapped her temple. "Because that's the disease, right? It's sneaky. Whispering all the time about how one drink won't hurt. About how you've earned it. That tonight's different."

She paused. Met eyes. Felt the weight of their silence within her.

"But I've learned better. I've seen the end of that road. It's not freedom or fun. It's a goddamn freight train, and I've been hit by it before. I'm not interested in doing that again."

A breath.

"I left the bar and came here. I thanked my higher power the whole drive. Because this"—she gestured at the room—"this is where I stay on the rails. One day at a time."

She stepped back, throat tight.

"Thanks for letting me share."

Applause came warm and soft. She sat again, wrapped both hands around her coffee. Two others shared before the meeting closed.

She refilled her cup, shook hands, gave a few hugs, and stepped out into the night, still tired but steady.

"Hey, Nolan, wait up!" Johnny Sanchez, a guy about her age who worked one of the other construction crews, trotted toward her from the church.

"What's doing?" Nolan said.

"I tried to catch you inside." Smiling, Johnny brushed a thick lock of jet-black hair off his forehead and grinned sheepishly. "Jo Beth needed a minute."

"Uh-huh." Nolan grinned. Johnny was good-looking, if deep dark eyes, dimples, and loose-limbed swagger were your thing—which they weren't, for her at least. But he was a steady guy, trustworthy, and she liked him. "What's up?"

She leaned against her truck, coffee in hand.

Johnny mirrored her, sticking a toothpick in his mouth. "I got a favor to ask. You know my cousin Maya, who lived in Chicago?"

"Not sure. Don't you have a bunch of cousins?"

"Only a dozen or so." Johnny laughed. "Anyhow, she was a little younger than us in school. I told you last year about her wife being killed in a car wreck."

"Oh, right." She sighed. "Effing tragedy."

"Yeah." He looked away for a second. "Well, she just moved back with her little girl. Bought a nice house that needs some work—more than she can handle. I took a look the other day, and she needs someone trustworthy and good. So I thought of you."

"You trying to flatter me?"

He held up a hand. "God's truth. She's family, Noe."

Nolan shifted. "I don't know, Johnny."

"I thought you wanted to get into home reno?"

"I do. Eventually."

"Then this is perfect."

"Where's the house?"

"Bungalow at the end of Sycamore. The one with all the acreage."

"No kidding? Pris's family's place?"

Johnny pointed a finger at her chest. "That's right. You dated her back in high school, didn't you?"

Nolan nodded. She wasn't getting into *that* disaster with Johnny. "I always liked the house. I even thought about buying it when it came on the market, but it sold fast. Now I know why. Your cousin, huh?"

Johnny removed the toothpick. "Think you can call her? At least walk through it?"

Nolan hesitated. Her current job was wrapping. Maybe it was time she started making her dream happen instead of just thinking about it. "Sure. I'll call her."

"Great." Johnny gave her the number, shook her hand, and headed off.

Nolan slid her phone into her pocket and climbed into her truck. She drove with the windows open, enjoying the silence, thinking about the house. Pris's parents weren't big on home maintenance even a decade ago. She could only imagine what it needed now.

Well, she could look it over and give Johnny's cousin an honest estimate. If there was one thing she knew, it was building. Her father had made sure of that.

She snorted. He hadn't been much of a father. Showing her the ropes had been about the only useful thing he'd done. The rest of the time, he was either tanked or cruel—or both. Bitterness and bourbon. A poison cocktail that had tainted her childhood.

They'd done better when they stayed out of each other's way.

She pulled into her driveway, shut off the engine, and sat for a moment. She didn't have to deal with him anymore. She couldn't conjure up much more than distant sympathy for the man who'd raised her. He'd told her at every opportunity she'd never amount to anything. That she was a millstone around his neck, and that when she hit eighteen, she was on her own.

She'd taken his edict to heart—maybe too much of the rest of it, too. But she'd walked out at eighteen and never looked back.

He'd died alone.

And thinking of him was a waste of her time. She dumped the rest of her now-cold coffee and walked to her house. The house she'd bought with her hard-earned money.

At the door, she paused and looked up at the sky.

Tomorrow held possibilities. She just had to leave the past behind.

Maybe one day she'd be able to.

CHAPTER THREE

The house was eerily silent as Maya unlocked the front door and stepped inside. Izzy had taken Emmie to the village playground to give Maya a few uninterrupted hours to meet with the contractor Johnny had recommended.

She dropped her keys on the small table by the door and paused. Even with the furniture delivered, the place still didn't feel quite real yet. It needed so much work—everywhere she looked, a new reminder, but at least the boxes were no longer threatening Emmie's safety at every turn. She'd spent the last few days sorting and stashing what she could into corners Emmie couldn't reach.

Still, the enormity of the renovation hovered over her like a low-pressure system. Finding a new preschool for Emmie was first on her agenda after she got the reno contracted. Emmie needed a structured space and a way to make new friends, and *she* needed a few precious hours of sanity for herself every day. Not to mention childproofing the house was going to be a joke once demolition started.

She flipped on the coffee machine in the kitchen, breathing in the faint scent of grounds left over from her last cup. The drip began its slow, sputtering rhythm as she leaned against the counter and looked outside. A big white extended-cab truck pulled into the drive.

Wright Contracting, written in black script on the door panel, identified it.

Maya checked her watch. Ten minutes early. A promising start.

She pulled open the front door just as the contractor reached the porch steps—and blinked, pleased to find a woman. A tall, broad-shouldered one with short-cropped blond hair, sharp blue eyes set into a surprisingly gentle face, and obviously plenty of muscle beneath her navy button-up. Johnny had only mentioned "his buddy" Nolan, and she'd just assumed he meant "guy." Dantas would have called her on that, and the thought made Maya smile.

"Maya?" the woman asked, her expression quizzical.

"Yes." Maya stiffened. She didn't mean to—her body just did it. Wary, on edge.

"Hi, I'm Nolan Wright."

Maya shook the extended hand. Nolan's was rough but warm, firm without posturing. The kind of grip that said she knew her work and didn't have anything to prove. Maya forced herself to relax. "Please, come in."

Nolan sidled past her with a polite nod. As she did, her shoulder brushed Maya's. The contact, so unexpected, so foreign, had her jumping away so quickly her back hit the door. Other than Izzy and Emmie, she hadn't touched anyone since…before.

"Oh, hey. Sorry." Nolan took a big step back and jammed both hands into the pockets of her tan canvas work pants. "If this is a bad time—"

"No." Maya felt the heat rush to her face. "This is great—I mean, you're right on time." She cleared her throat. God, Nolan must think she was a flake. "I'm not sure where you want to start."

"Here's just fine." Nolan gestured to the living room. "I see you're already moved in."

"For the most part." Maya motioned vaguely toward the hall. "I've still got a mountain of boxes to unpack—hopefully with no more unpleasant surprises."

Nolan regarded her intently. "Problems?"

Her serious expression somehow made Maya think Nolan was what her mother always called a fixer—the kind of person who wanted, needed, to solve everyone's problems. Maya mentally chided herself. Her imagination had joined the GPS in full-on fairyland. "My great-grandmother's clock didn't survive the trip."

"Sorry. Losing something like that's tough."

"Yes," Maya said as Nolan unslung a camera from the case at her hip. "Can I get copies of the photos?"

"Sure. Once I've done the walk-through and taken measurements,

I'll draw up my recommendations, and we can go over everything. No surprises."

"Good. I don't like surprises."

Nolan paused to study her again. Had she sounded as uptight as she felt? Who knew interacting with a stranger would be so hard?

"Then I'll try my best to be sure there aren't any."

Maya laughed. The sound, the feeling inside, startled her. When had been the last time she hadn't *pretended* to laugh, for Emmie's sake? For Izzy's? "Probably you'll need to see everything."

"That's the plan."

Nolan smiled. A very nice, warm smile that reached her eyes in a way that made Maya's chest tighten unexpectedly. She folded her arms around her middle and swallowed hard. "I'll just follow you. Go anywhere you want."

Nolan pulled a pencil from behind her ear and a small spiral notebook from her back pocket. She measured the entryway, making notes without comment, not needing to fill the silence with unnecessary chatter. She moved efficiently, quietly, in an oddly calming way—shoulders set with purpose, fingers precise, eyes missing nothing.

Caught up in just watching her, Maya slowly relaxed, the tightness in her shoulders easing for the first time in days.

Nolan photographed the foyer, then crouched to inspect the flooring, running her palm over the worn wood—caressing it almost—as if reading its history through touch.

"Normally I'd try to restore wood like this," she said, bouncing slightly as she stood, "but there's too much flex. You've got underlying damage."

"I agree. I'd prefer new flooring throughout."

"Have you picked a style?"

"Hard flooring, everywhere. Emmie—my daughter—she just turned five. Spills are a daily occurrence." Something about saying this aloud—this mundane, parental concern—struck her as strangely intimate.

Nolan chuckled softly. "Got it."

In the living room, Nolan ran her hand along the wall, apparently checking for warping, and glanced up. "You'll need a lot of drywall repair. And some ceiling patching."

"I figured."

"Anyone look at the roof?"

"Johnny. He said it needs some attention."

"I'm sure he's right, but I'll double-check."

Maya wasn't surprised. Nolan obviously left nothing to chance. Her whole approach seemed methodical, thorough, and solid. "I was hoping I could do a lot of the work myself."

Nolan's eyes widened for an instant. "Really?"

"Why not?" Maya's shoulders stiffened at her tone. Slightly incredulous. Did she look helpless, like just another fragile widow who needed rescuing?

"These kinds of projects eat time," Nolan said evenly. "And the heavy lifting parts take a team."

"I know. That's why you're here. But I still want to be involved." She needed this—needed to build something with her hands, create spaces that were fully hers. Not inherited, not shared with ghosts.

"Let's finish the assessment, and I'll have a better idea for you."

Nice diversion.

Maya nodded. That would be a battle for another day. "Fine."

Nolan walked around, checking the windows. "These look newer. Good shape."

"That's a relief. *Something* I won't need to worry about." Maya smiled, and Nolan returned it—quick and soft, almost like she wasn't used to smiling. Then, as if suddenly uncertain, she looked away with a flicker of vulnerability that vanished as quickly as it appeared.

Maya tilted her head, trying to read her. Was she shy? Reserved or just focused? Hard to tell. Something about her stillness felt deliberate—a practiced containment, holding something back or inside.

"I know a lot needs to be done," Maya said. "Johnny said you're good. And honest. That's what I'm counting on. That, and preserving the house's original design elements." She glanced toward the dining room. "That means a lot to me."

"I'd want to keep all of this, too." Nolan gestured to the crown molding, and her gaze met Maya's—a long second that turned strangely warm. Too warm. Crackling with electricity that had no place here, no place in her life. Not now.

Maya turned to look out the window, breaking the connection. "I've always loved this neighborhood—and this house. I wanted a quiet, safe place for Emmie to grow up. I was so lucky to get it."

"That explains it," Nolan said.

"Explains what?"

"Why it sold so fast." Nolan's gaze flicked to the crown molding above them again. "I was interested."

Maya blinked. "You were going to buy this house?"

"I thought about it. But I'm glad you got it." A pause. "Seems like it's in the right hands."

Something about the way she said it—the certainty in her voice—made Maya feel momentarily visible in a way she hadn't been in months. Which just showed how the absence of adult company for over a year had her off balance. Mentally shaking off the odd discomfort, she said brightly, "Where to next?"

"Kitchen. Need to check your plumbing."

Maya leaned on the counter while Nolan pulled a slim penlight from her back pocket and crouched to peer under the sink. How long since someone else had moved through her space like they belonged, so confident and controlled? And stranger still, *her* noticing the precise movements of Nolan's hands and the flex of muscle beneath her clothes was beyond her recall. And seriously discomforting.

"Pipes look okay," Nolan said, sliding back out and standing. "You've got good water pressure, but this faucet's on its last legs."

"I think the master bath is where you'll find the bigger problems."

Nolan jotted notes, then surveyed the cabinets. "What's your plan in here?"

"New everything. Sink, faucet, flooring, countertops—simple stuff, nothing over-the-top."

"Cabinet style?"

"I've got some links I can send you."

"Perfect."

They moved down the hall and into the master bedroom. Maya flipped on the bathroom light. Nolan walked in and rotated slowly, taking everything in, clearly assessing and calculating. Planning.

"Missing tiles, chipped sink, and that toilet's got attitude." She knelt and checked beneath the vanity. "Corrosion here. This needs replacement."

"I feared as much."

Nolan tested both faucets. "Yep. New everything. Want another tub in here?"

"Yes. And one in the hall bath, too." Maya laughed. "It's tough washing kids in a shower."

"I imagine it is."

"None of your own?"

Nolan, a shadow passing over her face, looked momentarily uncomfortable. "Me? No."

"They keep you busy," Maya said quickly. What kind of question had that been? Too personal—too assuming.

Nolan seemed not to notice, snapping a few more photos. "You want to replace all this tile with new tile?"

"Yes." Maya folded her arms again, suddenly cold. The room still smelled like drywall dust and mildew—and a little like old grief. She left quickly, leading Nolan on to Emmie's future room.

The ceiling sagged in one corner, and the wall beneath it showed water damage—washed-out yellowing that spread like a stain.

"You said this is Emmie's room?" Nolan made more notes.

"Will be, yes."

"Emmie," Nolan repeated. "Cute name." She glanced up and smiled, softer this time—transforming her entire face.

Maya blinked, unexpectedly moved. Maybe it was the sincerity in her tone or the lack of hesitation. No awkward pause that usually followed any mention of her daughter, as if people were afraid to ask too much.

"Thanks," she said. "She's a little firecracker."

She didn't mention the nightmares or the meltdowns. Or the way Emmie still sometimes woke up asking for Mommy D—eyes dark with confusion and loss, with a hurt Maya couldn't fix but would spend the rest of her life trying to.

They finished up in the third bedroom, which might someday be a den. Maya led the way to the porch and stepped outside. Nolan lingered, inspecting the exterior trim before retrieving a ladder from the truck.

"Last stop," she said, smiling that confident smile again.

Maya sat on the porch steps, listening to Nolan on the roof. Boots on shingles and the scrape of metal flashing set her teeth on edge. She really wasn't ready for more bad news—not now, not with the weight of everything else pressing down.

A few minutes later, Nolan descended and secured her gear.

"Well," she said, walking up the steps with her notebook, "your foundation looks good. Roof needs some repair. Found a few damaged shingles and the flashing needs replacing, but nothing major."

Maya let out a long, grateful breath. "Anything else?"

"Trim's rotted on the west side." She flipped through her camera and handed it to Maya.

She scanned the photos, handed it back. "I see what you mean."

"Mind if I join you?" Nolan motioned toward the steps.

"Not at all." Maya scooted over, and Nolan settled beside her.

They sat in silence for a moment. A breeze rustled the trees. Somewhere in the distance, a dog barked, the sound homey and comforting. Normal.

"How are you feeling about all this?" Nolan asked.

Maya laughed under her breath. "Right now? A little freaked out."

"That tracks." Nolan nudged a loose pebble with her boot. "But once it's done? You're going to feel amazing."

"You sound awfully sure."

"This house…" Nolan looked back at the house, then met her gaze. "It'll be yours. Fully. You'll raise Emmie here and watch her grow up. This place will hold her milestones, her birthdays and graduations. Someday, it'll be memories stacked wall to wall."

Her voice had dropped a little, her words not scripted or blithe. Just sure, with a quiet certainty that made Maya want to believe her.

The sunlight caught Nolan's eyes, a shade of blue with golden flecks Maya didn't have a name for, like the summer sky trapped in amber.

She looked away again, suddenly self-conscious. "You're really good at this, you know."

"I just like building things that last." Nolan pushed to her feet. "I'll work up your estimate along with a simulation for you to review. Then if you want to adjust anything—scope, cost, whatever—you can let me know when we go over it all."

"Okay." Maya stood, too, brushing her hands on her jeans.

Nolan offered her hand again. Maya took it. Warm, callused, and steady. Dantas's hands, used to touching hurt and injured people, had always been so soft—surgeon-gentle, satin-smooth.

Maya jerked her hand back. "Thanks for coming."

If Nolan noticed, she didn't show it. "Nice to meet you, Maya. I'll email you a detailed report—or if you want, I can come by?"

Maya hesitated, the flicker of anticipation in her chest confusing—and unwelcome. Of course, if she hired Nolan—and where was she likely to find a more likeable, competent, or honest contractor—she'd be seeing her on the regular. "Come by when you're ready. That way we can discuss anything I may have to put off for a while. That will be more efficient."

"Efficient." Nolan grinned. "I like it."

Maya felt her face heat again. She hated how easily she blushed around her. "Yes, well…"

"I'll call first." Nolan sketched a small salute and strode toward her truck.

Maya waved as Nolan pulled out of the drive and honked in farewell. Maya watched her disappear around the bend, unsettled by the odd pull of connection.

Inside, she poured herself a cup of coffee and sat at the table. The house felt different now. Like it had been seen, not just assessed, by someone who had finally found it worth saving.

She stared at her mug, steam curling into the air.

If she accepted Nolan's estimate, a lot was about to happen over the next few months. And Nolan would be there every day—a stranger in her private refuge.

She'd just uprooted everything. Wasn't that enough for now?

She closed her eyes, took a breath. Ready or not, it was happening. The house needed a lot more work than she'd anticipated, but she couldn't keep waiting for her life to magically restart. She and Emmie deserved a home they could shape together, brick by brick. A place that was whole and safe.

And a big check in the plus column, Nolan cared about the house. She'd heard Nolan's respect for its bones and its history in every comment.

She sipped her coffee. Nolan was respectful, steady, and clearly a great person for the job. Whatever little discomfort her presence stirred up was understandable. She just wasn't used to spending time with anyone, that's all.

Yes.

The time was now.

CHAPTER FOUR

Nolan checked the time on her dash as she drove away from Maya's house, white-knuckling the steering wheel. She could make the late morning meeting in thirty minutes. A lifeline, the meetings always gave her space to breathe when her mind wouldn't stop.

Her pulse hadn't slowed since she'd sat beside Maya on the porch steps, close enough to catch the faint floral aroma, bright and unexpectedly stirring. The scent hadn't left her since she'd said goodbye and walked away, wishing she could stay and not knowing why.

She hadn't seen Maya Sanchez coming. Should've known she wouldn't be much older than her. Johnny'd mentioned they'd been near contemporaries in high school, but her mind had fixed on the word "widow," which conjured the image of a withdrawn, remote woman.

Man, had she been wrong. Maya had been anything but that.

Captivatingly beautiful—small curvy build, wild shoulder-length black curls, and those hazel eyes that shifted like sunlight through whiskey. Quicksilver humor and a smile that shone like sunlight, all the more striking for its rarity. Assessing eyes that probably revealed more than Maya intended.

Nolan shook her head. That infrequent brightness had knocked the air from her lungs. Hell, she'd barely managed to get through her work list, too busy watching the graceful way Maya moved—cautious but determined—and how her whole face transformed when she mentioned her little girl. And there *she'd* been, trying not to show she was watching like some starstruck teenager.

She ran a hand through her hair and caught a glimpse of herself in the rearview mirror. Flushed, eyes a little glazed, definitely steamed up. For Christ's sake!

Maya was Johnny's cousin. That alone ought to be enough to kill any thought of getting up close and personal with her. But a bigger reason than that? Maya was still suffering from losing her wife. Her pain was written in the tight set of her shoulders, the shadows in her eyes, and the way she drifted off into some memory only to pull herself back to the present like a drowning woman struggling for air. A woman grieving—fragile, vulnerable, and rebuilding—with a child, no less.

Her sponsor would have a field day with any one of those reasons, let alone all of them.

Watching the road, keeping to a safe speed, Nolan rubbed her jaw and tried to calm her racing heart. Physical reactions were one thing—she could control those, but the ideas floating through her head? Another matter entirely.

What she ought to do was tell Maya she had a scheduling conflict, that something had come up on another job that she couldn't put off. Because she couldn't ask Maya out to dinner or suggest a walk along the trail in the woods behind Maya's new house—the very same trail she'd walked with Pris the first time they'd kissed.

"Fuck," Nolan muttered. If she was thinking of Pris, of all people, *now*, she really needed a meeting.

But the image of Maya standing in that crumbling kitchen, shoulders straight despite everything, flashed through her mind. Maya had jumped when they'd accidentally touched—raw and skittish but determined not to show it. Seeing Maya struggle like that had hit her with a fierce surge of protectiveness that surprised her still. Yes, Maya'd recently lost her wife in a violent, tragic way, and had a small child. She still needed someone honest, who would do good work. Nolan couldn't throw her to the wolves, where someone else might exploit her vulnerability and overcharge her for shoddy work. The thought of Maya being taken advantage of made her stomach clench. Anger and old memories of being left to find her own way tangled into something dangerous.

She had to do this for Maya. For them both.

As for this attraction… Nolan shifted uncomfortably in her seat. She needed to compartmentalize—lock these feelings away where they couldn't interfere. She'd spent just over a year driving straight ahead on her own road. Things were good. Smooth and predictable. Safe.

She wanted to keep them that way. Needed to.

Relationships were disasters waiting to happen, for her at least. Her father's legacy—an emotionally unavailable alcoholic who'd driven her mother away, who'd chosen the bottle over his family every single time—was a pattern that ran deep in her blood and her bones.

She *wanted* to believe she was different now, responsible and stable. But the evidence suggested otherwise. Until a few months ago there'd been a string of brief connections, physical but never emotional. She enjoyed women's company, but she'd never allowed anything meaningful to form. Couldn't risk it and wouldn't know how if she tried.

Blowing out a breath, she pulled into the church parking lot next to Johnny's truck and sat there a minute, letting her thoughts settle. The familiarity of the routine steadied her. Meetings, community, and a sense of purpose created the structure that had saved her life. She respected the process, and part of that lesson was to avoid putting herself in situations that would stress her fairly limited willpower.

Like beautiful, wounded women.

Right. Decision made. She'd do the work for Maya Sanchez. And keep a nice safe distance from anything personal. She hopped out and hurried into the church, then downstairs.

Johnny stood at the refreshment table, fiddling with the coffee maker. The normality of this quiet ritual before people arrived offered relief from the storm of her thoughts.

"Hey," she said, joining him. "Need help setting out the snacks?"

"Sure." He handed her a pack of cream-filled cookies. His trademark cinnamon toothpick danced in his mouth as he punched buttons on the coffee maker.

While arranging cookies and a stack of paper napkins on a serving tray, she pictured Maya's living room—the worn floorboards, the water stains on the ceiling, the warped molding—and beneath the wear and tear, the potential of it all. A house with good bones, waiting to be restored. Yeah—she wanted that job.

Johnny discarded his toothpick and grabbed a chocolate cookie, taking a bite. Crumbs cascaded down his shirt. He brushed them away casually, not bothering with a napkin. "What's happening?"

"I met with Maya this morning," she said.

"Oh, yeah?" Johnny's tone remained casual, but his eyes sharpened.

"She's really nice." Understatement of the century. More like kind of amazing. Strong-willed and tough and still…fragile.

He paused mid-chew. "Do I sense a 'but' coming?"

"No, I just…" Nolan shrugged. Telling Johnny about her storm of impressions, images of Maya she couldn't sort out herself, was maybe not the smartest move.

"Is it the house?"

"No, the house is fine. I actually love it, and I can do the work."

"Still hearing a but." He held up his palm. "Look, if it's the time—I can shift some of my jobs and pick up some of yours. We've helped each other out like that before."

"No, I'm clear." Nolan exhaled. "You know she wants to help with the work? Like hands on?"

Johnny's worried look turned into a grin. "Not surprised. Is that the sticking point?"

"Not really," Nolan admitted. "It *is* her house—she's the boss. I'm sure there'll be plenty of small stuff I can point her at. Shouldn't really be a problem."

Johnny snorted. "I'll remind you of that later. Look, I know it's a big job, but it's more than just making the house livable. Maya needs this. Dantas's death damn near destroyed her. But she kept going for Emmie, and renovating that house is a…a symbol, I guess…of her and Emmie rebuilding their life."

His words landed like a punch. The image of Maya crumbling, devastated and alone, made her chest ache. That she'd even consider backing out over her own confused feelings suddenly seemed cowardly.

"Well, when you put it that way." She tried for lightness but heard the strain in her voice.

"I mean it, Nolan. I know you'll do right by her, and she's good for the money."

"I'm not worried about that." Concerns about payment never crossed her mind. Only Maya's eyes—watchful and wary, wounded but undefeated—kept coming back to her, making her wish she could drive away the pain.

The coffee machine stopped gurgling.

Saved.

"There's no problem." Nolan grabbed a cup and turned away before he read the lingering uncertainty in her face. "I'm taking the job."

He clapped her on the shoulder. "Thanks so much, buddy. Now I won't have to worry about them. You're all right, Nolan."

She sipped her coffee, the bitterness matching her self-assessment. "Yeah, yeah. Just don't spread that around."

Johnny laughed, finished his cookie, and reached for another. Nolan followed him to the rows of chairs as people trickled in—familiar faces, friends traveling a common road.

Nolan sat quietly, choosing not to share. Instead, she closed her eyes, words of struggle and hope flowing past her, reminding her that challenges could be met, obstacles overcome, one day at a time. Now and then, an image of the small green bungalow on Sycamore Drive and a woman with haunted eyes flickered though her mind.

Maya needed help, and she could offer it. She could do the work, be of service to Maya and her little girl, without letting her baggage complicate their lives.

"You alright?" Johnny asked.

Nolan jerked upright and opened her eyes. The meeting had ended, and people were filing out while others folded chairs.

"Hmm? Oh. Yes. Just reconnecting with why I'm here." She stood. "Need any help closing up shop?"

"Nah, I got it." He clasped her arm. "I really do appreciate you helping Maya out. I promise you, it will be worth it. Especially when you see how happy it will make her."

Happy. The word landed strangely. Maya hadn't seemed happy—she'd seemed determined, resilient, and barely holding together the fragments of a shattered life. The chance that she might lift some of that weight off Maya's shoulders, make that rare smile appear, sent a dangerous warmth through Nolan's chest.

Nolan forced a grin. "I better get home and work up that estimate, then."

"Yeah, you better." He smiled. "I'll see you next time."

Nolan echoed his signature farewell. "Next time."

Outside, the afternoon air had warmed. She said goodbye to a few people in the parking lot and turned her mind to a safe topic. Schedules, materials, layouts, costs. The practical elements that would transform Maya's house into a home. This she could handle. This made sense.

Once home, she brewed coffee and carried a mug to the nook off the kitchen that she used as an office. She spread her notes across the table and fired up her laptop. After opening the new renovation software, she checked her email, smiling when she saw a new message from Sanchez. Not surprised that Maya didn't waste any time, she opened the message. Maya'd sent links for flooring, counters, cabinets, sinks. Nolan studied each carefully, noting the clean lines, the warm tones, the pleasing aesthetics fused with functionality that said a lot about Maya—practical and unpretentious, but sensitive to what made a house live and breathe.

With what Maya had sent her, Nolan envisioned the house transformed—walls repaired, floors restored, systems updated. She entered measurements, explored options, built the simulation room by room. A sanctuary taking shape around a mother and daughter who deserved peace. Maya's dream. One Nolan could make come true.

Two hours later, she leaned back, tapping the pencil she still used to scratch notes on a yellow pad she kept nearby on the table despite the fancy computer program, and reviewed all she'd done. Fair price, quality materials, realistic timeline—all within Maya's budget. Good work. Pleased that she had something that might make Maya happy, she replied to Maya's email and asked for a convenient time to meet to review the estimates.

Email sent, laptop closed, she drained the last of her now-cold coffee. The workday wasn't over—the medical office site still needed her attention. She locked up and headed to her truck.

At the site, Gruff's old beater pickup sat amid the construction vehicles. He glanced up from his crouch over a nail gun and waved. The familiar sight grounded her. Work—physical, demanding, and uncomplicated—was exactly what she needed. The job gave her a purpose, brought normalcy to her life.

Gruff removed his safety glasses to rub his eyes. "Didn't think I'd be seeing you today."

"How's it going?" She shouted to be heard over the construction noise—hammers, saws, drills. People shouting above the din. Ordered chaos. The medical offices were taking shape—framed, roof up. Gruff took the helm when she wasn't around. She couldn't be everywhere, and he wasn't just good at his job, he was scrupulously honest.

"It's going," he said.

"We on schedule?"

"About a day behind."

"That's not bad." She breathed relief. Schedules mattered. Deadlines resulted in progress, and that meant happy clients. "Good job, guy."

She headed for the work trailer, the morning's tension and disquiet melting away. Gruff followed her inside.

"Listen, Nolan. About the other night at the Roadrunner—"

"Hey, it's all good." The last thing she wanted was to dissect that uncomfortable evening. "Don't worry about it."

Gruff shook his head. "I didn't mean I liked you better when you drank. That's not what I meant. I just…you still don't seem happy is all."

Okay. They were going to talk about it. She met his worried gaze. "I'm working on it. I promise."

He nodded. "Well, maybe if you had someone…" He cleared his throat. "You know, special, you'd be happy. Not lonely, if you didn't feel like hanging at the Roadrunner, I mean."

His eyes lit up, hopeful and earnest, as if the solution was so simple.

Lonely. The word struck deeper than she expected—a direct hit on a truth she'd been avoiding. And of course her mind went just where she didn't want it to go, unbidden and unsettling. To Maya. "Hell, Gruff, don't throw that into the mix. I can only focus on one thing at a time."

He nodded, accepting her deflection.

Nolan shrugged away the unexpected reflex. She'd just spent the morning with Maya and most of the day thinking about making Maya's house a home. So naturally her mind went there. Nothing more than that. "Really, Gruff, I'm fine with the way my life is. No need to worry, okay?"

"Sure, boss." He backed out the door. "I better get back to it."

Nolan joined the crew working on the stucco, and the work absorbed her—spray, smooth, repeat. Physical labor that helped quiet her churning thoughts.

Still, Gruff's words echoed. *Maybe you'd be happy. Not lonely.*

For some people—some *other* people, that might be true. But for her? Work was safety, something she couldn't fuck up. Couldn't hurt if she fucked up. And she might.

The only life lessons she'd ever had came from a man who did nothing *but* fuck up—letting people down, lying, cheating, failing. And she'd been on her way to following in his footsteps.

Spray, smooth, repeat.

This was real, not fantasy. Not dangerous dreams that could lead to disappointment, failure, hurting someone else.

One day at a time—the only path forward. The only safe way through.

CHAPTER FIVE

"Em? You dressed, honey?" Maya poked her head into the master bedroom. Emmie sat where she'd left her, on the edge of the bed, her favorite sneakers on the floor and her unicorn T-shirt in her lap.

Uh-oh.

"Something wrong, sweetie?"

"I don't wanna go to school." The whining tone was a throwback to the first few months after Dantas had died—raw, vulnerable, painfully familiar.

Maya took a slow breath, picked up Emmie's sneakers, and sat on the bed beside her. As she slipped one of Em's favorite "light-up shoes" over her pink ankle socks, she asked casually, "Why not?"

"I want to stay here with you." Emmie's eyes radiated anxiety.

"Well, you will—every day after school, and every night, and," she hugged her, inhaling the sweet-shampoo scent of Emmie's hair, "every morning *before* school."

Emmie automatically lifted her other foot for Maya to slip on her sneaker—a small concession that gave Maya hope. "What if I don't like it?"

"How about we try it for—let's see—a week. You can tell me all the fun things you did every day when I pick you up, and after a week, if you don't like it, we'll talk about what we should do." Maya kept her voice light even as her stomach knotted with worry.

Emmie scrunched up her face. "Is that like family meeting time?"

Maya's heart dropped—a sudden freefall that left her dizzy. Whenever she and Dantas made plans, they always included Emmie, even when she was too young to understand. They told her it was family meeting time, and that often ended in something fun for Emmie. Now it would just be the two of them—a family diminished, incomplete. The weight of that absence pressed against Maya's chest with such force she struggled to breathe.

She swallowed the lump in her throat. "Yep. Just like that."

"It won't be the same," Emmie said in a small voice.

"I know, baby. But sometimes things change and can still be fun." Maya forced certainty into her voice—a skill she'd perfected over the past year. Strong for Emmie, even when she felt anything but.

"Okay." Emmie jumped off the bed and stomped her feet, making the lights in the soles flicker, red and purple bursts against the worn carpet.

"Look at that!" Maya clapped, grateful for the distraction. "I bet the kids at school will really like those."

Maya stroked Emmie's cheek. Thank goodness she had a referral for a new child therapist. Emmie was so much better, but the move had brought up a lot of her old anxieties—the fear of separation, the dread of loss, the creeping sense that nothing was permanent.

Maya's fears, too.

"Okay," Emmie said, "I guess I'll go to school."

"That's my girl." Maya took her hand. "Come on, let's go pick out your snacks for break time."

In the kitchen, Maya sat Emmie on the counter—her new favorite place when Maya cooked—and checked the food list the preschool had suggested for snack time.

"Apple slices, yogurt, trail mix, or string cheese?"

"All of them." Emmie's expression was so serious, so earnest, that Maya had to bite her lip to keep from smiling.

"Pick two for today."

Emmie regarded her solemnly. "What do you think?"

"Yogurt and apple slices."

"Okay."

Maya packed the food in the little rainbow-colored backpack with sparkles and stars scattered over it and held it out. "Time to saddle up."

Em tilted her head. "That's what Mommy D always says."

Maya's breath caught—a sudden, painful hitch. "Yes, she did." The words echoed in the hollow places inside.

"Is she ever coming back?"

Maya plucked her off the counter and hugged her—too tightly, perhaps, but she needed the anchor of Emmie's arms wrapping around her neck. "No, sweetheart, she's not."

"But why?"

Maya fought tears, trying to smile softly through her pain. "Remember we talked about the accident? She would never want to leave us, but sometimes things happen that we can't change."

So woefully inadequate—how could words explain something she still couldn't comprehend?

"I miss her."

"I do, too, baby. I do, too." Maya kissed her forehead and set her down. "It's okay to miss Mommy or to feel sad. And it's okay to talk about it."

"I know." Emmie kicked her feet, and her shoes lit up—small flares of brightness in the moment's gravity. "You already told me that."

"I did, didn't I? I'm glad you didn't forget." Maya helped Emmie into her sweater and handed her the backpack filled with everything the preschool instructions had suggested she bring. "So, ready?"

Emmie wiggled until she got her backpack settled just right. "Yep. Let's saddle up."

Maya laughed, and the pain, always present, seemed a little more distant. A shadow retreating, if only for a moment.

The preschool was less than a mile away and they arrived at exactly 8:00, precisely the time of their meeting with the director.

Maya led Emmie into a bright foyer with colorful drawings, obviously done by children, adorning the walls. A door down the short hall opened, and a white-haired woman wearing a blue and white checked dress, practical black flats, and round black eyeglasses strode briskly in their direction, a smile wreathing her pale pink, wrinkleless face.

"Good morning!" she said in a dancing soprano voice, one hand extended. "Are you Ms. Sanchez?"

"Yes, I'm Maya." Maya shook her delicate hand, surprised by its warmth and strength.

"I'm Annabelle Everett. The children all call me Ms. E, but you go ahead and call me Annabelle."

Instantly charmed, Maya smiled. “Wonderful to meet you, Annabelle.” She grasped Emmie’s hand and gently drew her forward from where she’d been hiding behind her leg. “And this is Emmie.”

Annabelle crouched with surprising agility and smiled. “Hello, Emmie.”

Emmie pressed her face to Maya’s leg, a familiar gesture that spoke volumes about her anxiety.

“She’s a little nervous,” Maya said, resting a protective hand on Emmie’s shoulder.

“That’s very understandable. I was always nervous on my first day of school, too.” Annabelle plucked a strip of glittery stickers from her dress pocket. “Would you like a sticker, Emmie?”

Emmie slowly turned to examine the stickers, her eyes widening with unmistakable interest. She nodded, still silent.

“Want to pick one out for yourself?”

Emmie nodded again and pointed to a pink and purple butterfly, colors that matched her light-up shoes.

“Very good choice,” Ms. E. said. “This one is special. It will keep you company all day while you make new friends.”

She removed the sticker from its backing and gave it to Emmie.

“Where do I wear it?” Emmie asked, her voice small but steady.

“Anywhere you like.”

Emmie stuck it to the front of her shirt—a badge of courage, Maya thought, her throat tightening.

“Oh, that’s a good spot. You’ve found your first friend, but there’s lots more inside.” Ms. E. straightened. “How about you and your mom come see your classroom now.”

“Okay,” Emmie said. “Will there be drawing?”

Annabelle laughed and met Maya’s gaze with a reassuring nod. “There most certainly will be.”

Maya held Emmie’s hand until they reached the classroom, where a young woman about Maya’s age in jeans and a smock covered with daisies sat with a half dozen preschoolers in a circle of miniature chairs. Several were empty.

“Would you like to join the other children while Lucy reads a story?” Annabelle said. “Later we’ll all finger paint.”

Emmie glanced up at Maya, her lower lip quivering. “Can you stay, too?”

Maya crouched beside her. "I have work I need to do, but I'm not going far. Remember how short the ride was?"

Emmie's eyes filled with tears, though she didn't let them fall. No matter how many times Maya and her therapist told Emmie everyone cried, and she could, too, Emmie fought not to. Maya heard the therapist's oft-repeated advice. *Give her time. Answer her questions. And go on living. She'll cry when she needs to.*

"I'll come get you after snack time," Maya said. "You're my special girl, remember? In a few hours, you can tell me all about your adventures."

Emmie glanced inside at the children, then back up at Maya—hesitant, uncertain, but with a flicker of curiosity in her eyes. "Okay. I want to finger paint."

Maya's heart swelled and tears threatened. God, Emmie was so brave—braver than she had any right to ask her to be. She smoothed Emmie's curls and kissed the top of her head. "I can't wait to see."

The young woman named Lucy came to the door, smiling warmly. "Hi, Emmie. I'm Lucy. Want to come pick out a seat and meet the other kids?"

And just like that, Emmie crossed the threshold and didn't look back. Maya eased away into the hall, her chest simultaneously lighter and tighter.

"She's been to preschool before, but I think this is harder on me, this time around." Maya tried to keep her voice steady, not entirely succeeding.

"She'll be fine," Annabelle said. "She's a beautiful child."

"Thank you," Maya said. "She might take a little time to adjust—the last year has been…hard." Maya mentally grimaced. Hard. Such a bland word to describe heartbreak—to describe the way life had been torn in two, how every day since had felt like walking through deep water, how even breathing sometimes required concentration.

A look of sympathy passed over Annabelle's face. "I saw in the personal statement on your application that you recently lost your wife. I'm so sorry."

Maya nodded, grateful for the woman's directness. "I thought it important that you know that—Emmie has adjusted fairly well, but she still has moments of insecurity."

"Understandable, of course," Annabelle said. "If she seems

distressed at any time, we'll call you. But I think she's going to be fine here."

"I do, too," Maya said, surprising herself with her certainty.

Resisting the urge to take one last peek into the classroom, Maya shook Annabelle's hand and hurried to the car. She'd done it. Emmie was in. And she hadn't cried. Not yet, anyway. She sat for a moment in the driver's seat, hands on the wheel, forehead resting against it—allowing herself a moment of weakness now that there was no one to see.

"Okay," she whispered. "That's step one."

A few minutes later, she walked into the kitchen with a free hour before lunch with Izzy. Sitting with the remains of the morning coffee, she pulled up the email from Nolan. She hesitated a moment before opening it, finger hovering over the trackpad.

This was really happening. She was probably about to hire a contractor to bring this house back to life.

Probably? Who was she kidding. Short of a sticker price high enough to send a rocket to Mars, she was hiring Nolan Wright. She'd known that when Nolan had climbed that ladder like she'd built the house herself—confident, capable, at home among the rafters and roofing in a way that had made Maya's chest tighten with admiration and something she couldn't name. Trust maybe? Yes, she'd trusted Nolan from the moment they'd met. Something in her directness, the way she'd looked Maya in the eye, listened, and commented—*hearing* her.

Still, she hesitated. What if Nolan had emailed to say she didn't want the job? Maybe she didn't like the suggestions Maya had sent. Maybe, maybe…oh, enough with the maybes. Really, Emmie was braver than her at times.

With a deep breath, she opened the message, and her nervous butterflies morphed into a buzz of excitement. A heady sensation she hadn't experienced in so very long—anticipation, possibility.

The message was short, and to the point, like Nolan. Clear. Professional. But with a hint of warmth.

Maya: Liked your ideas. They suit the place. I have the price list, labor estimates, and schedule ready to discuss. Contact me with a good time, when you're ready. Thank you for letting me bid on this job. It's a great house. N.

Maya hit reply without a second thought. *Thanks for being so quick. My time is flexible, so you pick the time. If you come after work, I can offer pizza. If you remember the state of the oven, I'm not planning to test it out. M.*

She sat back. There.

Step two.

Just before noon, Maya pulled into the gravel lot in front of Millie's Place, a restaurant in an old-fashioned diner car that boasted *Homestyle Cooking Like Your Mama Made* on a big sign on top. Izzy waved from a booth next to the window, her cropped hair freshly styled, wire-rim glasses catching the midday sun.

"How'd Emmie do?" she asked the instant Maya slid in across from her.

"A little rocky for the first few minutes, but she's there and I think she'll be fine. It's a great place." Maya hung her jacket on the hook beside the booth, feeling lighter than she had in days.

Izzy rolled her eyes. "Would I steer you wrong?"

Maya grinned. "Um, yes?"

Izzy tossed a straw at her. "Not in years. So how are *you*? Okay?"

"Leaving her was harder than I expected. I just want to wrap her up and protect her all the time. I always have, but since Dantas…" She looked away, past Izzy to the parking lot beyond—the words catching in her throat. "God, Iz, this sucks."

Izzy grasped her hand and squeezed, her grip firm and anchoring. "You're doing everything right, Maya. You're my goddamn hero."

Maya laughed, a little watery, but a real laugh. One that felt good, like stretching a muscle that had been cramped too long. "Not in a million years. But one thing I did right was to move home. Emmie needed it, and so did I. We needed family."

"Speaking of," Izzy said with an uncharacteristic frown, "Johnny stopped by. He said the house needs a *lot* of work. He sort of implied I should have known that."

"Oh, phooey," Maya said, waving away Iz's concern. "We *both* knew that—just not quite how *much* work it might need. I know now. It's fine. It will be, at least. When Nolan is done."

Izzy studied her over the rim of her coffee cup. "So, what's going on with that?"

Scanning the menu, Maya said absently, "Nolan is coming by

sometime soon to go over all the details. We should get started right after."

"What? Just like that?" Izzy's eyebrows shot up.

"Mm-hmm." Maya continued reading the menu, though she already knew she wanted the veggie omelet.

"Maya." Izzy waved a hand in front of the menu. "Hello?"

"What?" Maya looked up, feigning innocence.

"Shouldn't you get a few estimates? It's a huge project."

"Why?" Maya shrugged. "Johnny says Nolan's the best there is. I trust him. Besides, I get a really good vibe from her. She's the real deal, Iz. No need to worry."

"Well," Izzy muttered, as the waiter approached, "if Nolan doesn't do a good job, Johnny will kick her ass, I guess."

"Forget that," Maya said. "*I'll* kick her ass."

The waiter cleared his throat, grinning broadly. "Know what you're having?"

"Veggie omelet with cheese, sweet potatoes on the side," Maya said, handing over the menu.

"Biscuits and gravy," Izzy said, staring past Maya with a grimace. "Oh, hell."

"What?" Maya started to turn.

"Don't look," Izzy said as the waiter sprinted away. "Maybe she won't come over if we don't make eye contact."

"Who?"

"Too late." Izzy sighed.

An auburn-haired woman with killer cheekbones, dressed more for the country club than the diner with what Maya guessed had to be a five-thousand-dollar bag dangling from her shoulder, stood by their booth.

"Hi, Pris," Izzy said in a tone that seemed a little frosty.

"Hello, Isabelle. Sorry to interrupt." She glanced at Maya from beneath long, heavy lashes—assessing and somehow calculating. "I'm Priscilla Mendez—Pris. You must be Izzy's sister."

"Maya," Maya said. "Nice to meet you."

"I used to live in that house on Sycamore that you just bought."

"Oh," Maya said, polite but uncertain. Why did this feel like a subtle interrogation? "I'm sorry I didn't recognize your name. My real estate agent handled the house sale completely. I didn't even realize anyone lived there."

Pris laughed, an amused sound that didn't reach her eyes, as if Maya had just said snow was predicted overnight. "Oh, heavens. I haven't lived there in years, not since I was a teenager. My parents held on to it even after they moved away. Tried renting it for a few years, and then it just sat. Last I heard, it needed quite a bit of work."

"A fair bit," Maya admitted, flushing under the scrutiny. She couldn't shake the feeling that she was being appraised like a horse at auction and found wanting.

Pris smiled, a sharp, predatory curve of coral-glossed lips. "Well, it's in good hands now." She hesitated, her gaze calculating. "I heard you're working with Nolan Wright?"

Maya searched the icy eyes. The question felt pointed, personal. Definitely being interrogated. "We're discussing it."

Pris's smile dimmed, just slightly, a flicker of possessiveness crossing her perfect features. "Well. She and I go way back. I *do* hope the project goes well. She's good. When she shows up."

Maya bristled—not visibly, but somewhere under her ribs—with a spark of irritation, hot and unexpected.

Pris gave a small wave, manicured nails glinting in the diner lights. "Anyway. Nice to meet you."

"You too." Maya kept her tone neutral, though her heart was suddenly racing.

Pris walked away, hips swaying in an expensive pencil skirt, heels clicking against the linoleum. Whatever *that* was about, she didn't like the feeling it left in her chest. That Pris found something amusing, at her expense. Nothing overt—no raised voice, no dramatic insinuation. Just the way Pris said "when she shows up," like a subtle warning dressed up in a compliment.

Everything about the encounter irritated. A burr against her skin, small but impossible to ignore. News certainly traveled quickly through a small town. Of course, Johnny knew everyone, and telling him anything was as good as taking out an ad in the daily news.

Izzy stirred her coffee, gaze fixed on Pris's retreating back. "So. That was awkward."

Maya raised an eyebrow. "You think?"

"She's got that look." Izzy sipped her coffee with exaggerated nonchalance. "The 'I knew her before she had tool belts and boundaries' look."

Maya tried not to react, but heat crept up the side of her neck—a flush that had nothing to do with the diner's warmth. "She just said they go back."

"Mm-hmm. And that's generally code for they used to be an item."

"I don't care about Nolan's past." Maya picked up her water glass, needing something to do with her hands.

"Didn't say you did." Izzy gave her the same knowing look she'd given Maya since they were kids and Maya had sworn she absolutely wasn't bothered that Katie Reynolds had borrowed her favorite book and never returned it. "That was just typical Pris. Since she 'married up,' she fancies herself one of the social elite and always in the know." Izzy leaned back as the waiter set down their food. "Ignore her."

Maya intended to do just that. Nolan undoubtedly had more than one ex in town, if that's what Pris was. Of course, Nolan could be married now with a whole life she knew nothing about. Her stomach tightened at the thought, an involuntary reaction that she refused to examine too closely.

And whatever Nolan's situation? Certainly none of her concern.

She planned to hire Nolan to fix her house. That was the extent of her relationship with Nolan Wright. Simple, uncomplicated, and professional.

So why did her hands shake slightly as she cut into her omelet? Why had Pris's words settled in her chest like a stone? And why did she suddenly care about who Nolan had been before she showed up on Maya's porch with her toolbelt and her steady blue eyes?

Maya pushed the questions away. She had enough complications in her life. She didn't need to borrow more.

Chapter Six

Maya set the last plate on the long French peasant's table her mother had given her and Dantas as a wedding present. A kitchen big enough to accommodate it had been a selling point of the house when Izzy had sent her the video. The table was one of the few things she'd carried with her into this new chapter. Not much else remained, just the memories.

The ringing doorbell came as a welcome reprieve from revisiting the past.

She wiped her palms on her jeans and crossed the living room, nerves she hadn't expected rising with every step. Just a meeting to go over plans and numbers. She'd done this a dozen times back in Chicago when they'd added a bathroom after Emmie came along. With Dantas working twelve-hour shifts, Maya'd had to oversee the project—she'd even had a spreadsheet for contractor info, timelines, and supply runs.

But this was different, and not just because the project was ten times bigger. Nolan was different—from the moment she'd walked in, she'd given off the air of being in charge. Subtly, not the least bit condescendingly, but definitely self-assured and confident in her judgement. She wouldn't be needing Maya's spreadsheets. She'd made an impression, when nothing—no one—had really penetrated Maya's awareness for over a year. That alone was unexpected, and enough to make her uneasy.

Not something she really wanted to think about, either.

When Maya opened the door, Nolan, in work boots and cargo pants, sleeves rolled to the elbow, a pencil tucked behind her ear, looked slightly flushed, like she'd rushed over straight from a construction site—sun-kissed skin, hair tousled by the wind, gaze steady on hers. The evening light caught the golden flecks in her eyes, turning the blue almost luminous.

That quiet intensity sparked an electric pulse inside—like tectonic plates sliding against each other, impossible to ignore or explain.

"Hello." Nolan lifted a folder as the seconds passed. "Hope I'm not early."

Maya swallowed and put on what she hoped was a friendly but not *too* friendly smile. "Right on time." She stepped back to let her in, suddenly hyperaware of the threshold between them. "Come on in."

Nolan walked past her with her easy, grounded gait. The way she took in the space with a focused, respectful intensity made Maya's skin prickle. Uncomfortable with the strange reaction, Maya gestured toward the kitchen.

"Hope you don't mind working in the kitchen. It's presently the most habitable space."

"Sounds good," Nolan said, following her back. She settled in a chair at the big oak table and squared the file folder, bulging with papers, in front of her. The movement revealed the curve of her shoulders and the lean strength in her arms. Her fingers, calloused and careful, smoothed over the edge of the papers. She caught Maya looking and held her gaze for a long beat before looking away. "I can send you digital copies once we're settled on the details, but I like to work off the paper copies at this stage."

"That's great." Maya pulled her yellow pad and pen from a drawer under the counter, grateful for an excuse to turn away. Her pulse shouldn't be racing from something as simple as eye contact. "I'm a note-taker myself. I ordered pizza—it should be here soon. Can I get you something to drink? Water? Soda? Beer?"

"Any kind of soda's great," Nolan said quickly. "I've got to be up early. Demo day on another site."

"Sensible. Hope ginger ale is okay—I keep it on hand for sick days."

Nolan's brows rose. "Sick days?"

"Preschoolers are germ magnets. Dantas swore that ginger ale cured most ills." Maya stilled as the image of Dantas holding a crying Emmie on her lap while coaxing her to take "one little sip" of the warm soda rose unbidden in her memory. Her breath caught at the beauty of the remembrance and the unexpected absence of pain. She grabbed a glass, needing a moment to collect herself. Now was not the time to analyze the meaning of her conflicting feelings.

This was a business meeting. Nothing more.

She set the drink down on a coaster decorated with chickens, Emmie's current favorite animal, just as Emmie raced into the room in a blur of pink leggings and tangled curls.

"Mommy! Did the pizza come?" Emmie skidded to a stop and stared at Nolan, her entire body going still.

"Any time, sweetheart. This is Nolan. She's going to help us fix up the house." Maya waited. Emmie hadn't spent much time with strangers outside of preschool and therapy. There'd been no one new in their lives for months.

Nolan turned toward Emmie with a slow, genuine smile—not the quick, bright flash adults often used with children, but something softer, more patient. "Hey there. You must be Emmie."

Emmie blinked at her, uncertain, then moved behind Maya and clutched her leg, as if seeking safety.

Maya smoothed a hand over Emmie's head. "She's had a big week. She just started preschool a few days ago."

She offered the explanation not as an apology, but so Nolan would understand Emmie's reticence. Emmie's world had been shattered once already. Caution was her safety net now, and Maya would provide it as long as needed.

Nolan set her soda down, pushed back her chair, and crouched beside it. She didn't rush, didn't extend a hand. Just tilted her head like she was speaking to someone who mattered—who deserved time, and patience, and attention.

"Preschool, huh? That's a big step." Her voice dropped to match Emmie's energy, gentle but not condescending. "What's the funnest thing that happened all week?"

Emmie peeked out from behind Maya's leg, nodding slowly. "Lucy has a fish in a bowl named Glitter."

"No way. Glitter? That's awesome." Nolan's grin was bright, unguarded. "I always wanted a fish, but my dad said they were boring. I think he was just afraid he'd have to clean the tank."

Emmie giggled, the sound bubbling up, a little surprised, but genuine. "I painted her." She pointed to the fridge. "Look."

Nolan whistled. "Whoa—a purple fish with gold sparkles. Very cool."

The tightness in Maya's chest softened. Nolan's tone held no performance, no cloying sweetness or exaggerated interest. Just relaxed interest—natural and unforced, like breathing. Emmie's posture shifted. Still a little shy, but no longer closed. She was listening. Engaged. That hadn't happened with anyone outside the family since the accident.

The doorbell rang, and Emmie shot toward the hall. Maya caught her by the shoulder, suddenly protective again. "Let me get that, firecracker."

She paid the delivery driver and handed one of the boxes to Emmie. "Careful now. What do you do?"

"Not tilt it," Emmie exclaimed.

"Exactly. Give it to Nolan to put on the counter, okay?"

"Yes." Emmie took each step with care.

"Pepperoni or cheese?" Maya asked when she walked into the kitchen.

Nolan had already cleared space at the table, and Maya helped Emmie into her booster seat next to hers. Nolan sat across from her and started a conversation with Emmie about the merits of sparkly stickers versus the regular kind.

Maya passed out slices, laughing when Emmie tried to convince Nolan that unicorns were real and lived in the mountains behind the school. Nolan countered with a solemn "Only the invisible ones," which made Emmie squeal with delight.

Within minutes, Emmie turned into a chatterbox, and Nolan leaned in like she cared about every word. Watching them, that soft ache pressed behind Maya's ribs again. The ache of remembering who Emmie had been before the silence. Before the accident. Before the world taught her that happiness was fragile, that love could be taken without warning.

She wanted to freeze this moment, to preserve it and protect it. Keep it safe. She wanted to memorize the sound of Emmie's laughter mingling with Nolan's deeper chuckle. She wanted to hold on to the warmth blooming in her chest, unfamiliar yet exhilarating. Not something to dissect, just something to be happy for.

After Emmie polished off a second slice and a cup of milk, her eyelids started to droop. Maya lifted her from the booster seat before she was sound asleep.

"Okay, sweetie. Time for bed."

"Is Nolan going to fix up my room?" Emmie mumbled, eyes already half-closed.

"Yes, she is." Maya gently stroked a curl from Emmie's forehead. "That's the very first thing we'll plan."

Emmie cast a drowsy look at Nolan. "You're really coming back?"

Nolan's expression shifted from tenderness to a flash of something that almost looked like pain. "Definitely."

"Can you fix Mommy's clock? She cried because it got broke."

"Honey," Maya said quickly, "Nolan has to work on the house, and that's a big job."

"'Kay," Emmie murmured and closed her eyes.

Maya glanced at Nolan. "I won't be long if you can wait. I should have thought—"

"I'll be here," Nolan said. "Don't rush."

"Thanks." Maya carried Emmie down the hall, aware of Nolan watching them. She changed Emmie quickly into pajamas, helped her brush her teeth, and tucked her in with Sparkle the unicorn secured firmly under her arm.

Emmie was asleep before Maya even finished the first verse of her favorite bedtime song. That hadn't happened in weeks. Maya lingered, the steady rise and fall of Emmie's chest, the peaceful softness of her face in sleep, filling her with aching wonder. For a moment, she could almost imagine Dantas there beside her, whispering, "She's beautiful, isn't she?"

The ghost of that memory—sharp and sweet, sacred—made her eyes burn.

When she came back to the kitchen, Nolan had cleared the plates, stacked the pizza boxes neatly on the kitchen counter, and stood at the sink rinsing dishes. The folder sat open on the table beside a notepad and her ever-present pencil.

Maya blinked, caught off guard by the domesticity of the scene. "You didn't have to clean up."

Nolan glanced over her shoulder as she rinsed a plate and added it to the stack. "You cooked, I clean."

Maya laughed. "Hardly cooking, but I'll take it."

"Fair division of labor." Nolan shrugged, a fluid ripple of muscle beneath her shirt. "How bad is the clock?"

"What? Oh, sorry. She doesn't understand you can't just fix everything."

"I'm no clockmaker," Nolan said, "but if it's mostly outside damage, I might be able to."

"I can't ask you to do that," Maya said, flustered without knowing why.

Nolan shrugged again. "I've got a workshop at home, and I tinker when I have time. It might be fun."

"Thank you. I'll show it to you sometime, then." Maya sank into her chair, refusing to think about the oddity of having a near stranger in her space or why it didn't feel strange. "Okay. Hit me with the plan."

Nolan came around the table and sat beside her, her shoulder and thigh a breath away from Maya's. "We'll go room by room. I want to get the interior done so I'm out of your hair sooner."

Maya nodded, making notes as Nolan highlighted high-priority areas that required repair before the surface finishing—water damage, structural vulnerabilities, old wiring. The whole presentation was direct, focused, and orderly.

At each step, Nolan asked for her opinions, made some changes based on Maya's desires, and adjusted her notes.

Maya enjoyed every minute of the problem-solving. All a sign of moving forward.

"Look here," Nolan said, pointing to a floor plan sketched out on grid paper. "Emmie's room has no closet, which might not matter if this isn't her forever home, but if it is? A teenager will want their own place for clothes."

Maya looked at the plan, which now had a wall of closet space built in. "How could I have missed that?" She sat back, laughing quietly. "Believe me, I don't plan on doing this again. We're here for good."

"That's good." Nolan sounded so serious Maya turned in her chair to look at her.

And her knee ended up touching Nolan's. A jolt of warmth shot up her thigh. Nolan's eyes, this close, were not just blue but a flickering montage of indigo and gold. Stunning, and totally fixed on Maya's. Maya took a shallow breath, all she could manage, and eased away.

"What else did I miss?" Maya asked, barely recognizing the husky tone of her voice.

"Not much," Nolan murmured, leaning forward to pull up the plans for the den.

By the time they'd finished the last room, the clock on the microwave read 11:57.

Maya laughed under her breath. "We've been talking for four hours."

Nolan leaned back, stretching one arm over the back of her chair. The back of her hand brushed Maya's shoulder. "Didn't feel like it."

"No." Maya looked down at her notepad, suddenly unable to meet Nolan's eyes. "I don't remember the last time I did anything for that long without noticing time passing."

She didn't add how little she slept, or how damn hard it was to concentrate on something as simple as reading a book.

"You've got good instincts. That was a big help." Nolan grinned. "I can't remember the last time going over a proposal with a client was so much fun."

Maya's pulse quickened. Maybe it was the late hour, or the intimacy of sitting this close for so long, or the quiet hum in her blood, but she wanted to lean into it—and she wanted to run from it. She wanted distance between them, and the safety of space. She wanted something she couldn't name and didn't want to think about.

She pushed back her chair and stood, the room suddenly cooler without Nolan close beside her. "I should let you go. I bet an early start for you means first light."

Quickly, Nolan stood, too, and pushed the scattered papers back into the folder. She didn't look at Maya. "When you're ready to sign, I'll—"

"Give me that." Maya held out her hand, and Nolan passed her the proposal summary. She signed it and handed it back. "When can you start?"

"First thing Monday. If it's okay with you, I'll bring the dumpster over on the weekend so we can start the demo first thing."

"That's fine." Maya led her to the door. "Drive safe."

Nolan smiled. "I will. Thanks for dinner and the company."

"Same here."

Nolan paused on the threshold, the porch light casting flickering shadows across her face.

"You're doing a really good thing, you know," she said. "This house. A new school for Emmie. All of it."

The unexpected validation, simple and sincere, brought moisture to Maya's eyes, and she turned away. She couldn't remember the last time she'd felt something—anything—that wasn't grief or loneliness or the crushing weight of responsibility.

She swallowed the sudden lump in her throat. "I don't always feel like I am."

"Well…you are." Nolan's voice, so steady and certain, settled her.

"Thanks," she said.

Nolan met her gaze for another quiet moment before stepping out into the night.

Maya watched until the taillights disappeared around the curve, red pinpoints of light swallowed by darkness. She closed the door and leaned her forehead against it.

She was just tired—that had to be it. She'd driven God knew how many hours away from the life she'd known, and counted on, with her child and all her worldly possessions, less than two weeks ago. She'd spent months on an emotional ice floe where she'd refused to feel anything for fear she would crack.

Enjoying a few hours with a warm, kind woman was safe.

Wasn't it?

❖

Nolan didn't drive straight home.

She turned left instead of right at the light by the post office and let the road unwind beneath her tires without direction. Cool air rushed through the open windows carrying the sharp, almost metallic scent of spring growth and pine. It rushed over her, brisk and cleansing.

Not cool enough, though.

Her skin still too hot. Or maybe it wasn't her skin at all. Maybe the heat kindled inside, deep in some place the wind couldn't touch—

where embers glowed and sparked and threatened to consume what little peace she'd built.

She'd only meant to talk plans, timelines, and the material costs. Instead, she'd sat on Maya's table watching a little girl with glitter on her cheeks talk about invisible unicorns. She'd listened to Maya laugh—quiet, like the sound still surprised her—and something dangerous and undeniable inside had shifted. She'd gone in to discuss renovations and had come out with a storm in her chest.

She'd seen Maya. Really seen her.

As a mother who knew how to hold grief without letting it consume her daughter. As a woman who still smiled, even when it clearly cost her something. As someone who showed up, even when she was still finding her feet.

Maya wasn't pretending she was okay. She just kept going anyway. And God, she respected the hell out of Maya for that. She admired her strength, envied her endurance, and wished she had more to offer than a floor plan and a few words of cautious encouragement.

But that wasn't all the evening with Maya had stirred up. Not by a long shot.

She liked her. Liked her in a way that already kept her thinking about her way too much.

Too much, way too fast. And worse than that? Too real.

Where did that leave her? Keeping to her own damn side of the street, that's where. Doing the job Maya needed her to do and nothing more.

She turned onto Sycamore, Maya's street, and drove past the bungalow without slowing. She hadn't meant to be there, cruising past like some damn stalker, and she didn't mean to look. But she couldn't stop a quick glance.

The house was dark. Emmie was asleep, Maya maybe still awake, maybe not. Hopefully when she slept, some of the sadness she carried would lift.

Nolan wanted to go back just to sit on the porch. Just to be near that quiet she hadn't felt in years, to sit in the tranquil stillness that radiated from Maya even amidst chaos.

But she didn't. Wouldn't ask Maya to bear her problems, too.

She turned again, circling the back side of town past the shuttered pharmacy and the dark diner that would open in a few short hours. She drove aimlessly, the cold licking at her knuckles where she gripped the wheel—the steering wheel her father had once gripped just as tightly, driving home from bars with bloodshot eyes.

The town was asleep.

Stillness everywhere, no one moving. Except her. Always her, driving around alone, searching for peace and never finding it. But unlike *him*, she'd arrived home sober. She took a little pride in that as she pulled into the driveway.

She sat in the truck, engine ticking as it cooled, and stared at the darkened windows of her house, knowing exactly what waited inside.

Nothing.

No one calling her name as she opened the front door or to ask if she'd eaten. No one to miss her if she didn't come home.

She stepped inside and flicked on a light.

The house didn't welcome her. Only the emptiness yawned, all too familiar, like the cold reception of her father's place. That hadn't been her home, just the place she'd grown up in and left as quickly as she could. And here? Different paint, better bones here, but the same emptiness. Her boots echoed on the hardwood as she moved from room to room, each footfall a reminder of how alone she was.

She passed the second bedroom—still unfurnished, still waiting for a purpose it would never fulfill. Passed the hallway mirror and didn't look in it. She didn't need to see the echo of her father's face in her own. That image haunted her daily. She opened the kitchen cabinet where the bottle used to be.

It wasn't there and hadn't been in a long time. She scanned the shelves anyway, waiting for the need. When it didn't open like a hungry mouth inside her, she carefully closed the cabinet door and breathed out.

Reflex. That was all it was. Not temptation. Not desire. Just the ghost of what used to live in her like a thirsty shadow lurking beneath her skin. She filled a glass with water and drank half in one swallow while the unnaturally loud thump of the fridge compressor mimicked a mechanical heartbeat, the only living sound in the house.

The glass hit the counter harder than she intended.

She leaned on the counter, the wanting that still coursed through her veins a steady enticement almost too powerful to ignore. Almost.

She wasn't tempted. She was just tired. So fucking tired of fighting, of resisting, of wanting things she couldn't have.

She walked through the house turning off the lights. Pointless trying to illuminate a void, like trying to warm ice. She knew the way and what she'd find when she got there.

In the bedroom, she unlaced her boots, peeled off her shirt and pants, and sat on the edge of the bed, staring at the floor.

The space felt too big, even though the house was smaller than Maya's. Maya's house, with its warmth, and light, and the sound of Emmie's laughter, comforted rather than erased. The smell of pizza and ranch dressing said *people live here*. Maya, despite the exhaustion and sadness that shadowed her eyes and hollowed out her laughter, had managed to make her house come to life as Nolan's never had.

Nolan had sensed that life, had relaxed into it. Lying in the dark, she held on to the memory of sitting together, knees brushing, blueprints between them, silence humming like a shared song.

She exhaled into the dark.

That was enough. Had to be.

And this time, the silence didn't press but settled around her shoulders like a familiar embrace she'd never ask for. Like the comfort she'd never deserve.

Chapter Seven

Monday morning dawned crisp and clear. Nolan drove to Maya's a little before seven to start work on the house. Controlled chaos usually defined the first day on a new site, along with the anticipation of a fresh challenge. With new construction, the big equipment operators cleared the site and did initial grading before surveyors staked out the building perimeter. Home reno was a different animal. She'd have crews working in several rooms at once, diving in from the get-go. She pulled the Silverado onto the shoulder just past Maya's and sat organizing the paperwork—work permits, room layouts, and material lists—into a multi-pocket blue vinyl work folder she'd carry everywhere until job completion. She'd done plenty of contractor work in private residences, but nothing on this scale yet, so definitely an exciting opportunity. And then there was Maya.

Knowing she'd see Maya in the morning had made sleep elusive the night before. Silly, maybe, but real all the same. She'd half hoped Maya would come outside yesterday afternoon when she'd met the driver delivering the dumpster to the house, but no sign of her. Probably out doing something fun with Emmie. Nolan hoped so, despite the disappointment of not seeing her. Maya deserved all the happiness she could find.

And she would see her today, after all. Whistling softly, she climbed out of the truck, grabbed her tool belt and hard hat, and tucked the folder under her arm. Expecting an unusually warm afternoon, she'd layered a checked shirt over a blue tank top. Just as she reached the walkway, the front door opened and Maya and Emmie stepped out, hand in hand.

Nolan paused, trying not to stare. Maya's white, ribbed top was just form-fitting enough to accentuate her breasts without pointing a flashing arrow at them, and her slim-fitting khakis showed off shapely legs. She'd pulled her thick curls back into a careless ponytail and looked…terrific.

Nolan kick-started her brain and walked toward them. "Morning."

"Good morning. It's nice to see you again." Maya's smile, a little wan, still sent Nolan's heart racing. "Emmie and I were just going for a walk before school, weren't we, Em?"

Emmie twisted her foot and chewed on her lower lip, eyes downcast.

"Hi, Emmie." Nolan glanced at Maya. Not the same ebullient child she'd shared pizza with. Something was up. "Looking for unicorns?"

Emmie shrugged but finally met her gaze. "Are you fixing the house today?"

"Some of it. It will take me a while."

"The door's unlocked," Maya said. "Go ahead on in. Fresh coffee and muffins—store bought but pretty good—on the counter in the kitchen."

"Thanks," Nolan said. "I have to warn you, though, if you don't want my crew descending like locusts every morning, you'd better not offer food."

Maya laughed softly. "I rather like locusts."

Nolan grinned. "You've been warned."

"So noted." Maya's eyes met hers, alight for an instant, like the sun coming out after a storm.

Nolan couldn't look away.

Emmie continued to twist her foot into the gravel.

"Come on, Em," Maya said gently. "Let's go see what birds we can see today."

"Bye, Em." Nolan waved, but Emmie didn't, trailing a little behind Maya with her head down.

Nolan's chest ached. Maya and Emmie had both been wounded. She couldn't imagine the pain of losing a loved one, especially in such a shocking way. With nothing she could say, she at least had something she could do. She could help them make their new home what they dreamed of.

Resolved and more than ready to get started, she strode inside and stopped in the kitchen for a cup of coffee and a muffin. The latter tasted just fine, store-bought or not. Expecting Gruff and the crew any minute, she walked through the empty rooms, reviewing her work plan for the week. With Maya living in the house while the work progressed, they'd have to work in sections. The kitchen was a critical space and needed a lot of work. She'd have one crew start there while a couple of guys worked on Emmie's room, a smaller project. She'd told Emmie she would fix her room and didn't want to disappoint her.

Maya had already cleaned everything out of the kitchen cabinets. They could move the fridge and the table to the adjacent room. The dishwasher and stove were shot, so those they'd haul away.

"Nolan?" Maya called.

"Back here," Nolan said, walking down the hall. She checked the time. Not quite seven thirty.

Maya stood just inside the front door, her eyes reddened as if she'd been crying, or more likely, trying not to.

Nolan's stomach clenched. "Something wrong?"

"Izzy came by to take Emmie to school today so I could meet with you," Maya said. "Emmie didn't want to go, and it took both of us to get her to stop crying."

"That's rough," Nolan said softly.

"She clung to me, begged me not to go away." Maya shook her head, her lips trembling. "She didn't say it, but I could hear it in her sobs. Don't go away like Mommy D." Maya wrapped her arms around her middle. "Broke my heart."

Nolan planted her feet, resisting the urge to go to her and pull her close. Just to offer some comfort. "Why do you think it happened today? She seemed like she was having fun at preschool when she talked about it the other night."

Maya shook her head. "She had a nightmare and woke up crying, calling out for me. She hasn't had a night like that since Dantas—since my wife died." Maya scrubbed her face with both hands, a determined look replacing the fragile tears. "I think she's scared she's going to lose me, too. Maybe all the changes have been too fast—a new house, new school. So many adjustments."

Nolan shoved her fists into her pockets, forcing a calm she didn't feel. "Johnny told me a bit. I'm sorry. I can't even imagine what the two of you are going through."

"Emmie is so young," Maya said with a sigh. "All I can do is keep showing her I'm here, that I love her, that she doesn't have to be afraid."

"Looks to me like you're doing all that and more," Nolan said, "for what that's worth."

Maya met her gaze. "That's worth quite a lot. Thank you." She brushed her hair back from her face. "I was lucky that Johnny suggested you."

"I feel that same way. I'm glad Johnny trusted me to take care of you." Nolan flushed. "I mean—"

"Oh, you're not wrong. Johnny is a rough and tumble guy, but beneath all that, he's sensitive." Maya smiled, and the warmth of it hit Nolan like a lightning bolt to the heart. "After all, he must know a dozen contractors, but he knew *you* were just who we needed."

Hell. Maya didn't know they were AA buddies. Now wasn't the time to bring it up. That was her issue, and right now, Maya and Emmie were what mattered. She kept silent. What could she say? *You're so incredible, strong and kind and loving? I couldn't imagine a better mother?* Why would Maya believe her? If she knew…

"Emmie's made so much progress here recently," Maya continued. "I actually thought we were in for brighter days. But I guess not. Not yet anyway."

"I'm really sorry. If there's ever anything you need, just let me know." Nolan shrugged. "If you think we should delay getting started, if it's too much disruption, I can reschedule."

"No," Maya said firmly. "Just the opposite. Emmie was excited you were coming back. You were a hit the other night."

Nolan's face heated. "Well, I liked her, too."

"She needs new people in her life. Good, steady people. She—both of us—turned inward for too long, at least according to our family therapist." She laughed softly. "So you're apparently just what the doctor ordered."

Nolan's stomach soured. If Maya only knew just how much she was *not* that person. Good, steady, and reliable was exactly what she *hadn't* been until fifteen months, two weeks, and three days ago. And she was too damn selfish to tell her. She wanted to be the person Maya thought she was. She wanted to mean something to someone for once in her life. Cowardly to pretend she was who Maya thought her to be, yeah. But she already knew that.

"Like I said, anything you need, either of you, just say." She winced at the rumble of trucks pulling up outside. "That will be my guys. If you're sure?"

"Oh, I'm very sure." Maya took a step closer. "I want you to put me to work. I need that like Emmie needs you to talk to her about unicorns and glitter."

"I can do that."

"There's one more thing," Maya said.

Nolan breathed her scent—violets and sunshine. She recognized the subtleties of it now. She pushed her hands deeper into her pockets.

"Name it."

Maya glanced out toward the front yard where men and women called to one another and equipment clanged, adding hurriedly, "I haven't had a chance to explore the town too much, and it's been a few years since we visited. Know a good ice cream stand somewhere?"

"Sure. Scoops—fifteen minutes from here."

"Want to join us for a sundae after work tonight? Emmie would love it. If you don't have plans, I mean."

Plans? What could be better than spending an hour with an amazing woman and her little girl? "Nope. Calendar's clear. If you're sure."

"Absolutely," Maya said, sounding suddenly shy. "Emmie and I could use a little fun."

"Me too," Nolan said quietly.

"It's a date, then." Maya nodded, her shoulders lifting. "Then I guess we'd better get to work."

Nolan grinned. "You're the boss."

Maya's laughter settled in her chest like a small, bright flame.

❖

"You coming tonight, boss?" Gruff stopped next to Nolan as the rest of the crew piled into their vehicles and drove off with honking horns and waves. "It's Kennedy's birthday."

Nolan nodded. Flip Kennedy was a mainstay on the crew. If she didn't at least stop in for a while to celebrate, everyone would notice. And wonder. Keeping a bunch of guys and three women loyal and happy meant she needed to be one of them, as well as the boss.

"Yep. Got a few things to do, but I'll make it."

Gruff's wide smile said he'd been worried she'd bail. "Good first day. That Maya is a terror. Frannie put her to work stripping out that old carpet in the kid's room, and she didn't bat an eye about doing grunt work. I think she even had fun."

Nolan worked not to look as relieved as she felt. She'd been too busy to check on Maya more than a quick look-see all day, and in her spare moments, she'd worried about her. "Good to hear. And putting her with Frannie was a smart call."

Gruff ducked his head. "Thanks, boss. See you tonight."

Nolan waved as Gruff drove off and leaned against her truck, waiting for Maya to get back from Izzy's with Emmie.

The afternoon sun cast long shadows as the tension bled from her muscles in the warm air. She'd spent the morning ripping out old kitchen cabinets, carefully preserving any of the original hardwood trim that could be restored. She'd worked steadily, pausing only when her thoughts drifted to Maya—her quiet strength, the grace with which she shouldered her grief while still making space for joy with Emmie. And her amazement that Maya had suggested they all go out for ice cream.

She hadn't been this excited about anything in years. She shook her head. Maybe she was asking to be disappointed. She didn't exactly have a great track record in the relationship department, even though all Maya wanted was a friend. And even that was probably temporary. Eventually, Maya would make a new life with new people, and she would be part of the past.

Nolan's misgivings blew away on the breeze when Maya pulled into the drive and waved as she got Emmie out of the back seat. Now was what mattered.

Emmie spotted her and broke into a run. "Nolan! Mommy said you're taking us for ice cream."

Nolan crouched and caught Emmie in a hug before Emmie propelled herself into the street. "Sure am. You ready?"

"Yes!"

Maya rested a hand on Emmie's head as Nolan eased away. "Maybe Nolan will drive us in her truck."

Emmie stared at Nolan. "Can I sit up front?"

Nolan glanced at Maya. "It's a bench seat. She can sit between us."

"You'll get to wear a seat belt, Em." Maya took her hand. "Come on, I'll help you."

As Emmie raced to the truck, Maya turned to Nolan. "Is this okay?"

"It's great." Nolan brushed her arm lightly.

"Do you mind that she calls you Nolan?"

"Why would I? I answer to it." Nolan laughed. "Come on, let's go. We've got ice cream waiting."

Nolan drove with the windows down and the cab filled with Emmie's excited chatter. Nolan couldn't remember the last time she'd felt so relaxed. Or happy. "How was school today, Emmie?"

Emmie's smile faltered slightly. "It was okay. I painted a picture."

"Yeah? Of what?"

"A unicorn." Her voice dropped to a whisper. "With sparkles."

"Well, sure. No other kind, right?"

"Right!"

Maya said, "She did great today."

"Well, that sure sounds like ice cream is in order," Nolan said, meeting Maya's eyes over Emmie's head.

Maya smiled back, the quiet recognition of a shared victory.

"Can we get rainbow sprinkles?" Emmie asked.

"Absolutely," Nolan said.

The short drive to the ice cream parlor might as well have been a trip to another galaxy. When Nolan pulled into a parking spot in front of the roadside ice cream stand and watched Maya help Emmie climb out of the truck, contentment filled her, making her throat ache.

She circled the cab to join them, and Emmie held out her hand. She took it without thinking. Emmie's small fingers curling around hers knocked the breath from her chest.

Maya glanced down at their joined hands, a strange look passing over her face. "Let's eat outside at one of the tables. It's such a beautiful day."

"Sure," Nolan said.

They stood in line behind a boisterous trio of teens and a family with twin boys who looked to be about eight. Nolan had never done anything like this in her life. So simple. So stupidly perfect.

When their turn came, Emmie announced, "I want chocolate with sprinkles."

"Excellent choice," Nolan said. "I'm a chocolate fan myself."

Maya studied the flavors on the board by the server's window. "I'm thinking butter pecan."

"Sweet and a little salty," Nolan said. "That fits."

A faint blush colored Maya's cheek. "How so?"

Nolan's stomach dropped. Did she just blow it? Cross a line? "Just…you know. Complicated." That wasn't much better. "Not in a bad way. Layered."

Maya studied her as if she had three heads. "Okay. Thanks, I think."

Nolan wanted to punch herself in one of those three useless heads. Then Maya laughed, and the clouds lifted. Maya's gaze lingered on hers for a moment before she turned to order. The brief connection left Nolan feeling oddly exposed, like Maya had glimpsed something she hadn't meant to reveal.

They settled at a round picnic table with a rainbow-colored umbrella on the grassy lot beside the ice cream stand. Emmie attacked her ice cream in between chattering about Lucy's fish and how she helped change Glitter's water. Maya laughed, a real laugh, unrehearsed and light, and leaned over to wipe a smear of chocolate from Emmie's cheek. The sunlight played in her glossy hair and turned her bronze skin to gold.

Nolan couldn't look away.

"You've got a little…" Maya touched a finger gently to Nolan's chin.

Nolan dabbed at it.

"You missed," Maya said quietly.

Emmie giggled when Maya wiped Nolan's chin with another paper napkin.

"Thanks," Nolan said, the touch so unexpected her whole body tensed.

"Mommy says you're fixing our kitchen first," Emmie said. "Can I help?"

"Well," Nolan said, glancing at Maya for direction. Maya unhelpfully continued eating her ice cream. "I think, given your skill at painting, you can help pick the colors for the cabinets."

Emmie brightened.

"Purple?"

"Ah..." Nolan looked at Maya over Emmie's head and mouthed *help*.

Maya giggled. Actually enjoying the hole Nolan had dug for herself.

Nolan shot her a look. "What do *you* think, Maya?"

"For your room, absolutely," Maya said, taking pity on her. "For the kitchen, we might need something a bit more...kitcheny."

"Yellow," Emmie declared. "Like sunshine."

"Yellow could work," Nolan agreed. "Does that work?"

Maya's spoon paused halfway to her mouth, her eyes meeting Nolan's. "I think...yellow sounds perfect. Bright and warm."

"Like you," Emmie said, pointing her spoon at Nolan. "Your hair is like sunshine."

Nolan felt a flush creep up her neck. "Is it? Well, thank you."

"And Mommy's is like chocolate," Emmie continued, pleased with her observations. "And mine is like...like..."

"Caramel swirl," Maya supplied, twirling one of Emmie's curls around her finger.

By the time Emmie had nearly finished her ice cream, she'd grown quiet.

"Big day," Maya said as she wiped Emmie's face and hands and pulled her onto her lap. "About ready to go home, sweetie?"

Emmie nodded sleepily.

The drive back was quiet and peaceful. When Nolan pulled up in front of Maya's, she wished she had an excuse to stay.

"Thank you," Maya said softly when Nolan came around and opened Maya's door to help her out with Emmie. "For today. It was exactly what we needed."

"It was exactly what I needed, too," Nolan said, suddenly aware of how close they were.

Maya smiled, and for a heartbeat, the world seemed to still, possibility hanging suspended in the space between them.

"Are we home now, Mommy?" Emmie asked.

Maya blinked, and Nolan stepped back. "Yes, sweetheart."

Maya eased out of the truck, gathered Emmie into her arms, and looked at Nolan. "See you tomorrow?"

"Tomorrow," Nolan confirmed, the word feeling like a promise.

She watched them until Maya opened the door and stepped inside. Maya glanced over her shoulder for an instant and then was gone.

Nolan climbed into the truck and drove off, the sunset painting the sky in fierce oranges and gentle pinks. Something shifted inside her, subtle but unmistakable, as if a door had opened, just a crack, to a future she hadn't dared to imagine.

Chapter Eight

After a quick grilled cheese sandwich that Emmie barely stayed awake long enough to finish, Maya carried her down the hall. "Bedtime for you, sleepyhead."

Emmie, her head on Maya's shoulder, mumbled, "No bath?"

Maya laughed, making her way to the bedroom where Emmie's small bed sat against the wall opposite hers. "Not tonight. We'll have a morning bath tomorrow."

"'Kay." Emmie curled up, her favorite stuffed unicorn tucked close.

Maya kissed her forehead. "'Night, baby."

She paused at the door, waiting to be sure Emmie drifted off completely. The day had taken its toll—first the tearful morning drop-off, then the excitement of ice cream with Nolan.

"Sweet dreams," she whispered, heart swelling with tenderness.

When Emmie's face relaxed into peaceful slumber, Maya padded down the hall past rooms filled with ladders and drop cloths, the smell of sawdust and fresh paint lingering in the air. The house felt different. Still far from finished, but not so hollow anymore. As if the workers had awakened something dormant within its walls. Or maybe it wasn't just the renovation.

Maybe the work stirred something in her, too.

She grabbed a bottle of wine from the refrigerator and a glass from the cabinet, poured herself half a glass, and went out to the porch, leaving the door ajar in case Emmie called for her. The evening air held the last remnants of the day's warmth. Crickets chirped their nightly serenade in the tall grass beyond the yard. She settled onto the porch swing and took a sip, the swing creaking as she pushed it into motion with her foot. She couldn't remember the last time sitting alone had felt like peace rather than abandonment. Or when she'd forgotten the crushing weight of her grief even for a moment.

That answer came right away with a certainty that surprised her.

Earlier that day, with Nolan.

Maya closed her eyes, the afternoon replaying in her mind like a favorite movie. The way Emmie had warmed to Nolan so quickly, reaching for her hand without hesitation. The comfortable silence in the truck as they drove home, Emmie dozing between them. How Nolan had ducked her head and smiled when Emmie compared her hair to sunshine.

Innocent flashes of sweetness, unburdened by guilt or remorse.

And the moment—just a heartbeat, really—when Nolan had helped her from the truck, Emmie half-asleep in her arms. The shared look of recognition that had nothing to do with grief or obligation or the past. Something new. Something possible.

Even now, the memory electrified as some invisible tether loosened its grip. A terrifyingly unexpected and inexplicable sensation. She sighed, setting the confusion aside. Maybe she was just as tired as Emmie, and the wine had gone to her head.

Headlights swept across the yard, and Izzy turned into the drive in her ancient Subaru. Maya leaned her chin in her hand, elbow resting on her knee, as Izzy jumped out, balancing a covered dish in one hand.

"Thought you might need dinner," Izzy called softly as she climbed the porch steps. "Johnny said Nolan's crew worked you like a pack mule today."

"Tell Johnny, tell the world." Maya laughed, patting the swing beside her. "I helped tear out carpet. Hardly slave labor."

Izzy pointed to the dish. "Lasagna. Not as good as Mom's, but it'll keep you alive. You hungry?"

"Not now. Probably it will hit me at midnight."

"I'll put the food in the fridge," Izzy said as she walked inside. When she returned with a bottle of seltzer, she settled on the swing. "So. Tell me about your day."

Maya took another sip of her wine. How much to share? Especially when she couldn't sort it all in her own mind. "We sort of attacked the house on multiple fronts. The crew is great. Professional but fun. After

I picked Emmie up, we went for ice cream with Nolan." Maya smiled, recalling Emmie's happiness. "Emmie's already down for the count. She loved it."

"Ice cream, huh?" Izzy's tone carried a hint of something Maya couldn't quite place.

"Mm-hmm. After the rough morning Emmie had, I thought she needed a treat."

"And Nolan just happened to tag along?"

Maya shot her a look. "I invited her. She drove us over in her truck. Emmie loved that, too."

"Thoughtful of her." Izzy's voice remained carefully neutral.

"It was. And it helped. You should have seen Emmie laughing. I haven't heard her laugh like that since…" Maya swallowed hard. "In a while."

Izzy reached over and squeezed her hand. "That's good, Maya. Really good."

They sat in comfortable silence for a moment, the swing creaking softly beneath them.

"Johnny thinks highly of her," Izzy said eventually. "Says she's the most reliable contractor in the county."

"She seems to be. Very organized. Clear about everything."

"Mmm." Izzy set her seltzer bottle aside. "And you like her?"

Maya's cheeks warmed, and she was grateful for the evening shadows. "She's been kind to us. Emmie is comfortable with her."

"That's not what I asked."

"Iz—"

"I'm just saying, this is the most animated I've seen you in months."

Maya stared out at the darkening yard. "I barely know her."

"I don't want you to shut yourself away—that's the last thing I'd want for you. Nolan is just…" Izzy sighed. "Like you said. Practically a stranger. But I'm glad you're feeling…better."

"What I feel is grateful. For normalcy." Maya's voice caught. "For someone who doesn't look at me like I'm made of glass."

Izzy's expression softened. "Maya, honey. You're allowed to feel whatever you're feeling. Dantas would—"

"Don't." Maya held up a hand. "Please don't tell me what Dantas would want. I can't…I just can't."

Izzy fell silent, then nodded. “I’m sorry. That was stupid of me.”

Maya squeezed her hand. “No, it wasn’t. I just need space. A little time.”

“I know. I’m here.”

“And that’s why *we’re* here,” Maya said. “Because Emmie and I need you.”

“So now I’ll stop being the nosy big sister.”

Maya snorted. “As if.”

Maya relaxed as the stars emerged, and they talked of safer things—Johnny’s latest girlfriend, of whom Izzy approved, the summer play schedule at the theater in the park, enrolling Emmie in kindergarten in a few months. When Izzy finally stood to leave, she hesitated by the porch steps. “Johnny says she’s single. Has been for ages, apparently.”

Maya nearly choked on her last sip of wine. “Why would that matter to me?”

Izzy lifted a shoulder. “No reason. Just making conversation.”

“Good *night*, Iz.”

After Izzy left, Maya lingered on the porch, unable to shake the feeling that her sister had something on her mind she’d left unsaid. Izzy wasn’t usually the subtle type. Opinionated would sum up her usual approach.

Really, though, she was too damn tired, in body and soul, to worry about it.

Heaving herself up, she went inside, rinsed her glass in the kitchen sink, and headed to bed. Once there, with Emmie breathing softly across the room, sleep eluded her. She kept replaying snatches of the day—Nolan’s hand steadying her elbow as she climbed into the truck, the way the sunset had gilded her profile as they drove home, the inexplicable comfort of their shared silence.

It wasn’t *just* gratitude she felt. She knew that much.

What it was, exactly, she couldn’t define.

❖

The noise level in the Roadrunner was as headache-inducing as ever. Nolan slouched in a corner booth, nursing a Coke. She’d raised her glass with the rest of the crew to wish Kennedy a happy birthday, but that had been an hour ago. She had no reason to stay, but she had.

She knew why. For the same reason as always. To prove to Gruff and the others that she was fine, perfectly happy in her carefully constructed life. She stared at the melting ice in her flat Coke and called bullshit on that. She was there trying to prove to herself that *she* liked her life just fine.

That lie was getting harder to believe every day. Tonight, when all she could think about was the drive home from the ice cream stand, Emmie dozing between them and Maya's profile softened by the evening light, the lie shredded like petals in a thunderstorm.

She hadn't made a life so much as run from one.

She pushed the Coke aside and stood up. Time to leave.

"Yo, Nolan. Not going yet, are you?" Gruff shouted above the din. He crowded closer in the packed bar, an attractive brunette Nolan didn't recognize at his side. Somewhere in her thirties, a short-sleeved yellow shirt stretched to the limit over full breasts, a tight black pencil skirt, and skyscraper heels.

Nolan's stomach tightened. Gruff had that look that said he was over his limit and up to no good.

"Here she is," Gruff announced as he drew the brunette a step forward. "Janet, this is Nolan Wright. My friend Nolan. My very *single* friend. Nolan, this is Janet. She's also very single. And she's been dying to meet you."

Nolan forced a smile. "Nice to meet you."

Janet smiled. "Hi. Gruff's been telling me all about you. And he said it would be better if I just came right over here instead of waiting for you to come to me."

Gruff stared down at his feet. Had she missed something? When she had occasionally, very occasionally, sought female company, she sure didn't look for it at the Roadrunner. Not with all her crew around, for cripes' sake. Gruff must really be loaded. Damn it.

A few hours ago, she'd been sitting in the sunshine with Maya and Emmie, feeling more alive than she had in years. Now here she was, back in the same dark corner she'd occupied a hundred times before.

Nolan sidestepped. "Well, it's very nice to meet you, Janet, but I think I'm going to call it a night."

Janet looked surprised. “Oh, but I was hoping—”

Gruff cut in. “Can you hold the booth with Janet while I get us another round, Nolan? Won’t take but a minute.” He motioned for Janet to scoot into the booth and hurried back to the bar without waiting for Nolan to answer.

Faced with being a rude a-hole, Nolan relented and slid in across from Janet.

“So Gruff tells me you’re a contractor.” Janet shifted in her seat and toyed with the oversized beads that draped her chest.

“I am.”

“That means you build things, right?”

“Mm-hmm.”

“I bet you’re strong.” A hint of a smile appeared.

Nolan recognized the flirtation but, other than annoyance, had no response. Once, she might have found Janet’s suggestive gaze and playful smile interesting. Once, she might have welcomed the distraction, the mutual, if probably temporary, connection. But now all she could think of was the way Maya had touched her chin to wipe away a spot of ice cream, how that simple contact had sent warmth flooding through her. How she’d been more moved by that than the possibility of a night of sex that would leave her empty in the morning.

“You sort of have to be to do the work I do,” Nolan said.

“You look strong.”

Gruff came back with a fresh Coke for Nolan and a glass of beer for Janet. “Here you go. I just saw Randy come in. Gotta grab him before he disappears.”

With that, Gruff hightailed it into the crowd.

“He’s so nice,” Janet said.

Nolan nodded and sipped her new Coke.

Janet studied her quietly. “You don’t want to be here, do you?”

Nolan met her gaze. “Not really. No offense to you, I just—”

“I understand. Gruff said you didn’t really like socializing.”

Nolan leaned back. She was going to kill him. “He did, did he?”

“He said you’re a bit shy. That I would have to take the lead.”

Nolan laughed softly. If only it were that simple. How could she explain the growing realization that she wanted something more than what this familiar dance could offer?

"Is that true? Do I need to take the lead?"

Janet's dark eyes, heavy-lidded and faintly predatory, slowly took her in. Her gaze offered something wild, something that some other time might have been tempting. But the memory of Maya's eyes, so different with their depth of strength and vulnerability, held her captive.

"Not that I'd mind, if things were different, but I'm tired and was just about to head home." She fished some cash from her wallet and left it on the table. "I'm sorry I'm not up for company."

Janet gripped her hand. "It's okay. I'm not really wanting to stay either. Do you think you could give me a lift home?"

Nolan searched for Gruff, then reconsidered. He was in no shape to drive anyone home.

"Please? I'd really appreciate it." Janet smiled.

Nolan withdrew her hand. She couldn't very well leave a woman stranded in a bar after midnight. "Sure, let's go."

Nolan's phone dinged as she walked Janet across the lot to her truck. She checked the screen and grimaced. Gruff had sent her a thumbs-up emoji.

"Here we are," she said, opening the door for Janet.

Janet climbed in and closed her door. "Nice truck."

"Thanks."

"It suits you. All rough and ready."

As Nolan drove from the parking lot, Janet inched closer on the bench seat where Emmie and Maya had been hours earlier. The night, dark and cool, so different from the golden afternoon hours, closed in. Nolan gripped the wheel with both hands and followed Janet's directions, easing her discomfort by envisioning the morning's work—the lumber stacked in Maya's yard, the plans spread across the big oak table, Emmie's unicorn drawing Maya had made sure stayed taped to the refrigerator.

Eventually, Nolan found the small cottage where Janet explained she was house-sitting for an old college friend. Nolan parked by the front yard. A faint light by the door illuminated the small porch. "I'll wait until you're inside."

Janet didn't open the door. Instead, she released her seat belt and slid a bit closer, her hand curling over Nolan's thigh. "You think you might want to come inside? It's nice and quiet. I could make you a drink. Maybe even rub your shoulders, since you're so tired. I'm really good at it, you know. I'm a massage therapist."

Nolan glanced at the hand resting on her leg. Another night, she might have accepted the invitation, but her mind was elsewhere. Tenderness unfurled in her chest as she pictured sitting on a rainbow-colored picnic bench watching Maya throw her head back in laughter.

"I should probably get home."

Janet inched closer, close enough to kiss. "Another time?"

Nolan had nothing against a safe, uncomplicated time with a nice woman. She'd sought that simple comfort, maybe settled for that, enough times to know that wasn't what she wanted. Not anymore.

Nolan drew away. "I'm not looking for anything personal. Not right now."

Or maybe she was, just not with Janet. The thought ambushed her and left her reeling.

"Oh. Okay. 'Night then." Janet hurriedly got out and walked to the house without looking back.

Nolan waited until Janet was inside before driving away, trying not to feel guilty about making Janet uncomfortable. *Thanks a lot, Gruff.*

He probably thought he was doing her a favor.

Once upon a time, he might have been. Hell, if Janet had been Maya, would she have turned her down?

Nolan caught her breath. Maya would never be that woman. Maya would never be a casual fling.

Maya was a woman still grieving the love of her life. A woman with a child, with roots and responsibilities. A woman who deserved someone solid and whole, not someone patching themselves together day by day, meeting by meeting.

Nolan cursed as another thought buffeted her tired brain. About having a drink.

No. That wasn't who she was anymore either. She might not deserve Maya—might not deserve anything close to what Maya represented—but she'd worked too hard to throw away her sobriety over one confusing evening.

She held on to that conviction until she reached home and logged onto an online meeting. She talked about the challenges and cravings, but not about the real reason her heart raced in her chest. Not about the revelation that she wanted more than sobriety, more than work, more than the carefully constructed boundaries of her recovery.

She wanted a chance at something she'd never believed possible for someone like her—a family, a home filled with laughter, a future built on more than just avoiding the mistakes of her past.

She wanted Maya.

Chapter Nine

Spring, mid-May

Five minutes after Maya settled onto the porch swing with a glass of iced tea, Izzy pulled into the drive. Before the Subaru even completely stopped, Emmie's excited chatter reached her. With a soft groan, Maya rose to greet them. To her eternal gratitude, Izzy freed Emmie from her car seat and lifted her out before Maya had to assist.

She wasn't sure she had it in her to hoist forty pounds of squirming child. Her arms felt like noodles, and her back ached and burned. Six weeks. Six weeks of hauling, lifting, measuring, and learning. Six weeks of falling into bed bone-tired but satisfied in a way she hadn't felt since…well, since before. True to her word, Nolan had let her help every step of the way, making sure one of the crew took the time to show her what to do. Her muscles had adapted, somewhat. Her palms had calluses. And the ever-present constriction inside her chest had loosened, just a fraction.

Despite her pain and fatigue, she was in an incredible mood. So much of the major kitchen demo was already done. True, the kitchen was unrecognizable, but boy was it going to look amazing when finished. Emmie's room was done except for taping the new drywall, painting, finishing the trim, and putting down the new carpet. The carpet was not the bright purple Emmie had asked for but a nice lilac with a muted gray pattern that would hide the inevitable stains. She laughed to herself. Yeah, just all that left.

"Mommy." Emmie broke into a run as soon as Izzy set her down. Maya braced for impact.

"Easy there, hurricane," Izzy called, but it was too late. Emmie crashed into Maya's legs, nearly toppling her backward.

"Hi, baby." Maya crouched to give her a hug. Her thighs screamed. She tried not to.

"Sorry about that," Izzy said, Emmie's unicorn backpack dangling from one finger. "She's been buzzing about unicorns all day. Again."

Maya caught the speculative look in Izzy's eyes and felt heat creep into her cheeks. "What?"

"Nothing." Izzy shrugged, her lips twitching. "You just look… different. And I don't mean the dust in your hair or the—is that sawdust on your shirt?"

Maya brushed ineffectually at her clothes. Hopeless. "Drywall, actually. We're almost ready for the last round of major work in Emmie's room."

"We? As in you and Nolan?"

God, Izzy could be a noodge. There was no *her and Nolan*. Maya cleared her throat. "And her crew. They're all great."

"Mm-hmm." Izzy grinned. "I'm sure there must be a few more people involved, but you've mentioned Nolan at least seventeen times this week alone. I've been counting."

"I have not…" But the protest died in her throat. Had she? Possibly. Probably. Definitely.

Nolan *did* tend to appear whenever she was learning something new, but that was just natural. She was responsible, after all.

"She's just…patient. Shows me how to do things right." Like how to measure twice, cut once. Like how to swing a hammer without catching her thumb. Like how to laugh again, even covered in drywall dust and sweat.

"It's okay, you know." Izzy's voice softened. "To enjoy someone's company."

Maya's stomach tightened. It wasn't that simple. Was it?

Izzy checked her watch. "I've got to run. Brian is dropping the boys off tonight."

"Big weekend plans?"

Izzy grimaced and glanced at Emmie, who'd parked herself on the swing next to Maya with a picture book. "I suspect Brian has something special going on with his flavor of the month since he checked with me three times today to be sure I could take them." She rolled her eyes. "As if I wouldn't want to see my own kids anytime."

Maya had never much liked her brother-in-law, but he never shirked child support or seeing the boys. Izzy seemed happier after their divorce, too, and that's all she cared about. "Why don't you come over tomorrow, and we'll barbecue. The boys love exploring in the woods."

"I don't see a grill anywhere," Izzy noted.

Maya laughed. "So we'll get one."

"I'll bring food."

"Call me in the morning, and we'll menu plan."

Izzy snorted. "Um, beyond burgers and beans?"

"Maybe something for adults, like…oh, I don't know, chicken."

"Talk to you in the morning, then. Bye, Em," Izzy said.

"Bye," Emmie said quietly.

"How was school?" Maya asked Emmie as Izzy drove away.

Emmie didn't look up from her book. "It was okay."

"Just okay?"

"Uh-huh."

"Is something wrong?"

Emmie shrugged.

Maya mentally ran down the list of possible problems, which was short. "Something happen at school?"

Emmie shook her head.

"Are you still upset with me? Because I'm busy, and you have to go to preschool?"

"No," Emmie said, not the least bit convincingly.

Maya hugged her. "It's okay to be upset, Emmie. It's okay even to be mad at me. You can tell me. I promise *I* won't be mad."

"I don't ever want you to leave."

The words stabbed at her heart.

Emmie wasn't angry. Scared still. Going on two months since the move, and with the reno in full swing, they were still rebuilding more than just cabinets and countertops.

"I'm not going anywhere, Emmie."

"But Mommy D didn't come back."

God, it still hurt. A knife between the ribs, every time. Maya swallowed hard. "That was an accident. A terrible, tragic accident."

"I don't want you to get in an accident."

"Oh, honey. You don't have to worry about that. I'll be very careful. I'll be just fine." The words tasted like ash, like the lies they were. How could she promise safety in a world that had already shown its jagged teeth? But she said them anyway, because that's what parents did. They lied about safety and monsters under the bed and how everything would be okay, because the alternative was too much for small shoulders to bear.

"Promise?"

"I promise you I will always do everything I can to come back to you. Okay?" She held out her little finger. "I pinkie swear it."

Emmie's tiny finger wrapped around hers, a pact sealed in trust. Maya's throat burned. Somehow, she had to rebuild Emmie's trust in the world. "How about some dinner?"

"But we don't have a kitchen."

"We've still got a microwave. And we've got that leftover mac and cheese."

"Okay." Emmie jumped down from the swing and followed Maya into the kitchen. "Can I get a unicorn tattoo?"

Maya's brain hiccoughed with the change in subject. "I'm sorry. What? How do you know about tattoos?"

"Nolan has one," Emmie announced, as if that was all the reason necessary. "I saw it when she took off her shirt."

Maya nearly dropped the casserole dish. Nolan took off her…oh, right. The long-sleeved shirt she often arrived in and removed when it got warm in the afternoon. The image of Nolan in a tight tee, arms corded with muscle, and the small compass tattoo on her deltoid popped into her mind. And she just as quickly chased it away. "Tattoos are for grown-ups, sweetie. So not for a little while."

Like fifteen years or so.

"Okay," Emmie said. "Nolan said that, too."

Really? Of course Nolan would say the right thing. She had a natural way with Emmie. And was fast becoming Emmie's hero. Maybe that was a problem, but Maya just couldn't get worked up about it when Emmie needed positive people around her.

"Well, then, we all agree."

"She said maybe a magical unicorn, if I still wanted one later."

"Did she," Maya said, sliding the leftovers into the microwave.

A magical tattoo. Of course Nolan would play along with Emmie's unicorn obsession, because that made Emmie happy. Keeping Nolan firmly in the contractor box got harder every day, especially after weeks of coffee-bringing and late-evening planning sessions.

"Yep, she says unicorns like purple best, too," Emmie continued, oblivious to the tangle of thoughts behind Maya's carefully neutral expression. "She said we could make a special purple paint that sparkles."

"Wait—paint for what?" Maya set the steaming dish in front of Emmie.

Emmie gazed at her as if she should have been following. "For its house."

Oh, of course. What house? Clearly they had moved on to another conversation.

"Mommy, are you listening?"

"I am, I swear!"

"That's what you always said when Mommy D asked, too." Emmie's voice held no sorrow, just matter-of-fact acknowledgment.

And there it was—that casual mention that could still steal Maya's breath. But the sharp pain had dulled, somehow. Maybe the demolition had stripped away more than just the damage on the walls.

Maya sat beside Emmie and ate, although her appetite had fled. Emmie seemed to be taking the changes better than her sometimes, and for that she was grateful. Grateful for Nolan.

"Can Nolan come to the barbecue tomorrow?" Emmie asked suddenly.

So she'd been listening to that conversation with Izzy. Of course she had. She heard everything.

"It's the weekend, sweetie. She's probably busy." And why wouldn't she be? Nolan was single and great-looking. She must have better things to do than hang around with a woman and her child.

"You could ask her," Emmie said stubbornly.

Maya sighed. She wouldn't mind help dragging a barbecue grill home, and she couldn't ask Nolan to do that without offering to feed her, could she?

"We'll see. Finish your dinner, then it's bath time."

Later, with Emmie tucked safely into bed, Maya stood in the ruins of what would eventually become their kitchen again. When she'd made the decision to leave Chicago a year after the accident, she'd been drowning in grief and responsibility. Now she was still drowning, maybe, but there were moments—moments like this—when her head broke the surface and she could breathe.

Tearing down was cathartic, but building back up…that was something else entirely. Something that felt dangerously close to hope.

And what was hope if not change?

Eight o'clock. Not too late to text.

Hi. I need to buy a barbecue grill in the morning. Assistance requested. Payment: food from said grill. Interested?

The answer came back instantly.

You bet. 9 too early?

9 is perfect. Maya smiled at the thumbs-up response. So Nolan. Direct, no games, always reliable.

Just what she needed in a friend.

The Saturday afternoon sun beat down on Maya's backyard, warming her shoulders as she set out paper plates on the rickety card table Izzy had unearthed from her garage. From her perch on the back porch, she had a perfect view of the scene unfolding on the patchy grass below—Nolan cross-legged on an old blanket, surrounded by parts of the new grill, with Emmie and Izzy's boys, Manny and Luis, circled around her like eager disciples.

"Hand me that Phillips head, buddy," Nolan said to ten-year-old Manny, who scrambled to find the right screwdriver in the small toolbox on the ground beside them.

Eight-year-old Luis peered at the instruction sheet. "It says to put the wheels on first," he announced with authority, pushing his glasses up his nose.

Nolan gave a serious nod. "You're absolutely right. Good catch."

Emmie, determined not to be outdone, pointed to a small metal piece. "What's this for?"

Nolan turned it over in her hand. "That's the thermometer. Very important."

"Can I hold it?" Emmie asked, eyes wide.

"Absolutely. You're my official parts manager."

Emmie clutched the piece to her chest, beaming.

"She's good with them," Izzy said quietly, appearing at Maya's side with a bowl of potato salad. "I didn't expect that."

Maya glanced over. "Why not?"

Izzy shrugged in that way she had of not saying what she was thinking. "I don't know. Just…kids require special handling. Respectful, but with boundaries."

"That sounds just like Nolan to me." Maya heard the defensiveness in her tone but didn't care. Izzy seemed to have something against Nolan. Subtle, but there.

"Maybe you're right." Izzy shook her head. "'Cause look at her now."

Maya did look. She'd been stealing sneak peeks for an hour. Nolan had tied a dark blue bandana around her unruly hair, as she often did when she worked, and stray strands escaped to frame her face. Her worn jeans had a hole in one knee, and her faded blue T-shirt had ridden up slightly as she leaned forward, revealing a strip of tanned skin at her lower back. When she laughed at something Manny said, the sound carried across the yard, warm and genuine. All three kids giggled.

"She's been great with Emmie from day one," Maya said, setting out plastic cutlery with more focus than the task required.

"Yeah, so you've mentioned. Several times." Izzy bumped her shoulder. "I'm glad it's working out."

Maya busied herself arranging napkins. "She's a good contractor."

"Mm-hmm. And I'm the Queen of England."

"What exactly are you implying, Your Majesty?"

Izzy sighed. "Nothing. I just…" She paused, apparently choosing her words carefully. "I want you to be happy, but…" She sighed. "Never mind."

"It's not…" Maya swallowed the reflexive denial.

What wasn't it, exactly? What Izzy suggested? Appropriate? Possible?

What was *she* denying? And why? She'd spent a lot of energy pretending not to notice what had been there the whole time. The flutter in her chest whenever Nolan walked into a room, chalking it up to gratitude, to relief, to anything but what it might actually be. Oh, maybe not right away, and maybe not even now, but something. Something more than simple.

Below them, Nolan showed Emmie how to tighten a bolt, her hand covering Emmie's tiny one on the wrench, guiding the movement with gentle patience.

"She put the grill together faster than Brian ever did," Izzy commented. "And without swearing once. So she gets points for that."

Maya smiled despite herself. "Low bar."

"The lowest. But still." Izzy studied her for a moment. "She surprises you, too, doesn't she?"

Maya considered the question, watching as Nolan effortlessly lifted the heaviest piece of the grill into place, used to the way her muscles flexed when she worked, but still enjoying the sight.

"Yes," she admitted finally. "She does."

She didn't want Izzy to know Nolan more than surprised her. Nolan intrigued her.

Something about Nolan didn't quite add up. Most of the time she exuded confidence and competence, but glimpses of vulnerability darkened the depths of her eyes at unexpected moments, too. She always seemed to be holding something back. Nolan had secrets. Who didn't?

The more Maya was around her, the less she knew, and the more she wanted to. She wanted to know what lay beneath the surface, to understand that quiet strength and where she went when the shadows crossed her face.

Admitting that set off warning bells about moving too fast, about betraying memories still fresh and raw. Despite the uncertainty, the guilt that rose up even now, she still wanted to know. That was enough to keep her thoughts from Izzy. For now at least.

"Done," Nolan called triumphantly, standing back to admire her handiwork.

The boys high-fived each other while Emmie danced in circles around the assembled grill.

"We did it," Emmie announced, racing up the porch steps. "We built a barbecue." She threw herself into Maya's lap, face flushed with excitement.

"I saw." Maya laughed and stroked Emmie's wild curls. "You were a very good helper."

"I was the parts manager," Emmie said solemnly. "It's 'sponsible."

"Very responsible." Maya's spirits soared to see Emmie's joy.

These moments of pure, uncomplicated happiness, unshaded by grief or worry, had been absent for over a year.

Nolan crossed the yard, wiping her hands on a rag. Manny and Luis had already disappeared around the side of the house, shouting about exploring the woods.

"Ready for the inaugural grilling?" she asked. "I'm about to do a test run and fire it up."

"Better you than me," Maya said. "I'm terrible with grills."

"Good thing I'm here, then." Nolan's gaze lingered on hers, and Maya felt that now-familiar warmth spreading through her chest.

"Yes," she said quietly. "Good thing."

The moment stretched between them, taut with unspoken words, until Izzy cleared her throat. "I'll get the burgers."

Maya stretched and glanced at her watch. "I think I'm ready for a glass of wine. I don't expect to be driving anywhere for a few hours."

When she looked at Nolan questioningly, Nolan held up her screwdriver with a grin. "None for me. I may still be required to operate heavy equipment here."

Maya laughed. "Very responsible of you."

"Safety first," Nolan said, looking over to Izzy. "I brought Coke in the cooler. I'm good with that."

Izzy's expression blanked for an instant before she said, "You two stay out here and listen for any bloodcurdling screams from the direction of the woods. Libations on the way."

Emmie tugged at Nolan's hand. "Can we roast marshwallows?"

"Marshmallows," Maya corrected automatically.

"Maybe later, after dinner, if your mom says." Nolan crouched to Emmie's level. "I'll show you how to make them just perfect—golden brown on the outside, all gooey inside."

"Promise?"

"Pinkie promise." Nolan held out her little finger, and Emmie linked hers with it, their faces mirroring the same solemn expression.

Watching such a poignant moment, Maya accepted the joy that had seemed impossible when she'd arrived from Chicago, when the weight of loss had eclipsed everything else. But now…now she stood in the warm afternoon light, watching her daughter laugh with a woman who could build things with her hands and fix what was broken. A woman Maya suddenly, startlingly, realized made her happy, too.

Emmie ran inside to find Izzy, leaving Maya and Nolan alone on the porch. Nolan leaned against the railing, the sunlight catching in her hair.

"Thank you," Maya said. "For coming today. For all of this."

Nolan shrugged, but Maya could see the pleasure in her eyes. "Building things is what I do. I'm still waiting for that clock, you know."

Maya flushed. "All right, I'll get it for you before you leave. But I meant with Emmie and the boys. You're good with them."

"They make it easy. Emmie's a special kid. Smart. Resilient." Nolan looked out over the yard. "Like her mother."

"Tougher than her mother," Maya said without thinking.

Nolan's gaze snapped back to hers, intense and unreadable. "You're the one who teaches her to be strong."

Electricity passed between them, a current Maya couldn't name and didn't dare examine too closely. All she knew was that for the first time in longer than she could remember, she felt fully present in her own skin, awake to possibilities she'd thought were closed to her forever.

Izzy burst back onto the porch with a plate of burgers, Emmie on her heels. "Let's fire this baby up!"

As Nolan took the plate and headed down to the grill, Maya soaked in the easy flow of her movements, admiring the confident set of her shoulders. She allowed herself, just for a moment, to acknowledge the truth she'd been sidestepping for weeks.

She was drawn to Nolan. Fascinated by her. She wanted to know her stories, her thoughts, what made her smile…and what kept her awake at night. She wanted more than just a contractor-client relationship. Maybe more than ordinary friendship.

The realization should have frightened her, should have sent her retreating behind the walls of grief and obligation that she thought would always define her world. Instead, the possibility of more, even just carefree time like this, opened a window in a too-long shuttered place inside her—terrifying, yes, but also finally allowing her to breathe.

"Are you coming to help?" Nolan called from the yard, the late-afternoon sun haloing her silhouette.

Maya took a deep breath and stepped off the porch.

"Yes," she said. "I'm coming."

CHAPTER TEN

Nolan hummed as she drove up the road to Maya's, the barbecue still lingering in her mind almost a week later—the rich scent of charcoal, the sound of laughter, the feeling of belonging, however temporary. How Maya and Izzy moved around each other with the ease of sisters, anticipating each other's needs, sharing glances that carried whole conversations. How Emmie's sticky fingers gripped hers as they toasted marshmallows over glowing coals and the boys roughhoused in the yard, their untamed energy vibrating through the air.

The afternoon had felt like family. Like home. Like everything she'd never had and never thought she'd want.

Seeing what she'd never known awakened a hunger so deep she hadn't even recognized it until last night, lying in her empty house with the silence pressing in from all sides. She'd tried to push down that foolish longing. What did she know about family? The closest she'd come to having one had been in the Army, and even then, she'd kept her distance and her secrets. Even then, she'd escaped her pain and confusion with alcohol. People like her—people who'd never learned to love—didn't get happy endings with ready-made families. They got silent houses and solitary meals and the cold comfort of knowing they were paying for their sins.

But the memory of Maya stepping off that porch, eyes locked on hers, saying "I'm coming"—those two simple words had kept her awake half the night, heart hammering against her ribs.

Nolan drummed her fingers on the steering wheel. Maya had looked tired lately, and Izzy had teased her about being out of shape. Maybe Maya was overdoing the apprentice thing a little. When she'd started, she'd barely had any hands-on experience, but anything Nolan had asked her to do, she'd done without complaining. Just another thing she admired about Maya: her unwillingness to give in, even when things were hard. Maya had said she needed to work, and Nolan got that, too. When the devil plagued her, she'd work. Sweat and sore muscles, along with the satisfaction of making something with her own hands, often chased the demons away. For Maya, too, she guessed.

She pulled into the drive, the first to arrive, as usual. She grabbed her thermos and her tool belt and climbed out. Emmie hopped down the porch steps with a purple backpack on, carrying a matching nylon lunchbox.

"You're up early," Nolan said.

Emmie jumped off the last step and looked up at her. "Hi, Nolan."

"And how are you today?"

"Good." She swung her lunchbox. The dings and scratches suggested it was a favorite.

Nolan pointed to the cartoon images on the side. "Who are they?"

Emmie studied her lunchbox. "It's My Little Pony."

"Right," Nolan said, totally clueless.

"See this one?" Emmie pointed to a blue pony. "She's a unicorn. She's my favorite."

"Well, sure. Does she have a name?"

"Uh-huh." Emmie's face clouded. "Trixie Lulamoon."

"Wow, that's a cool name."

"Uh-huh." Emmie rubbed her toe on the ground. "My mommy said she's magical."

"Must be true, then," Nolan said as Maya walked out.

"That's right," Maya said, her voice strained. "Mommy D said Lulamoon was one of a kind, just like you, sweetie."

"Do I have to go to school today?" Emmie asked suddenly.

Nolan's stomach dropped. Damn it. What had she stirred up? How was she supposed to know talking about cartoon horses would make Emmie sad? She glanced at Maya and grimaced.

Maya shook her head. "Yes, Emmie, you have to go to school. Today is numbers day, remember? And you'll get to show everyone how high you can count."

"But I was going to tell Nolan about all the other ponies."

"You can do that another time. Right now, we've got to go to Izzy's, or we're going to be late."

Emmie slouched. "Alright."

"Hey." Nolan crouched to eye level. "You can show me later today, okay?"

"You'll still be here?"

"I'll wait for you."

Emmie's smile blossomed. "Okay."

"You don't have to do that," Maya said. "But it's really nice of you."

"No problem. I happen to love my little ponies."

Maya laughed. "Do you now?"

"Sure do."

Maya's eyes sparkled. "Well then, you should know they're called My Little *Pony*."

"Oh. I knew that."

Laughing, Maya took Emmie's hand. "Let's go, you."

Nolan waited to go inside, watching them drive away, the now-familiar ache blooming inside. Emmie and Maya had had a whole other life before she'd met them. An obviously full, spectacular life. She'd do herself a favor remembering that, because nothing she could offer them would ever compare. She'd never be more than a temporary fixture in their lives. The contractor who fixed their house, who made Emmie laugh, who sometimes caught Maya looking at her with an expression that made her palms sweat and her mouth go dry.

But being temporary didn't stop her from wanting. Didn't stop her at all.

Waiting for the crew to arrive, she did her usual walk-through, examining the work so far. The kitchen walls were prepped and, after the painting was done, ready for cabinet installation. Once the base units were in, they could measure for the stone countertops Maya wanted. With luck, the counter guys could get them done and delivered in two weeks on the outside.

Emmie's room needed carpet once the final coat of paint went on, slated for early next week. Satisfied they were mostly on schedule, she walked outside to meet the delivery that was due at eight. Fran's crew arrived, and she sent them to start on the hall bathroom. Just as the delivery truck backed into the driveway, Maya pulled to the side of the road in front of the house.

Maya hurried up, face flushed. "What are we getting?"

The morning light caught in her hair, turning the dark curls to mahogany. Her face glowed, and when she smiled, Nolan's entire body responded like a tuning fork struck against stone. Damn, she was beautiful.

"Uh, cabinets," Nolan said, trying to pull her gaze away and failing miserably.

"You want it all in there?" The driver, a middle-aged guy in a neat blue uniform, pointed to the open garage.

"Yep."

A younger guy, looking faintly bored, climbed down from the cab, and the two men hauled the boxes into the garage.

"I need to check these," Nolan said, trailing them inside, Maya at her heels. She pulled the order list from her back pocket and the pencil from behind her ear. "I'll be a few minutes, guys."

"Take your time," the older one said, and the two sauntered back to the truck.

"What can I do?" Maya asked, and Nolan tried not to imagine all the answers to that question that had nothing to do with cabinets.

"Here." Nolan handed her the list. "I'll call out the part numbers as I inspect them, and you mark them off."

"I can do that."

Nolan opened the boxes, checking that each item was as ordered and undamaged, calling out part numbers as Maya ticked them off.

Maya peered inside one of the boxes. "Oh, my God, they're beautiful."

"That's just the base. Take a look at the doors."

Nolan pointed to another open box, and Maya ran her fingers over the gleaming cherry. The reverent touch of her fingertips on the smooth wood made Nolan's throat tighten.

"Nolan, they're going to look so good."

"Your decision to replace everything meant we could order

standard sizes. That saved you a ton of money." Nolan's voice sounded rougher than she intended.

"That was your call," Maya said. "Which is one of the many reasons I'm happy Johnny sent you my way."

"I think I owe Johnny, too," Nolan said, the words escaping before she could stop them.

Maya stared at her for a long moment, her dark eyes wide and searching.

Nolan had to force herself to look away, her pulse pounding. "Come on, you've got some painting to do so we can measure for these babies."

"Why did I hear *you* and not *we*?" Maya teased as they walked inside.

"Because I'm going to go find something I can pound on, or at least rip out." She needed the physical release, needed to channel this energy into something other than looking at Maya.

"Oh? Is painting too tame for you?" Maya shot her hip, brow raised.

Nolan's throat went dry. Maya couldn't be flirting, but damn, her gut reacted as if she was. A steady pulse beat low in her belly, and she had to fight to keep from swaying toward Maya like a tree bending toward sunlight.

"Uh, too fussy."

Maya laughed, the sound sending warmth cascading through Nolan's chest. "Color me surprised. Okay—point the way, so you can go off and do sweaty work."

Three hours later, Nolan stuck her head into the gutted kitchen. Maya stood on a ladder cutting in the last wall along the ceiling. The pale yellow, subtle but fresh, glowed in the late-morning sun. "Looks great."

Maya turned on the ladder, and Nolan laughed.

"What?" Maya frowned.

Nolan tapped her nose. "Yellow looks good on you."

"Oh damn." Maya pulled up the tail of her oversized T-shirt, baring a good three inches of toned midsection, and swiped at her nose.

Nolan's heart took a dive off a cliff. The exposed skin—smooth and golden-brown—sent heat racing through her veins. She wanted to reach out, to feel that warmth beneath her fingertips, to trace the curve where Maya's waist dipped in.

Maya dropped her shirt, her gaze finding Nolan's. Color crept into her face. "Did I miss a spot?"

"No," Nolan croaked. She cleared her throat. "All good."

Maya turned on the ladder, set her brush down on the paint tray, and started to back down.

Maya stumbled, arms flailing, and Nolan grabbed her around the waist. "I've got you."

Maya's back pressed to Nolan's chest, and her T-shirt rode up in front. Nolan's bare forearms rested on the warm skin of her midsection. Her cheek brushed Maya's hair, and she caught the scent of her—the familiar violets mingled with the tang of paint. Her heart didn't just race, it threatened to pound its way through her ribs. Maya must have felt that, but she didn't move. Didn't pull away.

"You okay?" Nolan murmured, her lips close to Maya's ear.

"Yes, thanks." Maya shivered. Her fingers drifted over Nolan's arms, just about the sexiest goddamn thing she'd ever felt. Soft, almost tentative, tracing a path from wrist to elbow and back again.

Nolan shuddered, every nerve firing at once.

"You can let me go now," Maya said softly, but her fingers continued their slow exploration.

"Right," Nolan said, hastily stepping back, her body protesting the loss of contact.

Maya turned, carefully not looking at Nolan. "I'll see what I can find for lunch."

"That'd be great," Nolan said. "I'll just go wash my hands." And maybe dunk her entire head in cold water while she was at it.

"I want to change into a clean T-shirt," Maya said, skirting around her without touching her.

On her way back from cleaning up, Nolan met Maya in the hall just as a black Mercedes pulled into the drive.

"Who is that?" Maya peered out the open door. "Oh, it's Pris."

"You know her?" Nolan clenched her jaw as Pris stepped out, carrying a designer bag, wearing oversized sunglasses, a sleeveless shirt open between her breasts, and tapered pants that hugged her Pilates-toned thighs. What the hell?

"I met her recently at the diner in town," Maya said. "I wonder what she's doing here?"

Nolan didn't know, but it couldn't be good. She hadn't seen Pris in nearly two years. They didn't run in the same circles. Pris had dropped into the Roadrunner one night, a place she never frequented, and since Nolan had had a few too many beers already, the evening had ended with them…well, it had been heated. She regretted it immensely.

"Hello," Pris said brightly as Maya opened the door. "I hope you don't mind me stopping by. I was in the neighborhood, and I thought I'd just swing by and see what you're doing with the old place." She stopped, looking surprised. "Oh. I didn't know you'd be here, Nolan. How are you?"

Nolan wasn't buying it. Her truck was right out front and had been every weekday for more than two months. The town wasn't that big, and news got around, especially when half the subcontractors in town were in and out of the place all the time.

"I'm fine, Pris. How are you?"

She tugged off her sunglasses and slid them into her purse. "Oh, you know. I'm doing well. I was surprised to hear you were doing work here, with you recently taking over your father's business and everything."

"Thought I'd try something new."

"I see." She took a moment to look around before very obviously sizing Nolan up from head to toe.

"You look well," she said. "Fit as ever." She laughed a little and set her shopping bag on the dining room table.

"I was just about to make some sandwiches," Maya said, her discomfort obvious to Nolan but clearly not to Pris. "The menu is limited these days, but you're welcome to join us."

"Oh, I wouldn't dream of putting you to the trouble. In fact, I just happen to have take-out from Billy's Barbecue right here. Have you eaten there? He has the best barbecue in Northern Arizona." Not waiting for an answer, she set down her purse and dug in the take-out bag, pulling out wrapped sandwiches and sides. "I've got everything here. Napkins, silverware, wet wipes."

Maya smiled thinly. "That's so generous of you. What would you like to drink? I've got bottled tea, water, and soda."

"Anything diet. I'm watching my figure." She winked at Nolan.

Nolan turned away. What the hell was she really doing here?

Maya got them all drinks, and they settled at the table. Pris ate her sandwich with a knife and fork, carefully carving out each delicate bite, while asking Maya between nibbles about the house.

"So, you're actually *working* with Nolan on the renovations?" Pris asked, pretending as if she didn't know.

"Mm-hmm." Maya lowered her bottle of tea.

"What on earth for?" Pris laughed at her own question, as if the notion was absolutely ridiculous.

"It's fun. I'm learning a lot."

"I suppose," Pris said, sounding unconvinced.

"It never hurts to be able to take care of the routine problems," Maya said mildly.

"If you're into that sort of thing," Pris said. "Although you're a widow, aren't you?"

Maya froze, and the color left her face. "Yes, I am."

"Your wife? She was killed?" Pris dabbed the corners of her mouth with a napkin.

Nolan shot Pris a look. What was she doing?

"Yes. She was," Maya said coolly.

"Has it been a while?"

Maya blinked. "A year and a half."

Pris merely smiled. "That *is* a long time to have to manage on your own. Of course, you have Nolan to help, don't you."

Maya's eyes blazed. "*Nolan* is renovating the house. She won't be here forever."

Nolan's chest tightened. Maya's tone had turned to steel.

Pris continued as if she hadn't noticed. "I've been known to be a good matchmaker from time to time, in case you're interested."

"I'm not."

Pris patted Maya's hand. "Of course not. Not yet." She cleaned up her half-eaten sandwich, sipped carefully from her can of Diet Coke, and checked her watch. "I should be off. I've got a hair appointment in twenty minutes, and Raul is a stickler for punctuality. Do you have a hairdresser yet, Maya? Raul is fabulous." She dug in her purse and plucked out a business card. "Give him a call. I'm sure he'd love to have you as a client."

She stood and gathered her bag, easing on her sunglasses once again. "It was nice to see you both again. Good luck with the house. I just know it's going to look fantastic. God knows Mama and Daddy never did much with the place." She sighed. "Nolan, walk me out, won't you?"

Nolan followed her out to her Mercedes. "What are you doing here?"

Pris laughed and placed her hand on Nolan's shoulder. "Easy there, Nolan. I just came to see what it was *you* were doing."

"Working."

"Is that all?"

"Give it a rest, Pris."

Pris laughed. "Oh, come now. I know you, remember?" She ran a finger down the center of Nolan's chest. "Look at you, being all protective. Don't tell me you're not interested."

Nolan struggled not to slap her hand away and stepped back out of range. "You don't know me, Pris. Not anymore."

Nolan turned and walked away.

Maya stood in the doorway, an unreadable expression on her face as Pris zoomed off.

"I'm sorry," Nolan said. "I don't know why she came here."

"This used to be her house."

"Well, it's not anymore. She was rude, and you don't have to be polite to her."

Maya looked up at her. "What did she want with you?"

Nolan shrugged. "To stir up a little excitement. She's probably bored."

"You two know each other that well?"

"*Knew* each other." Nolan strapped her tool belt back on, no longer hungry enough to finish Pris's offering. "A long time ago."

"Were you two…" Maya grimaced. "I'm sorry, that's none of my business."

Nolan sighed, wishing she could say it *was* Maya's business. But that was just her wish, wasn't it? She wanted Maya to ask, to care, to be jealous even—anything to confirm that the tension crackling between them wasn't all in her imagination. "What we were a long time ago was a couple of kids. Her parents…let's say they didn't approve of me. Or us. Whatever, Pris ended up marrying a college guy a couple of years older who her parents *did* approve of. That didn't last, and like I said, she's probably bored. End of story."

"I'm sorry," Maya said, the softness in her voice making Nolan's heart stutter.

Nolan met her gaze. "I'm not."

"I should get back to the painting." Maya didn't move, her eyes still locked with Nolan's.

If Nolan had her wish, she would have rewound to the moment she'd been holding Maya, even if it had been just to keep her from falling. But the past couldn't be recaptured, no matter how beautiful the dream.

CHAPTER ELEVEN

Maya peered into her bathroom, where Nolan bent over the half-disconnected sink. For a second, appreciating the way Nolan's canvas pants and cotton T stretched over her muscular frame, she forgot what she intended to say. When her brain clicked back on, she mentally chided herself. Since when did she ogle women? "I'm headed to Izzy's to pick up Emmie. You're sure you want to wait?"

"I told her I would," Nolan said. "You don't mind, do you?"

"Of course not."

"Good, because I want to pull this sink out before I leave today anyway."

"Can you do that by yourself?"

Nolan turned, grinning. "It shouldn't be a problem."

"Okay, I'm off, then." Maya hurried out to the car. Of course Nolan could handle ripping out a sink by herself—she'd just been admiring the muscles that proved it. *Admiring*, not ogling.

Ogling was more Pris's style.

Okay, that was petty, but every time she considered Pris and her impromptu visit, her annoyance doubled. She didn't mind the unannounced visit, but she seethed at Pris's entitled attitude and superior manner. Every glance seemed like an assessment. A comparison that deemed Maya the loser. Really. Did Pris actually think she'd missed those thinly veiled insults, hidden behind a veneer of false politeness? Worse, Pris was good at putting her off-balance. Like with that matchmaking offer. Her stomach clenched at the memory. Did Pris honestly think there was some time limit on grief, that she could just replace Dantas like swapping out a broken appliance?

What was she supposed to do when Pris insulted her while smiling? Call her out and look thin-skinned? Let it slide and look like a doormat?

She white-knuckled the steering wheel, anger still roiling in her middle. If she'd asked Pris to leave, *she* would have looked like the rude one. The overly sensitive one. She took a breath as she turned onto Izzy's street. Pris had probably been a mean girl in high school, and this was just the adult version. At least *she* hadn't regressed to that stage. But Lord, what had Nolan ever seen in her?

Maya snorted as she pulled to a stop. Um…let's see. Flirty, pretty, busty…probably smart, but *really*. That wink Pris had given Nolan? And the way she'd told Nolan she was looking "fit as always."

Okay, now she was back to petty.

But the familiarity in Pris's tone, the way she'd touched Nolan when they were standing outside. That image had set something uncomfortable churning in Maya's gut.

Was there something between them? Nolan had said there *had* been, past tense, but she hadn't seemed thrilled to see Pris show up. That suggested something more recent than a teenage romance, didn't it?

Maya cringed, imagining Nolan and Pris together, the wrongness of it surprising her with its intensity. Nolan was so solid, so forthright. Honest—yes, that was a word that fit Nolan. How could she have ever been interested in someone so…so condescending and manipulative?

Maya frowned. Everyone had a past, and what did she really know about Pris—or Nolan, for that matter?

What's more, why did she even care who Nolan had been with, or how she spent her time now? She was working herself up over nothing.

Nothing at all.

Emmie was probably wondering where she was. Putting thoughts of Pris's visit aside, she went in search of the one person who mattered most.

"Hello," she called when she walked into Izzy's Spanish revival house—two bedrooms and a third bath larger than hers. For the family Izzy had always wanted and now had—minus the cheating cur of a husband. "Anybody home?"

"Out back," Izzy called.

Izzy and Emmie sat at a table on the patio, Emmie coloring and Izzy with a book.

"Hi, you two," Maya called.

Emmie raced to her, hugged her around the middle, and asked, eyes wide and hopeful, "Is Nolan still there?"

Maya laughed, pushing aside her complicated feelings. "Yes, she's still there."

"Let's go, then." Emmie tugged on her hand.

Izzy rose to walk them out. "Well, I guess we know where we stand."

Maya rolled her eyes. "Yesterday's news."

Laughing, Izzy gave her a hug. "Just wait till they're all teenagers. We won't even exist then."

"Please." Maya hastened after Emmie.

"Have a good weekend," Izzy said as Maya got Emmie settled in the car.

The entire drive home, Emmie chattered about showing Nolan her My Little Pony collection. No talk about her day, no requests for ice cream—just Nolan, Nolan, Nolan.

"You like Nolan, don't you?" Maya studied her in the rearview mirror.

"Yes. She's nice and super strong. Like Thor." Emmie's eyes lit up. "My friend Carter at school wore a Thor T-shirt. Nolan has muscles just like him. I bet she could lift you up, Mommy."

Maya blinked, recalling Nolan's arms around her when she'd so ungracefully tripped down the ladder. Firm body, hard muscles in her arms and thighs. Heat spread up her neck to her cheeks. Nerves, or something else, stirred in her stomach. Nolan *did* have a sort of superhero persona—intense, focused, and probably capable of leaping tall buildings. That would appeal to a child, but what did it mean that it appealed to her, too? She swallowed, needing to deflect the conversation away from Nolan and her muscles and whether or not Nolan could pick her up. Or leap tall buildings. "Carter? You have a new friend at school?"

Thankfully, Emmie moved on to stories of her new friend. The thought of Nolan picking her up and carrying her away had left her head spinning.

"Mommy? You passed our house."

"What? Oh, I did, didn't I?" She forced a laugh and stopped to reverse and pull in the drive.

Emmie raced toward the house as soon as Maya got her out of the car. When Maya followed inside, she found Emmie's backpack, lunchbox, and Hello Kitty sweatshirt abandoned just inside the front door. She automatically picked them up on her way down the hall. Emmie stood in the doorway of the en suite bathroom, chattering to Nolan.

"Are you done yet?" Emmie said. "All my ponies are in the living room."

Nolan wiped her hands on a dark blue bandana she'd pulled from her pocket, grinning over at Maya. "Yep, all done for today."

Emmie grabbed her hand and tugged. "This way."

Nolan followed her past Maya, her woodsy scent lingering in the air. "Duty calls."

Maya folded a basket of laundry on the table in the dining room, listening as Emmie introduced each pony to Nolan by name while explaining their special quality. Nolan asked thoughtful questions that showed she'd actually been listening, apparently much to Emmie's delight. No wonder Emmie was enthralled. Nolan was special.

"Look what I got." Nolan held up a toy pony when she and Emmie joined Maya. "My very own magical pony."

"I gave her Rainbow Dash, the pegasus," Emmie announced proudly. "Rainbow's my second favorite. Plus, she has wings like Thor's helmet."

"That was very nice of you, Em." Maya's heart did a little dance to see Emmie so excited and genuinely happy. A moment of panic followed. How would Emmie feel when Nolan finished the job and disappeared? Her stomach dropped. How would *she* feel?

"Super nice," Nolan said. "I'm honored that you trust me with her, Em, and I'm really happy that I remind you of Thor."

"You're better than Thor." Emmie spun around to Maya. "Can Nolan stay for dinner?"

Maya squeezed the dish towel she'd been about to fold. This was too much, too fast, for her and Emmie. "Oh, sweetie, I don't know—"

"Can't tonight, Emmie," Nolan said, as if sensing her hesitation. "I have someplace I have to be."

"Like a…'pointment?" Emmie asked.

"Yep, just like that."

Emmie pouted. "Are you sure?"

"Nolan has other plans, honey." Maya smiled, doubting it reached her eyes. Damn it if she didn't instantly think of Pris. That picture made her grimace.

"You okay?" Nolan asked.

"Fine." She forced another smile, hating how she bounced from one emotion to the next all of a sudden. What was wrong with her?

"Take it easy this weekend," Nolan said, studying her intently. "You worked overtime this week."

Maya nodded, not trusting her voice.

Nolan paused a moment longer before pushing the toy horse into her pocket and glancing at Emmie. "I'll see you next week, sport."

"Sport?" Emmie giggled, her disappointment forgotten. "Okay."

Nolan straightened and gave a playful salute. "Thanks again for my pony."

"Welcome," Emmie said and ran off toward the living room.

She looked at Maya. "Will you be okay without the bathroom sink?"

"We have the other bathroom."

Nolan retrieved her tool belt, and Maya walked her to the door.

Nolan hesitated. "I'll push the supplier to get the new sink and shower parts here as soon as possible."

"Thanks."

"Have a good weekend," Nolan finally said.

Maya watched through the screen door as Nolan climbed into her truck, secured the pony on the dash, and backed out of the drive. Friday night. Of course Nolan would have plans. Plans that were absolutely none of her business.

"What's for dinner?" Emmie said, tugging on her sleeve.

Maya stood at the door, watching the truck disappear. "Hmm?"

"Can we have pizza?"

Maya focused on Emmie rather than on thoughts of Nolan with Pris. She warmed up the leftover pizza, praying the new stove would come soon so she could actually cook again, and ate a few obligatory bites. After she got Emmie settled into bed, she paced the living room, unable to shake the disquiet that had plagued her all evening. Finally, she grabbed her phone and texted Izzy.

What are you doing?

Thinking about washing my hair, Izzy texted back.

Come over—I need sister time

On my way

"What happened?" Izzy said fifteen minutes later as she came flying up to the porch.

"Nobody is sick." Maya pointed to the porch swing. "Sit. I need an emergency sister talk."

"Okay." Izzy, sounding relieved, plopped down next to Maya. "I love the boys, but I'm glad Brian has them this weekend. So…tell me."

"Pris dropped by today."

"Huh—just out of the blue?"

"So she said, but the whole visit seemed…planned."

"Spill." Izzy kicked off her sandals and curled her legs beneath her.

Maya recounted the visit in detail—Pris's condescending comments about the house, the not-so-subtle digs about Maya being foolish for wanting to help, the ridiculous suggestion about matchmaking.

"And then," Maya continued, her voice rising, "she has the nerve to practically flirt with Nolan right in front of me. Like I didn't even exist."

"That sounds like Pris." Izzy narrowed her eyes. "Why were you bothered?"

The question brought Maya up short, and she swallowed hard. Izzy *would* ask that. "It was just…it was inappropriate. And disrespectful."

"To you? Or to Nolan?"

"Both."

Izzy was quiet for a moment. "Maya, how well do you actually know Nolan?"

"She's been working here for over two months. I know what I need to know." The words came out more forcefully than Maya intended. "She's kind and sensitive and caring. You should see her with Emmie—she treats her like she actually matters, not just some kid to be humored. And she's skilled and honest and—"

"Whoa, okay," Izzy interrupted. "I get it. But everyone has a past. People can be all those things and still have darker sides."

Maya's stomach tightened. "What does that mean?"

Izzy leaned forward and squeezed her arm. "I just mean…you seem really upset, and I worry about you getting hurt."

"I *am* upset. I'm angry about Pris showing up here making snide comments and…just being Pris."

"Did Nolan tell you she and Pris used to have a thing?"

Maya stiffened. "Yes. She did. Like I said, this is about what Pris was like today."

"Are you sure?"

Maya fell silent, the question hanging between them. Was that all it was? Or was she upset because she was…jealous?

"I only want you to be careful," Izzy said gently. "You're just coming out the other side of something horrible, and you're doing great. Don't dive headfirst into something when you don't know what's really going on."

"I'm not diving into anything," Maya protested weakly.

"Good. I'm on your side, no matter what."

Maya smiled. "I know. Thanks for being you."

"I was born your big sister. I take the job seriously." Izzy rose and kissed her forehead. "'Night, baby sis."

"'Night," Maya called.

She sat on the darkened porch for a while after Izzy left. Maybe Izzy was right. Maybe she'd gotten too involved with Nolan without even realizing it. Had she already taken a dive into deep waters? Why should whatever was going on with Pris and Nolan bother her?

Too many questions. Questions about Nolan, questions about Pris, but most of all, questions about herself.

Who was she now? Was she still the same person she'd been before Dantas died? Or was she someone new, someone who could feel this strange pull toward another woman?

Maya hugged herself, suddenly cold despite the warmth of the late spring night. Nolan and the renovations were changing her home.

Maybe they were changing her, too.

Chapter Twelve

The next few days dragged by like a weight chained to Nolan's ankle. Maya had been distant all week, hardly talking, let alone laughing and joking as she usually did when working on the house. Nothing had been quite the same since Pris had shown up, but what Nolan couldn't figure was what bothered Maya so much about that visit. Pris had been pushy and intrusive, but Maya had handled her well enough. Something still nagged at her, though.

Nolan adjusted the final pipe beneath the new farmhouse sink, checked the inset with the level, and asked Maya, "What do you think?"

Maya turned from putting the primer coat on the wall beneath the window, brush in hand, her expression distant. "It's great."

"But?" Nolan pressed. Maya wasn't right, and if she had to push to find out what was going on, she would. The silence was lethal.

"No buts."

"You don't sound happy."

"I'll be happier when the floor is finished and the rest of the cabinetry is in." Maya's tone was flat, matter-of-fact.

The floor was half finished, up to where Maya was painting. As soon as that wall dried and the final coat went on, they could install the rest of the flooring. The upper cabinetry was next on the list for the following week. Maya knew all that. That couldn't really be the cause of her mood, could it?

"I just wanted you to have the sink for the weekend so you'll have a semi-functional kitchen." Nolan wiped her hands with a towel and tossed it into the corner with her tools. She went to the fridge and grabbed a bottle of water, her throat parched from crawling under the cabinet all morning.

"Thank you." Maya finally set the paint tray down and went to inspect the sink. "It's nice."

Nolan drank from the chilled bottle. "It's big."

Maya kept her back turned. "As I recall, you enjoy hard labor—you didn't have any trouble with the bathroom sink."

Nolan stared, struck by the icy tone. "What?"

"Nothing." Maya brushed past her and headed out the front door.

Nolan silently cursed and grabbed another water before following her onto the porch. Maya sat on the far end of the swing, staring out at the empty street. Since the house sat at the end of the cul-de-sac, traffic was rare. A breeze rattled the hummingbird wind chime Nolan had hung a couple of days earlier. The soft melody seemed at odds with Maya's dark mood.

"Mind if I sit?" Nolan offered her the water.

Nodding, Maya took the bottle.

Nolan sat at the opposite end of the swing. "You want to talk about it?"

"I'm fine. I'm sorry I snapped at you."

"I don't care about that. I know something's bothering you."

"It doesn't matter."

"Of course it matters." Nolan took a chance. "Is this about Pris's visit?"

"No. Maybe. Indirectly, I guess. Ever since I decided to leave Chicago and buy this house, and work on the reno, I told myself this would help me…help Emmie…move on." Maya sighed. "Sometimes I wonder what I'm really doing. Pris was wrong about pretty much everything, as well as being, well, a bitch, but she wasn't wrong about one thing. I've mostly been hiding here, pretending I'm doing something important. Making a new life. But I'm not sure I really am."

"It seems to me," Nolan said, choosing every word as if a misstep would land her in quicksand, "you have accomplished a hell of a lot already. And I don't mean the demo, painting, and drywall work either. You picked this place, you planned the changes, you got Emmie here where she has family. She's happy in a new school and excited to go to kindergarten soon. From where I'm sitting, you're amazing."

"It seems like so little," Maya said softly. "Sometimes I wonder… why was it Dantas who was taken and not me? She'd be a lot better at all of this than me."

Nolan's stomach rolled. She couldn't even imagine a world without Maya in it. She swallowed, searching desperately for the right words. She was probably the absolute wrong person for Maya to be confiding in. A big part of her wanted to jump up and run for the truck. Before she fucked up. Again. But Maya was so unhappy. "Accidents have no logic. They just happen."

Maya's eyes blazed. "Accident. No—that's not what it was. A drunk driver *killed* her. What would *you* call that?"

Nolan flinched. Johnny hadn't told her the details. A drunk driver? How must Maya feel now about people like that? People like *her*? Bile burned in the back of her throat, but she forced herself to hold Maya's raging gaze. "I'd call it manslaughter. And I hope they paid for it."

Maya waved her hand and looked away. "Not enough. Never enough. But that *is* something I refuse to let poison the rest of my life."

"Good for you." Nolan pressed her hands on her thighs before she reached for her. She ached to touch her, to comfort her. She was so damn bad at this. "I'll tell you what you're amazing at. Giving Emmie everything she needs to be happy. And not just happy, but the chance to be anybody, do anything she wants. Because you're who she'll look to as an example."

"Sometimes I'm not sure."

"Well, I am. I know you're brave and strong. And I can see the changes in Emmie since you've been here. She's not as scared as she was."

Maya studied her for so long Nolan's breath got shaky. Had she screwed up?

"Thank you. For saying that. For listening."

"I wish I could do more," Nolan muttered. Wished she could give Maya more. Take away her pain.

"You do plenty." Maya smiled, a real if small smile. "I'm sorry to dump all this on you. I didn't even know it was simmering."

"I'm glad you did. I wish I could make everything better for you."

Maya's eyes widened. "You've helped. That means a lot."

"Then I'm glad."

"I suppose I should thank Pris, too," Maya said.

"What?"

Maya laughed. The sound, competing with the wind chimes, was just about the best thing Nolan had ever heard.

"If she hadn't poked me about what I was doing with my life, I might not have asked myself the same question."

"You would have," Nolan said. "And if Pris shows up again, tell her you're way too busy to entertain her."

"It sounds like you two have some unfinished business," Maya said.

"Pris might, but I don't." Nolan sighed. Honesty, right? Atonement. "I haven't always made the best choices when it comes to relationships. My father wasn't any kind of example, but that's on me…I've made some mistakes. There's nothing between me and Pris now, but she isn't the kind of person who wants someone else to make that choice."

Maya picked up her untouched bottle of water. "I apologize, Nolan. It's really none of my business."

"Nothing to apologize for," Nolan said. "I'm sorry about Pris."

"Don't be sorry on my account. Pris is far from the worst thing that's come along." Maya squeezed Nolan's arm as she passed on her way inside. "You're a good listener. Thanks again. I need to head over to Izzy's to pick up Emmie."

"I want to check a few things. I'll close up," Nolan said. "Have a good weekend."

"You too."

Maya came out a few minutes later and drove away without saying anything more. As Nolan checked the faucet and pipes, confirming everything worked leak-free, she replayed the conversation, berating herself for all the things she probably should have said better. Satisfied about the work at least, she collected her things and left. The weekend stretched ahead, holding nothing but empty hours. She'd rather be working. Or spending time with Maya and Emmie.

She shook her head, driving away. Lying to herself was something she'd been working not to do. Maya had needed a friendly ear, and she'd been handy. That was all. Maya and Emmie did not need her, and even if there was the slimmest chance they might, which there wasn't, she was lousy at relationships—if she could even call the few times she was with a woman more than a week or so a relationship. Even when she'd tried, she'd heard the same complaints over and over.

Why was she so distant? Why didn't she care? Why didn't she try harder?

Questions she still couldn't answer except to blame her father. He'd raised her that way, so she'd turned out just like him—a loner, refusing to open up about her feelings—if she could even sort them out herself. Until she'd learned not to try. Recovery had taught her that her father's ways weren't healthy and didn't have to be hers, but she still struggled with how to change those patterns. Maybe it wasn't that she didn't know how—maybe she just hadn't had the chance to try a different way.

Fear choked her.

Maya mattered. Emmie mattered. What if she tried and failed? What if she lost the joy they'd brought into her life because she wanted more? Something she wasn't capable of feeling, or giving?

Nolan pulled over and texted Tim. She usually checked in with him every week or so, mostly because she liked him, but times like this, when fear and confusion curdled inside, talking with her sponsor was the smart thing to do.

Got time after the meeting for coffee?

You bet, he replied right away.

The tension in her chest eased a fraction.

One step at a time.

❖

Maya sat in the car in Izzy's drive. What had she just done, dumping all that on Nolan, who didn't deserve her black mood or her confessions of inadequacy? She never would have let herself be so vulnerable six months ago. Or trusted anyone enough.

Who was she becoming?

For over a decade, although she'd never really thought about it, she'd known who she was: Dantas's wife, Emmie's mother, and a woman waiting for the next phase in her life to begin. When Emmie started regular school, she would put her college English degree to use and get an editing certification. Freelance work would suit her. Then the future had changed, but even in grief, those roles anchored her—widow, single mother, keeper of Dantas's memory.

Until now. Lately, something had shifted. The move and the renovations had awakened a desire in her to create, to build, to transform. And Nolan…

Nolan made her feel things she wasn't prepared for. She looked forward to seeing her, enjoyed working with her, admired her skill and humor and basic kindness. And she adored the way Nolan had helped Emmie come out of her shell.

Oh, who was she kidding? Those were all things she might feel for a good friend. But that was the problem—there was more. Attraction. Interest. Possibility.

And that's where she stumbled. How could there be more?

Was she allowed to want more? To be more than Emmie's mother and Dantas's widow?

Guilt pressed down on her chest like a weight. Dantas had only been gone a year and a half. Wasn't it disloyal to be thinking about someone else? To be feeling…whatever this was?

Her phone buzzed with a text. Izzy.

Are you going to sit out there all night?

Sorry. I'll come get her.

When Maya let herself in the front door, Izzy called, "We're in the kitchen."

"Mommy," Emmie cried as soon as Maya walked in, "we're making cookies."

"I see." Emmie, Manny, and Luis knelt on chairs around Izzy's kitchen table, mostly covered in cookie fixings—splashes of flour on their shirts, a smear of chocolate on Emmie's cheek—and huge smiles.

"Having a party?" Maya asked.

"Game night," Izzy said. "We're making hoagies next. You should stay."

"Can I stay tonight, Mommy?" Emmie asked. "We can have a sleepover."

Maya glanced at Izzy. She'd been set up. Game night meant people. Conversation. Pretending to be okay when she still felt so…adrift.

Emmie gave her a hopeful look.

"Besides, if you stay, you can have some of the cabernet I just opened. Otherwise you get lemonade." Izzy grinned, damn her. She already knew Maya couldn't refuse.

Maybe something to take her mind off her self-examination was a good idea. When was the last time she'd spent an evening with adults who weren't contractors or Izzy? Since Dantas died, she'd retreated into her cocoon of grief and motherhood, venturing out only to take Emmie to therapy and preschool. Maybe that explained why Nolan had become such a focus—the woman was literally the only new person in her life since moving to this town.

"Okay, baby. We'll all have a sleepover." Maya glanced at Izzy. She'd left the house in faded jeans and a plain short-sleeved linen shirt. "I should run home and change."

"Pfft." Izzy waved a hand. "You look fine. And the guest bathroom has everything you'll need. Come on, we have to feed the masses."

Outnumbered, Maya set to work, and an hour later, the kids had been fed, a tray of sandwiches waited for Izzy's game group, and Emmie and the boys were tucked up in sleeping bags in the family room watching a movie. Considering how much they'd all eaten, they'd be asleep before it was half over.

"That was sneaky," Maya said as she and Izzy set up two oversized card tables in the living room.

"Sometimes trickery is required." Izzy bumped her shoulder. "It'll be fun."

Maya silently repeated those words a half hour later as she joined the group of six other people settling around the two tables.

"Everybody, this is my sister Maya," Izzy said. "There's wine in the kitchen, and lemonade or seltzer for the designated drivers. "

Maya smiled, did her best to put names to faces, and headed for the vacant seat next to a woman about her own age with collar-length black hair and dark brown eyes wearing jeans and a green polo shirt with a Puma logo on the chest. Her grip was firm, her smile genuine.

"Aisley, right?" Maya said as she sat down.

"Yep. Nice to meet you."

"You too." Maya leaned closer. "I have to confess, I have no idea what I'm doing here. The only board game I've played in the last few years is Candy Land."

Aisley laughed. "Don't worry. We're an easy bunch, and the game this table is playing tonight is Wingspan. A friendly, not super-competitive game."

"Help her out, will you, Ais," Izzy said as she stopped by. "It's Maya's first time."

"All set here, Iz," Aisley said, sipping from a glass of lemonade.

"Aisley is a new coach at Preston High," Izzy said. "And she coaches the peewee soccer team the boys play on."

"That sounds like fun," Maya said.

"It is," Aisley said, sounding like she meant it.

Maya studied the colorful game board, the tray of beautifully rendered bird images, and the miniature bird feeder with actual little plastic food bits inside. "This looks…complicated."

"Don't worry," Aisley said. "It's actually pretty straightforward once you get started."

Aisley explained the rules, and Maya relaxed. Aisley's explanations were nice and clear, and as the game progressed, she provided a running commentary—a mix of strategic insights and wry humor.

"So basically, I just sacrificed my blue heron to get more eggs, which sounds terrible ecologically," Aisley said at one point, making Maya laugh.

Halfway through the game, Maya caught Izzy watching her with a pleased expression. She smiled back. She *was* having fun.

"Izzy mentioned you moved back recently," Aisley said as they waited for Anton, another player, to take his turn.

"Yes, from Chicago. I've been renovating a house on Sycamore."

"Big project?"

"Pretty much top to bottom."

"Sounds like a challenge. Are you enjoying it?" Aisley really seemed interested.

"I am. I'm learning a lot working with the contractor."

"Nice," Aisley said.

Aisley's response couldn't have been more different—or refreshing—than Pris's condescending dismissal.

"What about you?" Maya asked. "Have you always coached?"

"Right out of college. I relocated here…" She grimaced, shrugging sheepishly. "Old story…for a relationship that didn't work out. But I got lucky. I love the area, and the school is invested in sports."

"I like a story with a happy ending," Maya said, setting aside her empty wine glass.

Aisley tapped the Puma logo on her shirt. "I've got the mini-warriors tomorrow morning."

"She's being modest," Anton interjected. "Her high school team made state finals this year."

Aisley shrugged. "The kids did the work. I just yelled from the sidelines."

"I doubt that," Maya said.

They exchanged a smile, and Maya felt something unexpected—a flicker of connection. It had been so long since she'd met someone new, someone who didn't know her as the woman whose wife died.

The evening flew by, and Maya ended up placing third in the game.

"Not bad for a beginner," Aisley assured her, and before Maya knew it, everyone was saying good night.

"I hope I'll see you again," Aisley said as she was leaving. "Maybe at one of the games? We could always use more team parents, even honorary ones."

"I'd like that," Maya replied, surprised to find she meant it. "My daughter is five. She'll love seeing her cousins play."

"Great," Aisley said. "Well, I hope I see you soon, then."

After everyone left, Maya helped Izzy load the dishwasher.

"That was nice," Maya admitted. "Thanks for the push."

"You're welcome," Izzy said casually, though her eyes sparkled. "Aisley is nice, too, don't you think?"

"She is," Maya replied noncommittally.

"The boys have a game tomorrow morning. Since you're staying overnight, we should all go together."

Maya hesitated. "I don't know, Iz. I've got so much to do with the house."

"The house will still be there Sunday." Izzy handed her a towel to dry her hands. "It's good to see you connecting with people again. Emmie will love going to the game."

Maya sighed. Outmaneuvered again. "All right, but Emmie and I have to go home in the morning. I'm not showing up there in the same clothes I was wearing tonight. Emmie can stand a change, too."

"No problem. I'll pick you and Emmie up on the way. Then we won't have to take two cars. It can get crowded at the field."

"Then I guess I'm joining the cheering squad."

Izzy hugged her. "Good. Now go to bed. You look tired."

Maya winced. "Thank you so much for pointing that out."

"What else are sisters for?" Izzy laughed.

Alone in the spare bedroom, Maya replayed the easy conversation with Aisley, the laughter, and the simple pleasure of being around others. Aisley had been charming and funny. Attractive, too, in an athletic, confident way. When their hands had brushed reaching for the dice, the brief contact surprised her. She hadn't touched anyone other than Nolan, and then only by accident, since Dantas.

Nolan's face floated into her mind. Intense blue eyes, strong hands, that rare, transformative smile. The touches they'd shared, no matter how casual or accidental, were different. More unsettling.

Maya got up to open the window, letting the cool night air wash over her. The sound of Izzy's wind chimes carried to her on the breeze, reminding her of the ones Nolan had hung for her on the front porch.

Almost a year and a half since Dantas died. Was she even ready to think about someone new? Did she even *want* to? Maybe all she really needed was simple friendship with someone easy to be around like Aisley.

And Nolan? The pull she felt toward Nolan was far more complicated and confusing.

She couldn't just be Emmie's mother forever, but something more didn't necessarily mean *someone* else. Someone who wasn't Dantas.

For the first time in longer than she could remember, the questions didn't terrify her. Just maybe she was ready to start finding the answers.

CHAPTER THIRTEEN

The morning was clear and bright, a perfect day for soccer. Maya sat on the aluminum bleachers beside Izzy, watching as a dozen kids in matching green jerseys chased the ball across the field. Manny and Luis were easy to spot. Both had their mother's dark curls, mischievous brown eyes, and boundless energy.

"Go, Manny," Izzy shouted as her older son took possession of the ball. "Pass it, pass it."

Manny ignored his mother's advice and attempted to dribble past two defenders, promptly losing the ball in the process.

"They never listen," Izzy sighed, but she was smiling.

Maya laughed. "He gets that from you."

"Probably." Izzy nudged her. "Thanks for coming. I know you've got a million house things to do."

"It's good to get out." She hadn't realized how true that was until they'd arrived at the field adjacent to the recreational center. The morning felt fresh and, for a change, simple. Uncomplicated in a way her life rarely was these days. Nothing for her to question, control, or solve. Just kids playing soccer under a cloudless sky.

Emmie sat on Izzy's other side, excitedly pointing to her cousins when she wasn't explaining the rules to her stuffed unicorn. Emmie's imagination never failed to amuse Maya. Her heart lifted with quiet relief that Emmie could still find magic in the ordinary.

On the sidelines, Aisley paced, calling out encouragement to her team. She wore shorts that revealed toned legs, her dark hair pulled back in a small ponytail. When she caught Maya's eye, she grinned and gave a little wave.

Maya waved back, unexpectedly self-conscious. How would it feel to be that comfortable in her own skin again? To not carry the weight of grief and single parenthood with every step. To have someone to share the ordinary joys and decisions with. She caught up short, her musings taking her down a road she wasn't ready to travel.

Her phone buzzed. Nolan.

Appliance delivery rescheduled for next Fri. unless they can come this AM. OK if I arrange that?

Maya hesitated, staring at the message, a dose of reality she probably needed. She'd been looking forward to a day away from the renovation chaos. A quiet house, and hopefully, a quiet mind. A chance to breathe without drywall dust or the sound of power tools. But until the appliances arrived, the kitchen was a nonstarter. She and Emmie had both had enough of microwaved food and take-out.

How soon?

11:30. Sorry for short notice. I can meet them

Maya glanced at her watch. The game wouldn't be over for at least another half an hour.

I'll be late. Go ahead if you're free

No problem. Would need to be there anyhow

Maya tucked the phone away, oddly flustered by how the short exchange rattled her. She'd been irritable all week, snapping at minor inconveniences, yet Nolan had been her usual steady self. Dealing with scheduling snafus, coordinating deliveries, and keeping the crews out of Maya's way as much as possible. Listening to her complain and soul-search, even. Basically making her life easier wherever possible.

And again today, Nolan stepped in without hesitation or a hint of annoyance. Maya wrestled with a little guilt over her mini-meltdown the previous day, on top of all the crankiness leading up to it. Nolan was just doing her job, but her unflappable presence reassured and unsettled at the same time. Maybe because Maya had started to depend on Nolan being there. Letting herself get used to it. A mistake.

"Everything okay?" Izzy asked.

"Yes, just Nolan. The appliances are coming this morning instead of Monday."

"Ooh, functioning kitchen. Progress." Izzy paused, studying Maya's face. "You know, for someone getting most of a new kitchen today, you don't look all that thrilled."

Maya shrugged. "I am. It's just…change of plans. That's all. I'm not as flexible as I thought."

"Change is good," Izzy reminded her gently. "That's the whole point, isn't it?"

Before Maya could point out that not all changes were good ones, a small commotion erupted on the field as Luis scored a goal. His team erupted in cheers, and Aisley pumped her fist in the air.

Her jubilant voice carried to the stands. "That's how it's done, team. Great assist, JJ."

Maya smiled. "She's got great energy. I guess she'd have to with that bunch."

"Mmm," Izzy said. "She's amazing in a lot of ways."

The rest of the game passed in a blur of small victories and comical mishaps. When the final whistle blew, the green team was victorious by two goals, and the kids swarmed Aisley for high-fives.

"Hey," Aisley said, joining Maya once she'd released the team to their parents. She was slightly flushed from the sun, eyes bright. "What did you think of your first soccer experience?"

"Exciting." Maya smiled. "Your kids are good, and they seem to love it."

"They make it easy. They're at that age where it's all fun, and if they score a goal or two, it's a bonus." Aisley took a seat beside her. "Plans for the rest of the day?"

Izzy interrupted. "Let's take the kids for ice cream to celebrate. You should join us, Ais."

"Actually, I have to get home." Maya glanced at her watch. "Unexpected delivery."

"Can't I go for ice cream, Mommy?" Emmie said.

"Aunt Izzy has to drive us home. We don't have time for ice cream first," Maya said. "Next time."

"I can give you a ride home," Aisley said. "I'm done for the day."

Maya hesitated, but Izzy was already gathering Emmie and the boys.

"Perfect. Thanks. Ais. I'll bring Emmie home later, Maya."

"If you don't mind," Maya said to Aisley, giving Izzy a side-eye. Izzy's satisfied smirk convinced Maya of what she already suspected. Izzy was pushing her in Aisley's direction. She did *not* need her sister matchmaking.

"No problem at all," Aisley said, tucking a clipboard into her gear bag.

As they walked across the field toward the parking lot, Maya tried to remember the last time she'd made a new friend. Before Dantas died, certainly. Now the simple act of getting to know someone seemed foreign and unexpectedly exciting.

"I need to be educated," Maya said. "What do you do in the summer when school's out?"

"Some administrative stuff with the athletic director. Budgets and personnel and whatnot. Mostly I divide my time between youth development programs and training camp sessions." Aisley's love of her work was obvious in her animated tone. "High school kids are competing for soccer scholarships at the collegiate level, so we want to get our athletes prepared." She pointed to a maroon SUV and opened the doors remotely. "I'm over here."

"I guess I never thought about how early these kids need to start preparing," Maya said, sliding into the passenger seat. The car smelled pleasantly of vanilla and citrus. "I'm on Sycamore, by the way."

"I know where that is." Aisley nudged into the long line of departing cars. "You've got a little while before you need to worry about college. Emmie's, what, six?"

"A few months past five," Maya said. "She's tall for her age."

"And very verbal," Aisley said with a grin.

"You noticed."

"Pretty sure I heard her down on the field." Aisley laughed. "Good age, though. Old enough to have personality, young enough to still think you're amazing."

"I'm hoping that lasts a few more years." Maya pushed a stray strand of hair behind her ear. "Do you have kids?"

"Me? No. My sibs do, though." Aisley glanced at Maya. "I'm single, no kids, one dog, no other pets, and no, uh, attachments."

Maya smiled. With Aisley, what you saw was what you got—open, friendly, and uncomplicated. Refreshing.

Unlike Nolan. For all the time she'd spent with Nolan, she remained a mystery in so many ways. Reserved, intense, private in the extreme. Sometimes she thought she caught glimpses of something more, a question in Nolan's eyes when Nolan looked at her. But then the distant look would slip back into place, and she'd wonder if she'd imagined it.

"So this renovation," Aisley said. "How far along are you? Sounds like a major undertaking."

"It is. The house is nearly a hundred years old and needed...well, everything. New kitchen, bathrooms, floors, paint. The roof."

"Brave undertaking."

"That's what everyone keeps saying. I'm not sure if it's brave or just stubborn."

"Little of both, probably." Aisley turned onto Sycamore. "Which house is yours?"

"All the way down, on the right. The green one with the white trim."

They pulled into the driveway behind Nolan's truck. For some reason, seeing it there sent a little flutter through her stomach. The familiar white pickup with its neatly organized tool racks had become a fixture in her life these past months.

"Nice place." Aisley let the SUV idle as she looked around. "Great location, too."

"According to Nolan—that's my contractor—we're two-thirds there. Barring a million potential unforeseen events."

Aisley laughed. "Sounds like an experienced contractor."

"She's terrific." Maya unbuckled her seat belt, suddenly eager to get inside. "We were supposed to get the major appliances delivered Monday, but somehow that got bumped to today."

"Early delivery? That *is* a rarity." Aisley turned in her seat. "I'm kind of a sucker for old houses. Would it be too much trouble for me to get a peek at what you're doing?"

Maya hesitated. Would Nolan mind? But that was silly. Why should she? This was *her* house, after all. "Sure. I have to warn you, though, some areas are still more demo than reno."

"Awesome." Aisley's eyes lit up. "That's the way to see the bones of the place."

"Exactly what Nolan said."

Aisley smiled, her gaze warm and gently searching. "My lucky day all around, then."

Maya flushed, caught between her easy connection with Aisley and, waiting inside, Nolan, the complicated woman who was never far from her thoughts.

❖

Nolan double-checked the stove specs against the space between the lower cabinets for the third time, even though she knew it was correct down to the sixteenth of an inch. She'd brought in an extra fuel line coupler from the truck, just in case. Half the time the installers showed up with something missing. She didn't plan on letting them leave until everything was in, connected, and running.

The call from the delivery company had been a welcome distraction that saved her from ruminating any longer on her conversation with Tim the night before. She hadn't planned to get into anything specific about Maya, but that hadn't worked out so well.

"So what's the trouble?" he'd asked, pulling out his vape pen as they sat on the steps outside the church. Scarecrow thin, gray-haired and sun-creased, somewhere in his sixties, his laid-back attitude belied a keen perceptiveness that made him the perfect sponsor for her. He'd just keep prodding until she finally got around to what was bothering her.

"No trouble."

He'd laughed at that. "Bullshit. You've been radio silent lately. Got something to unload?"

She'd hesitated, feeling like a teenager caught coming in late and stoned. He always had that effect on her—making her feel both safe and exposed at the same time.

"I'm not sure. I haven't done anything I need to report."

"Not drinking?"

She shook her head. "No. Not close, even."

"So something else you're thinking about doing."

"Yeah." She'd stared at her hands, steady now, where once they'd trembled every morning.

"Well, best spill it."

So she had. "It's the woman I'm doing the house renovation for. I'm, uh, I'm thinking a lot about her. Like I might like to get to know her better. Personally."

"Date her, you mean."

"Yes." The word had hung in the air. Getting out what she'd been trying to hide from herself had left her lighter, but scared.

His response had surprised her. "Tell me why that's a problem."

"I'm just closing in on my eighteen-month anniversary."

"Yes, and?" Tim exhaled a thin stream of scented vapor. "Do you feel your sobriety is threatened?"

"No, but…she's a widow. She's trying to pick up the pieces and raise her five-year-old daughter."

"Ah."

"And…" Nolan had swallowed hard. "She doesn't know about my past or that I'm in recovery."

He'd raised a brow. "And you don't want to tell her?"

"I haven't figured out how."

"Why is it complicated?"

"Because she lost her wife to a drunk driver."

Tim had studied her face, his gaze penetrating even behind his glasses. And then, more gently than she'd expected, he'd said, "You're obviously aware of the problems. So you don't need me to tell you that acting on your feelings isn't the best idea."

"Come on, Tim. You know it's not that simple."

"Isn't it, though? You know what's best for you and your sobriety. Keep in mind what might be best for her."

"I just don't know what to do about her," she'd confessed. "I have to see her every day. And I think about her. She's not like anyone I've ever known."

His advice had been simple. "Service. Start there and do your best to help her. That's the clearest path forward."

Now, standing in Maya's kitchen, Nolan tried to focus on the measurements rather than the churning in her stomach. Service. That's what she was here for. To help, not to complicate Maya's life with her own baggage. Maya deserved better than having to deal with someone else's problems.

She heard the front door open at the same time as Maya called out, "Nolan? You here?"

"In the kitchen," Nolan called back, quickly tucking away the measuring tape and straightening her shoulders.

"I've brought a visitor." Maya sounded different—lighter, almost buoyant—as she walked in with a dark-haired woman. "The delivery hasn't arrived yet?"

"Should be here any minute." Nolan masked her surprise with a professional smile. "Sorry, I thought they'd be here and gone by now."

"It's no big deal." Maya indicated the woman with her. "This is Aisley Mancuso. She coaches Izzy's boys in soccer. Aisley, this is Nolan Wright, the renovation magician I told you about."

Told you about? When had Maya and this woman been discussing her?

"Nice to meet you," Aisley said, extending her hand. "I begged Maya for a quick tour. It sounds like you've got an amazing project going on here."

Nolan shook, cataloging the firm grip, the confident stance, the easy smile. Mancuso was attractive and sure of herself. The kind of person who probably never had trouble connecting with others. The kind who didn't need to count days sober or attend meetings or wrestle with sleepless nights and dark memories.

And she'd *begged* Maya? Where had she even come from? Maya had never mentioned her before. But then, why should she? Nolan was just the hired help. The person who fixed things. The temporary person who'd be gone from Maya's life in another month.

"It's Maya's project," Nolan said flatly. "I'm just the builder."

Aisley's gaze flickered for a moment. Speculatively. "Right."

There was a moment of silence, which Nolan was happy to let grow. After all, this was Maya's house and Maya's *friend.*

"Aisley was kind enough to give me a ride home from the game," Maya explained, a slight nervous edge to her voice.

"Game?" Nolan said.

"This morning," Aisley said, leaning casually against the counter like she belonged there. In Maya's space. The space Nolan had been carefully rebuilding piece by piece. "Youth soccer."

"Ah." Nolan glanced at Maya. "Manny and Luis both played?"

"Yes." Maya turned to Aisley. "And I bet Emmie will want to play next. How old does she have to be?"

"Six," Aisley said, smiling at Maya in a way that made Nolan's jaw tighten. "Though we make exceptions sometimes for siblings."

"Oh, good," Maya said. "If she still wants to when she's old enough, I think that would be good for her."

"It is for most kids," Aisley said. "Builds confidence, teamwork, all that good stuff."

"Where is she, by the way?" Nolan asked.

"Still with Izzy. They're all getting ice cream."

"Ah." Nolan turned back to her measurements, feeling suddenly like an intruder. The easy rapport between Maya and Aisley was obvious. They'd probably spent the morning laughing, enjoying themselves, free from the weight of renovation problems, grief, and complicated pasts. The things she and Maya shared.

She pushed aside thoughts of what it would be like to be someone carefree and uncomplicated, like this soccer coach seemed to be. To be someone worthy of Maya.

Service, Tim had said. *Focus on service.*

"Ready for that tour?" Maya asked Aisley as the silence stretched.

"Absolutely." Aisley pushed off from the counter, her smile directed at Maya. "Lead the way."

As they left the kitchen, Nolan exhaled slowly, shaking away the tightness in her shoulders. None of her business who Maya's friends were. Her phone buzzed—the delivery company. She answered and confirmed the address, grateful she'd be able to escape soon. She really wanted to get the install done and get the hell out of Maya's house. The space, one she'd usually found comfortable, a place where she and Maya had spent countless hours making decisions and solving problems together, was suddenly too small and too weighted with emotions she didn't want to deal with.

Maya's happy, excited voice floated down the hall. Nolan hadn't heard that lightness before, at least not directed at her. Something sharp and dark twisted in her chest, a feeling she couldn't—wouldn't—name.

It shouldn't matter who Maya spent time with. It shouldn't bother her that Maya had brought someone here, to what Nolan had started to think of as their shared project. Their shared space.

But it did.

When they returned to the kitchen, Nolan was careful to keep her expression neutral. "They should be here in ten minutes."

"Oh, that's perfect," Maya said. "Aisley, I'll walk you out."

"Great." Aisley nodded to Nolan. "The house looks amazing. Really impressive work."

"Thanks." Nolan kept her response brief and professional. The way it should be. The way it had to be.

After Maya walked Aisley to the door, Nolan heard the murmur of their voices, though not the words. A laugh—Maya's laugh, bright and genuine. Being in Maya's space while Maya spent time with another woman left her with an uncomfortable mixture of tension and irritation. Which she had absolutely zero reason or right to feel.

Today was just another day on the job. Nothing more.

Chapter Fourteen

Maya cleared the last of the construction dust from the kitchen counters. The silence in the room had stretched taut as a wire since Aisley had left.

"Did you know Aisley growing up?" Nolan said. "I don't recognize her, but I didn't go to the same school as you and Izzy."

"Iz and I lived just across the town line and ended up bussing to Granger." Maya leaned against the counter, watching Nolan fiddle with the outlet for the refrigerator. "But Aisley hasn't lived here long, a year or so I guess. I met her at Izzy's yesterday."

Nolan looked over her shoulder. "After we talked."

Maya winced internally. What Nolan meant was after she'd had her crisis of confidence and cried on Nolan's shoulder, thank goodness, not literally. "Mmm. Last night."

"Ah."

"Izzy finally talked me into joining her game group." Maya wiped the same spot she'd already cleaned twice. Needing to fill the oppressive dead air, Maya added, "Then Emmie wanted a sleepover, and that ran over into the boys' game this morning."

"Huh." Nolan pulled paperwork out of one of her many folders, not looking at Maya. "Good coach?"

"I can't critique the soccer. First game I've ever watched. I had no idea what was going on other than where the ball was supposed to end up. But the kids seemed to really like her." Maya set down the cloth. The sharp line of Nolan's jaw seemed tighter than usual, and she was avoiding looking directly at her. "Is everything okay?"

"Why wouldn't it be?"

"You've been quiet."

Nolan shrugged, still not meeting her eyes. "Just focused on making sure everything's ready for the installation."

The doorbell rang, and Nolan strode toward the hall as if she couldn't wait to escape. "That'll be them."

The next hour dissolved into a flurry of activity. Delivery men in coveralls hauled in massive boxes. Nolan directed traffic with calm authority while the rip of cardboard and plastic wrap accompanied the scrape of appliances sliding into place over the plywood Nolan had put down to protect the new floorboards. Through it all, Maya wisely stayed out of the way. Nolan took charge, as she had dozens of times before with self-assured efficiency.

"Hold it." Nolan crouched and examined the gas line hookup on the range. "This coupling isn't seating right."

One of the delivery men sighed. "That's the one they sent us."

"That's the one for the residential model. This is the commercial stove." Nolan straightened and reached into her toolbox. "Lucky for us, I brought the right one."

The man looked ready to argue, but something in Nolan's steady gaze must have stopped him. He stepped back, hands raised in surrender.

"You're the boss."

"No," Nolan said, glancing briefly at Maya. "She is."

The simple statement warmed Maya in unexpected ways.

By the time the delivery crew departed, leaving behind gleaming stainless-steel appliances in place of the gaping holes, the earlier tension had eased. Nolan moved around the kitchen, checking each installation one final time, while Maya stood in the doorway, marveling at the transformation.

"It's starting to look like a real kitchen."

Nolan ran her hand along the inside of the refrigerator door, adjusting it a fraction of an inch. "Still need to finish the backsplash and install the ceiling lights, but yeah. Getting there."

"Emmie's going to flip when she sees this. She's been begging to bake cookies for weeks."

"Sport's got a sweet tooth, huh?" Nolan smiled, the curve of her mouth eclipsing the allure of the new shiny kitchen for an instant.

"You know, she's telling everyone that's what she wants to be called now," Maya said.

"Uh-oh. Are you mad?"

Maya tilted her head. "Why would I be?"

Nolan shrugged. "I just kind of came out with it when I called her that. I didn't mean to interfere with your daughter."

Maya frowned. "You've never interfered. You must know me well enough by now to know I would have said something if I was bothered by anything."

Nolan grinned, the most relaxed she'd looked all day. "Yeah. I got that."

"She's five," Maya said, relief washing through her as the atmosphere in the room finally lightened. Being at odds with Nolan had been unsettling. As if the day had gone wrong and she didn't know how to fix it. "One day it's all tutus and tiaras, the next she's digging for worms in the woods. This week she'll be Sport, next week, who knows."

"I'll try not to call her Snuffleupagus."

Maya laughed. "Thank you. Was that a favorite show of yours growing up?"

"Kids' shows weren't a thing in my house," Nolan said flatly, breaking eye contact again. "But the reruns show up everywhere, even after midnight when not much else is running."

"Night owl, are you?" Maya tried to sound casual rather than curious. They so rarely talked about anything beyond the plans for the house. Any personal revelation felt like a gift, one she coveted.

"Not by choice." Nolan adjusted a shelf in the refrigerator. "This is all set."

Maya crossed to the refrigerator, opening and closing it just to hear the soft, satisfying *thunk.* She wanted to ask what kept Nolan awake at night. She wanted to ask how she filled all the hours they were apart. She wanted to ask her a million things that were none of her damn business. "You're really good with Emmie, you know. Most adults don't take five-year-olds seriously."

"Kids are just people, only smaller with less filter." Nolan removed and reset a knob on the stove. "My sergeant in the Army used to say that. He had four kids. Taught me more about dealing with people than any officer."

Maya paused, absorbing this new piece of information. Another small victory.

"How long were you in the Army?"

"Eight years." Nolan seemed to be choosing her words carefully. "Enlisted right after high school. Best escape route I could find at eighteen."

"Escape from what?"

A shadow crossed Nolan's face. "Home wasn't a great place. My father and I…we didn't have much of a relationship. I was glad to get out, and he was glad to see me go."

Maya's heart hurt. How could a parent not make a child feel wanted? "I'm sorry. That sounds awful."

"I've heard a lot worse stories," Nolan said. "But growing up like that, you learn to read people. To watch for the signs. When to be invisible, when to speak up. Kids are always paying attention, even when adults don't think they are."

"That explains a lot about how good you are with Emmie."

"More luck, probably." Nolan drummed her fingers lightly on the counter. "I didn't want to come back here, but then he left me the business." She grimaced. "That was a huge surprise. But relocating—I won't say coming home because I never thought of it that way—forced me to ask where my life was heading. When I really looked, I saw too much of him in me. The anger, the way I pushed people away just like he did. So I've been working to change that."

Maya moved closer, drawn by this rare glimpse behind Nolan's careful reserve. "Trying to change takes courage."

"Not courage. Desperation." Nolan's gaze fixed on some distant point. "When you hit bottom, you have to choose to stay there or start climbing out."

"Is that what you did? Started climbing?"

"Working on it. Some days are harder than others."

The vulnerability in Nolan's voice made Maya's chest tighten. She'd never heard her speak this way, so open, so unguarded. Nolan's willingness to change resonated with the part of her trying to rebuild her own shattered life.

"For what it's worth," Maya said softly, "I think you're doing a pretty amazing job."

Nolan met her gaze then, her expression startled. "Yeah?"

"Yeah." Maya smiled. "Look at what you've helped create here." She gestured to the kitchen, gleaming and new, full of promise. "You're giving us our home back."

Nolan's expression warmed, an openness that hadn't been there before. "It's a good house with a solid foundation. All it needed was someone to see what it could be. Someone like you to take a chance on it."

The words hung between them, layered with meaning that made Maya's heart beat faster. She wondered if Nolan was still talking about the house. She turned slowly in the center of the kitchen, astounded by the transformation. The quartz countertops, cool and elegant. The gleaming stainless steel appliances, catching the sunlight and reflecting it back in slivers of silver. The new farmhouse sink, deep and roomy, just as she'd wanted, anchoring the space. The cabinets, with their simple handles and clean lines, exactly what she'd envisioned.

"Nolan, it's perfect." Joy bubbled up inside her, unexpected and bright. For the first time in longer than she could remember, hope and possibility overshadowed grief and the dull weight of responsibility. "I can't believe how beautiful it is."

Nolan watched her from the doorway, her expression soft. "You had the vision. I just executed it."

"No." Maya shook her head. "This is so much more than what I imagined. This is…" The words caught in her throat. For so long, nothing had felt like home, not since Dantas. But as she stood there, surrounded by the signs of renewal, the first stirrings of belonging filled her. "This feels like home again."

"I'm glad for you and Emmie," Nolan said. "You deserve it."

Maya crossed to Nolan. "You understood what I needed, even when I couldn't quite explain it."

Nolan's eyes held hers, steady and certain. "That's my job."

"No." Maya stepped close enough to see the flecks of gold in Nolan's blue eyes and to catch the faint scent of cedar and clean sweat that clung to her skin. "Your job was to fix the house. You've been fixing so much more than that."

Happiness, gratitude, and wonderment collided, and Maya wrapped her arms around Nolan in a sudden, fierce embrace. "Thank you."

In the next second, she registered Nolan's solid warmth pressed against her, Nolan's heart hammering against hers. Heat rushed through her, quicksilver fast. Nolan stiffened for an instant, and when Maya didn't move, *couldn't* move, Nolan's arms came up, tentative at first, then tightening around Maya's waist.

Maya gasped, the sound loud in the stillness. She hadn't been held like this, hadn't felt safe in someone's arms, surrounded by strength that asked nothing in return, in so long. The simple human connection cracked open a door inside her she'd kept locked since the funeral.

She pulled back just enough to look into Nolan's face. The unguarded longing there mirrored her own yearning. Without thought, without planning, Maya kissed her. Nolan's lips were soft and warm, with a subtle peppermint taste. New, but somehow right.

She could stop. She could question. She could search for the guilt and remorse that might surface. But she didn't move, and Nolan's hands slid up her back, pulling her closer. Their bodies seemed to fit together as if by design. Nolan's touch brought a hunger, a need she'd thought had died with Dantas, to life. She pressed closer and kissed her again, threading her fingers into Nolan's hair, tangling them in the soft strands, anchoring herself to the moment and the sensations flooding her.

Nolan deepened the kiss, her mouth insistent. Maya lost herself in the gentle pressure of Nolan's hands at her waist, the urgent groan that escaped Nolan's throat, and the way her body trembled. Maya reveled in the taste of her and the way she responded to every touch, as if she'd been waiting for this exact moment.

When they finally broke apart, both breathless, Nolan's eyes had darkened, pupils wide. Primal hunger lurked there, carefully restrained but unmistakable. Maya leaned in again, drawn by that look, needing that intensity and the singular connection that had been missing for so long.

More hurried now, the kiss carried an edge of desperation, of need too long denied. Nolan caressed her back, settled her palm at the base of her spine, holding her close. A claiming touch. Maya's entire body responded, every nerve coming alive after months, years of numbness. She gripped Nolan's shoulders, wanting more, needing more than this stolen moment in her kitchen.

Then, abruptly, Nolan gently pushed her away.

"Wait," Nolan said, voice rough. "Maya, we can't do this. Not like this."

Ice washed through her, suffocating the heat. Maya stepped back and folded her arms over her chest, suddenly cold in the space where Nolan's body had been.

"I'm sorry. I thought…" Her throat closed around the words, humiliation rising hot in her cheeks. "I misunderstood."

"No." Nolan reached out, then let her hand fall. "You didn't misunderstand. I want this. I want you. But there's something you need to know. Something I need to say."

Maya's heart raced. Nolan had said she'd been with Pris. She'd never intimated she didn't prefer women. She couldn't have been wrong about that. What then? God, was Nolan attached? Married?

"I'm in recovery." Nolan's words came out steady and deliberate. "I'm an alcoholic."

The world tilted sideways. Maya's lungs forgot how to draw breath. The words echoed in her head, incomprehensible at first, then suddenly, brutally clear.

"You're a recovering alcoholic." Her voice sounded distant, as if it belonged to someone else. "And you didn't tell me."

"I should have told you sooner, when I first realized…" Nolan's face was pale now, her shoulders squared as if bracing for impact. "I didn't expect this would happen. But when I started wanting it to, I should have told you. I know that."

"You wanted…" Maya shook her head. "You knew what happened to my wife. You knew what happened to Emmie's mother."

"I knew Dantas died in an accident. Johnny told me. I didn't know a drunk driver killed her until you told me." A muscle in Nolan's jaw twitched. "I didn't tell you right then because I was afraid. Afraid you'd look at me and see her killer."

The mention of Dantas's name struck like a knife twisting inside. The kitchen, so bright and new moments ago, seemed to shrink around her, the air thinning until she could barely breathe. Her mind flooded with memories—of the deputy's voice on the phone, the hospital corridor, and the closed casket at the funeral. The words "drunk driver" repeated in her head, a vicious mantra.

"What happened, exactly?" The question emerged flat, clinical, despite the chaos inside her. "With your drinking."

Nolan drew a breath. "I ran my truck off the road. Wrapped it around a tree. Blood alcohol was twice the legal limit. That was my wake-up call."

"Was anyone else hurt?" Maya's heart pounded so hard she could feel it in her fingertips and her temples.

"No. I was alone. It was late, empty road." Nolan's gaze never wavered. "I got lucky. Could have killed someone. Could have killed myself."

Maya nodded mechanically, processing. A drunk driver had taken Dantas. Now here stood Nolan, who had spent months in her home, around her daughter, earning their trust, becoming essential, confessing she could have been just like the person who destroyed Maya's world. How could she have missed it?

"How long have you been in recovery?"

"Eighteen months." Nolan cleared her throat. "Seventeen months, three weeks, five days and," she glanced at her watch, "seven hours."

Maya, her voice unnaturally calm despite the storm raging inside, said, "So you were already sober when we met."

"Yes."

"And you never drink now?"

"No. One day at a time, but no, I don't drink."

Maya's stomach twisted, nausea rising. The taste of Nolan's kiss, so sweet moments before, turned bitter on her tongue. Nolan had witnessed Emmie's fear, her own grief. And had hidden the truth about herself, might have kept hiding it if she hadn't thrown herself at Nolan in a moment of weakness. The betrayal cut sharp, nearly as vicious as her own self-loathing. *Her* betrayal, far worse than Nolan's, tore at her. She'd betrayed everything that had ever mattered in her life.

She recoiled from the absurd, terrible irony of it all and took another step back, needing air and distance. The room seemed to spin, the gleaming appliances that had brought her such joy moments ago now mocking her naïveté. She felt exposed and vulnerable, as if the floor beneath her feet might give way at any moment.

"I appreciate your honesty." The words tasted like ashes. "But I think I'd like to be alone now."

Nolan flinched, the hurt flashing over her face before she rebuilt the mask.

"Of course. I'll go." Nolan packed up her tools with slow, deliberate movements. "I can have Gruff take over finishing in here on Monday if that works for you."

"That's fine." Maya barely recognized the detached, distant tone, as if her voice belonged to someone else.

Nolan lingered at the kitchen doorway, toolkit in hand. "Maya, I…"

"Please." Maya shook her head, not trusting herself to hear whatever Nolan might say next, not when her control was hanging by such a fragile thread. "Just go."

After the front door closed, Maya stood alone in her gleaming new kitchen, surrounded by polished surfaces that she'd thought had represented progress and renewal. Instead, she pressed her palms against the cool stone countertop and tried to breathe through the tightness in her chest.

It might have been Nolan who'd killed Dantas. Nolan, who had become a fixture in her life. Nolan, whose quiet competence had become a cornerstone of her rebuilding. Nolan, whose kiss still burned on her lips.

How could she ever trust her again?

How could she ever trust herself?

The tears, when they came, surprised her. She hadn't cried in months, had thought perhaps she'd forgotten how. For once, she simply let the grief and anger and confusion pour out of her, unchecked and raw.

She cried for Dantas, for the life Dantas had never had a chance to live, for the future that had been stolen from them. She cried for Emmie, who would grow up without her other mother. She cried for herself, for the fool she'd been to even think she could start again, trust again, feel again.

When there were no tears left, only the hollow ache of exhaustion, she splashed cold water on her face. Emmie would be home soon. She couldn't let Emmie see that she'd been crying. The beautiful day, bright and filled with promise, had lost its splendor, tarnished along with her hope.

She would have to face Nolan again. The work was not finished, and Emmie…God, Emmie was so attached to her already. How had she let that happen? She should have been more careful.

She would be now.

Chapter Fifteen

Nolan gripped the steering wheel until her knuckles went white, the truck's engine growling as she pushed it harder than necessary down the winding road, away from Maya's house. But she couldn't outrun the look in Maya's eyes—the shock, the betrayal, the disgust.

How had she been so fucking stupid?

She'd known better. Known from the moment she stepped into Maya's house that first day that she had no business being there. Maya needed someone whole, someone without the kind of baggage that turned a life into a minefield. Someone who hadn't almost killed themselves with a bottle, someone who wouldn't bring that shadow into a house where a child lived, where a woman was trying to rebuild after losing everything to someone just like her.

The memory of Maya's lips against hers crashed into her thoughts, and she slammed on the brakes, pulling onto the shoulder with gravel spraying beneath the tires. She sat there, engine idling, hands shaking.

Maya had kissed her. What was she supposed to have done? Pushed her away? She didn't have the strength for that, not when she'd wanted to touch her for weeks. She'd kept telling herself she couldn't have her, didn't want her, wasn't half-crazy over her already, but she'd been lying to herself. She couldn't break that habit any more than she could resist the taste of her. The way Maya's body had moved against hers, soft and inviting, was better than any drink. She'd kissed her back and Maya had pressed closer, fingers threading through her hair, breasts full and firm against her chest. Maya's every move had said yes, and in her weakness—*her* weakness—she'd pretended that kissing her, that wanting more, was something she could have. She'd let herself believe until Maya's racing heart and trembling body had whispered she could have all that. That Maya wanted her, would have her. And it would all be based on a lie. Because Maya didn't know her.

And when Maya did know her—all of her—Maya had done exactly what she'd expected. Maya had turned away from her. Whatever Maya had seemed to feel was gone now. Dead the moment the truth left her lips.

Maya had rejected her. As she'd feared. As she deserved.

She grabbed her phone, scrolled to Tim's number, and stared at it. He'd told her a thousand times: When you're struggling, reach out. Don't isolate. Don't let the shame win.

But she couldn't. Not yet. Those moments with Maya—the wonder in her face as she looked at the completed kitchen, the joy in her laugh, the way she'd melted into her arms—those were hers. Sacred in a way she couldn't explain. Telling Tim would make them part of the wreckage, part of the mistake, part of the mess she'd made of everything.

She shoved the phone back into her pocket and pulled onto the road, driving aimlessly, heading out of town past the neat suburban developments and into the industrial district where the road opened up. Muscle memory must have taken over, and, before she knew it, she recognized where she was.

The Rusty Anchor, a low-slung cement block affair with a sagging roof and blacked-out windows, sat at the edge of town like a scar on the landscape. The gravel lot in front was half-empty, motorcycles and pickup trucks older than hers parked haphazardly. She'd driven past it a hundred times on her way to job sites but had never even slowed down. Now she pulled in and parked between a Harley with chrome that gleamed under the last slanting rays of the sun and a Ford pickup with more rust than paint.

She sat there, key still in the ignition, staring at the neon beer signs flickering in the darkened windows. The place looked exactly like what it was—a dive bar where people went to disappear for a while, to drown whatever was eating at them. She knew places like this. Had been a regular at places like this.

A bearded man in a black leather vest festooned with patches and illegible script ambled out of the bar with the telltale gait of a seasoned drunk, even though the sun wasn't even down yet. He got on his bike with the kind of practiced ease that said this wasn't his first time riding under the influence. Nolan watched him weave out of the parking lot and wondered if anyone would miss him if he didn't make it home.

One thing she'd never had to worry about. Still didn't.

She could go in. Order a beer with a whiskey chaser, maybe two. Welcome that familiar burn, that temporary quieting of the noise in her head. Maya would never have to know. Nobody would have to know. She was good at keeping secrets, after all.

She clenched her jaw until her temples throbbed. Eighteen months. Eighteen months of meetings, of counting days, of building something that felt like a life. Eighteen months of learning that the bottle didn't solve anything, just postponed everything until the hangover lifted and the problems were still there, bigger than before.

She could drink, of course she could. Just a dozen steps. And lose everything, again.

But God, she wanted it. Wanted to wash away the taste of Maya's rejection, wanted to stop seeing the shock in her eyes, wanted to forget how right it had felt to hold her.

A couple walked past her truck, laughing about something, the woman's hand on the man's shoulder. Music spilled out when they opened the door—some country song about heartbreak and whiskey. They disappeared into the bar, and the music echoed in her bones.

She started the truck.

She couldn't do this. Not to herself, not to Gruff and the others who counted on her, not to the life she'd fought so hard to build. She had jobs scheduled out for months, and she'd need to see the reno through at Maya's, even if Maya didn't want her there. She could stay out of her way, but she'd already hurt her enough without adding drunk calls or showing up at her door with alcohol on her breath.

She drove home just under the speed limit and pulled into her driveway as the sun was setting, painting the sky in shades of pink and orange that reminded her of the light in Maya's kitchen when they'd kissed. Inside, she made coffee she didn't really want and sat at her kitchen table, staring at the cup until it grew cold.

She texted Gruff. *Need you at Maya's Monday early*

Her phone buzzed a minute later. *Problem?*

She typed back: *No something came up.*

The silence said he was wondering how hard to push. She never missed work.

I'll be there, he finally replied.

She deleted the message thread without responding. Better to let him draw his own conclusions than to explain what couldn't be explained.

The house was too quiet. She walked through the living room she rarely used, past the second bedroom that was supposed to be an office but was just empty space and the bathroom where she sometimes caught glimpses of her father in the mirror.

Finally, she grabbed her jacket and headed out to the workshop. The smell of wood shavings and varnish usually calmed her, but tonight it just reminded her of the clock she'd started working on for Maya. Another mistake, inserting herself into a life where she didn't belong.

She pulled a piece of pine from the rack and brushed its smooth surface with her palm. She could start something new. A fresh start. A way to keep her hands busy and her mind occupied. Maybe in a few hours, the ache in her chest would fade enough for her to think clearly.

As she sketched a design on the pad she kept on the bench, her phone rang. A call from Tim. She almost didn't answer, but eighteen months of recovery had taught her that the times she least wanted to talk were exactly when she needed to most.

"Hey," she said.

"Missed you at the meeting tonight."

"Yeah."

"Guess that means you wanted to miss it, huh?"

"Look, Tim, it's kind of a crap night."

"I figured that much out, kid. Want to talk about it?"

Nolan closed her eyes. "Not really."

"But you need to?"

She leaned against the workbench, suddenly exhausted. "Yeah. I fucked up."

"Guess we should visit, then. Want me to come by?"

"I'll come to you."

"Drive safe."

After she hung up, she locked up the workshop. The wood could wait. The projects could wait. Everything could wait except figuring out what she was going to do about Maya, the conversations she needed to have, and the steps she needed to take to keep from losing everything she'd fought to build.

❖

Maya heard Izzy's car before she saw it, the familiar rumble of the old Subaru announcing the arrival of her family. She quickly splashed water on her face at the kitchen sink again, checking her reflection in the window. Her eyes were still red, but maybe Izzy wouldn't notice.

"Mommy!" Emmie burst through the door like a small hurricane, chocolate streaked on her shirt, baby-fine strands of black hair escaping from her purple barrette. "I had chocolate sprinkles!"

"I see." Maya forced a smile as she hugged her. "Did you eat it all?"

"Yes, except the very bottom of the cone. I was full."

"Hmm. Too full for supper?"

"No!"

Maya laughed, for a moment forgetting the pain. Emmie was her joy. Emmie mattered above all. Izzy crowded into the kitchen with Manny and Luis, their eyes bright and faces glowing with identical grins.

"Wow," Izzy said, looking around. "This is amazing. I love that stove."

"Did you see us?" Luis asked. "We won!"

"I did." Maya ruffled both boys' hair. "You were both great."

"Can we go outside?" Manny asked.

"If you stay within sight," Maya said. "That means you have to be able to see the house. No woods today."

"Okay," the boys chorused and stampeded for the back door.

"Can I go, too?" Emmie asked.

"How about you take your new coloring book and crayons out to the back porch," Maya said.

"Okay," Emmie exclaimed and darted away.

Maya let out a breath. Normal things, that's what she needed.

The minute the kids were gone, Izzy said, "You've been crying."

Not a question, and no sense denying it. Izzy had always known, from the first time Maya had snuck in after curfew to the moment she'd known she was into girls and not boys.

"It's nothing," Maya said automatically.

"Bullshit." Izzy's voice was quiet but firm. "What happened?"

"Nothing critical. Just tired. I—"

All three kids thundered back into the kitchen, cutting off any answer Maya might have given.

"It's really hot out," Manny declared.

"Can we go swimming?" Luis demanded.

"Yay," Emmie yelled.

"You know what?" Izzy said suddenly. "It's such a beautiful day. Why don't we take these maniacs to the pool? Let them burn off some energy."

"The pool?" Maya glanced at the clock. It was almost six.

"It's open until dark. Remember we used to go with Johnny and hang out until they chased us out when we were kids?"

Maya did remember. Long summer evenings at the community pool, the smell of chlorine and sunscreen, the exhaustion that felt good instead of the bone-deep weariness that had become her constant companion.

"I don't have swim stuff that will work for the boys," Maya said.

"They can wear their soccer shorts," Izzy said. "Come on. It'll be fun."

"I have *my* suit," Emmie said. "Can we go swimming, Mommy? Please?"

Emmie's hopeful expression and the boys already making swimming motions with their hands sealed it. Maya nodded. "Sure. Let's go swimming."

An hour later, Maya sat on a picnic bench in the shade of a large umbrella watching the kids splash in the shallow end of the public pool, their shrieks of delight echoing off the water. The pool area was busy but not as crowded as it would be in another few weeks. Parents who looked as tired as Maya felt sat in lounge chairs, and teenagers hung around the refreshment booth, pretending to be bored.

"So," Izzy said with forced casualness, "want to tell me what really happened?"

Maya watched Manny cannonball off the side of the pool, sending water splashing everywhere. Emmie paddled about with her water wings in the cordoned-off section for the under-sixes. "Did you know about Nolan?"

"Know what about Nolan?" Izzy's false-innocent tone was a dead giveaway. Izzy wasn't the only one who knew her sister well.

Maya squeezed her water bottle, fighting the anger building inside. "That she's an alcoholic."

Izzy went very still. "How did this come up?"

"That's not an answer, Iz."

"You first, Maya. What the hell happened?" Izzy's hushed tone vibrated with urgency. "Don't make me drag it out of you."

"She told me today. After..." Maya's voice caught. This was her sister, the woman who'd saved her sanity when Dantas died. Not the enemy. "After we kissed."

"She kissed you?" Izzy's voice rose, then dropped quickly as she looked around. "Maya, holy shit."

"*I* kissed *her*," Maya said, the words feeling strange in her mouth. "I was so happy about the kitchen, so grateful for this new start, and Nolan has been there every step. I just...I kissed her. And then she stopped it and told me the truth."

Izzy took her hand. "Oh, honey. That must have been a shock. Especially then."

"She could have been the one who killed Dantas." The words came out in a rush. "She drove drunk, Izzy. She wrapped her truck around a tree. She could have killed someone."

"But she didn't."

"That's not the point." Maya pulled her hand away, frustration and shame warring inside. "I should have had the choice—whether I wanted her to do the work, whether I wanted her in my house, around my daughter."

"Are you saying you wouldn't have hired her if you'd known?"

"How could I have known I could trust her? She might be just like the man who killed Dantas!" Maya's throat filled. There it was—the terrible fear. That Nolan, who'd somehow become so central to her life these past few months, was really a stranger who represented everything she hated.

"Maya, stop." Izzy's voice was firm. "She's in recovery. She told you that, didn't she?"

Maya stared. "You knew, didn't you?"

"I assumed," Izzy said. "Johnny talked about her. Might have mentioned they were friends from outside work."

Maya reeled from the sense of betrayal all over again. How could Izzy of all people not understand? She'd witnessed the destruction of Maya and Emmie's world. "You knew, and you didn't tell me?"

"It wasn't my secret to share," Izzy said. "And honestly, I didn't think it would matter. She's building your house, not dating you."

"Well, apparently the line got a little blurred."

"Are you going to tell me how that came about?"

Maya sighed, watching Emmie teaching her ponies how to swim. "I don't know."

"Guess." Izzy's tone held just enough sarcasm to make Maya laugh.

She hadn't expected to be able to laugh—possibly ever again. "Nolan is a complicated person—hard to get to know if you're waiting for her to tell you anything. But being around her? Her kindness, her patience, her reliability? That shines through."

"I suppose her being sex on a stick doesn't hurt?"

"*Izzy*." Maya shook her head.

"What? I'm not allowed to think a woman is hot?"

Maya tilted her head. "Are you trying to tell me something?"

Izzy waved a hand. "Don't change the subject."

"Fine, but I'm not forgetting that little remark." Maya stretched her legs, her muscles cramped and aching. "The kiss just happened. It wasn't planned, and if I'd had a minute to think about it, I wouldn't have done it."

They sat in silence, watching the kids play. The boys were teaching Emmie the basics of water polo, helping her hit the inflatable ball. Every time she connected, she laughed.

"She's wrong for you anyway," Izzy said finally.

Maya tensed. Part of her, a small but persistent part, wanted to argue. To defend Nolan, to say that Izzy didn't understand, that there was more to the story than just Nolan's past mistakes. But the logical side of her knew Izzy was right. Nolan represented everything Maya should avoid. She wasn't in a place where she could sympathize with Nolan's challenges.

"I know," she said, but the words left her hollow.

"Do you?"

Maya didn't answer. She couldn't. Because watching Nolan with Emmie, seeing the careful way she treated both of them, the way she'd kissed Maya like she was something precious—none of that fit with what she feared. None of that erased her guilt for wanting anyone other than Dantas, either.

"She lied to me," Maya said instead.

"She kept something private. That's different."

"Is it?"

Emmie climbed out of the pool and ran over to them, dripping and grinning. "Mommy, look!" She pointed to a complicated arrangement of pool noodles and kickboards the kids had constructed. "We made a boat!"

"It's beautiful, baby," Maya said, managing a smile.

"Maybe we can make a horse." Emmie ran back to the water.

"She's happy," Izzy observed.

"She is."

"You could be, too."

Maya turned to Izzy, surprised by the gentle tone. "What?"

"I'm not saying Nolan is right for you. I'm saying you're allowed to be happy. You're allowed to want things. You're allowed to kiss someone if you want to, even if it's complicated."

"But not her."

"Probably not her," Izzy agreed. "But someone. Someday."

Maya felt tears threatening again and blinked them back. "I don't know if I'll ever be ready."

"I know."

They sat quietly, watching the kids play as the sun sank lower in the sky. The pool lights came on, casting ripples of blue light across the water. The boys helped Emmie out of the pool and wrapped her in a multicolored beach towel.

"They're good with her," Maya murmured.

"Manny said she's like having a little sister."

Tears filled Maya's eyes, and she brushed them away. "I wanted another."

"You have time."

Maya met Izzy's gaze. "I can't see it, Iz. With Dantas, I knew what my whole life would be like."

"When you can see the picture again, you'll know it's time." Izzy squeezed her hand. "You still have the house to finish. What are you going to do about Nolan?"

"I have to see her again," Maya said eventually. "She said Gruff would be by on Monday, but I need…I want Nolan's input. She's the best."

"Gruff could—"

"No. Besides, Emmie would notice. She'll ask questions if Nolan disappears."

"You could tell her the truth."

Maya shook her head. "That Mommy kissed the house fixer and now things are weird? I don't think so."

Izzy laughed despite everything. "Good point."

"I just need to get through the rest of the renovation," Maya said. "Keep things professional. Pretend today never happened."

"Is that what you really want?"

The question hung between them as the kids played in the gathering dusk. Maya didn't answer, couldn't answer, because she wasn't sure she knew anymore.

All she knew was that Nolan had awakened something in her that she thought had died with Dantas. And now she had to figure out how to bury it again.

CHAPTER SIXTEEN

Maya stood at the kitchen window, her third cup of coffee growing cold as she watched the empty driveway. Monday morning, seven fifteen. Nolan was usually there by now, tool belt slung over her shoulder, that easy stride carrying her toward the house like she belonged there.

But she wouldn't be coming today. Or any day, maybe.

Maya's chest tightened until breathing became an effort. Hands shaking, she set the mug down and pressed her palms flat against the cool stone countertop. Even with the windows open, the air in the kitchen was still, lying heavily on her skin. The kitchen sparkled, new and bright. The same kitchen where she'd imagined a shining new future to match just forty-eight hours ago. Before she'd thrown herself at Nolan, and everything had changed in the space of a heartbeat.

I'm an alcoholic.

The words echoed in her mind for the thousandth time, each repetition a fresh wound. She understood why Nolan hadn't told her—God, did she understand. The shame, the fear of judgment, the terrible weight of carrying such a secret. But the betrayal still burned through her like acid. Not just that Nolan had hidden it, but that *she'd* been so blind, so ready to trust, so desperate to feel again that she'd missed all the signs that Nolan wasn't just a private person, but that she was hiding something.

Had there been signs? She'd replayed every conversation, every shared moment, countless times since she'd asked Nolan to go, searching for clues she might have missed. Nolan's careful way of declining wine at dinner or a beer at the barbecue. She had just assumed Nolan simply didn't drink much. Nolan's habit of never mentioning where she was going when she left Maya's. Looking back now, what she'd attributed to reserve was likely Nolan not mentioning the AA meetings. The way she'd deflected personal questions with jokes or work talk. The careful distance she maintained even as they grew closer.

She'd read it all as shyness, as professional boundaries or the kind of emotional walls that people built after being hurt. And the shadows that sometimes crossed Nolan's face when she thought no one was looking? She'd attributed them to fatigue or the stress of running a business.

She couldn't blame Nolan for everything. Nolan had every right to her privacy. But *she* should have been more wary. She hadn't *missed* the signs that Nolan might have secrets, might not be the woman she thought she was. She'd willfully ignored anything that threatened the fantasy.

Lord, she'd somehow managed to ignore the red flags when Pris showed up, fawning over Nolan and insulting her. Was Nolan even done with Pris?

"Stop it," Maya muttered. Now she was guilty of overthinking everything and assigning blame where there was none. Nolan had held back the truth, and Maya couldn't agree with her reasons why, but Nolan was not a liar. Izzy'd been right about that. That and everything else.

Maya sighed. Izzy had tried to warn her that Nolan was not someone she should build a fantasy around. Had she listened? Obviously not.

But then Izzy had said other things, too. That Nolan was in recovery, that she'd been sober when they'd met, that intent mattered. That people were more than their worst moments. But the echo of her screams in the hospital corridor the night Dantas died drowned out all reason with fury and fear.

Maya paced the length of the kitchen. Without Nolan's presence, everything seemed smaller somehow, less alive. Every gleaming surface seemed to mock her with its perfection. They'd created this together, piece by careful piece, decision by careful decision. She'd trusted Nolan's judgment about everything from grout color to cabinet hardware.

She'd trusted Nolan without knowing her, and that was a

monument to her own naïveté, to how desperate she'd been for any kind of connection. Nolan's secrets, her shame.

And no one to blame.

A truck rumbled up the drive, and her heart lurched before reality prevailed. Different engine sound. Wrong rhythm of gravel under tires. A flash of red rolling past the window, not a white truck. Not Nolan.

Gruff climbed out of his dusty pickup as a second vehicle pulled in behind. The sounds of men and women calling greetings, tools clanging, tailgates banging, so familiar after all these weeks. But Nolan's strong, resonant voice was missing. Relief and disappointment warred inside.

This was what she wanted, wasn't it? A few days to rebuild her shields. To exterminate the fantasies she'd had no business imagining. To stop missing her.

To stop wanting her.

Maya caught her breath. Did she want her? The way Nolan had kissed her back with such desperate hunger had haunted her all weekend. When she tried to sleep, when she pretended to Emmie she was fine, when she ran her hands over her body in the shower, the wanting simmered like a barely banked fire in her depths.

She took a long breath, resolved. She couldn't control what her body or her fractured emotions desired, but she could damn well control what she did about it. Which was going to be exactly nothing.

Time, everyone said, would heal even the deepest pain. She knew that wasn't true, but time would at least dull this craving.

She opened the door before Gruff knocked, forcing a smile she didn't feel. "Morning, Gruff. Coffee's fresh when the crew wants refills."

"Much obliged." He wore his usual red bandana around his neck, the same faded blue work pants, the same T-shirt that had been washed so many times the words were illegible. But today the sharpness in his gaze was new. He studied her face with those piercing brown eyes.

What would he make of the circles under her eyes and the weariness she'd seen in the mirror that morning? What did he know?

"Nolan asked me to take the lead this week," he said. "We'll be finishing up the backsplash and getting started on the trim work in the hallway."

Maya nodded, not trusting her voice. So that was it. She'd asked

Nolan to leave, and she had. Nolan had said she would send Gruff today, but she'd hoped…

There it was again. Hope. Perhaps her greatest enemy and worst failure.

"Did she say when she'd be back?" The question slipped out before she could stop it.

"Didn't say much of anything, to be honest. Just that something came up and I should handle things for a while." Gruff frowned, the creases around his eyes deepening. He rocked on his heels, clearly wrestling with something. "Ain't my business what the boss decides."

Maya waited.

Gruff cleared his throat. "Nolan missed the Monday morning planning meeting we always have and didn't return my texts since Saturday. I swung by the medical center job this morning, and her truck was there. She didn't have anything to say. Looked like she hadn't slept much. If there's some kind of problem with this job—"

"There's no problem," Maya said quickly. Too quickly. She'd been so focused on her own hurt that she hadn't fully considered what Nolan might be going through. The image of Nolan hurting made her ache. "We've made so much progress here. Maybe Nolan just wants to check up on the other jobs."

Gruff's expression said he didn't buy that for a second, but he nodded anyway. "Right. Well, if you need anything changed or have questions, I'm your man. Been working with Nolan since she took over the business. Know her methods pretty well."

"Thank you. I appreciate that."

After Gruff rejoined his crew, Maya retreated to her bedroom to shower and dress. Standing under the hot spray, she let herself imagine for just a moment that this was all a misunderstanding. That she and Nolan could somehow find their way back to the easy partnership they'd built over the past months. But even as she indulged yet another fantasy, she knew it was impossible. Too much had been said. Too much revealed. The trust between them, so carefully built, lay in pieces on her kitchen floor.

Gruff's crew worked quietly and efficiently, and Maya tried to lose herself in small tasks—organizing Emmie's toys, looking at online editorial classes, and researching kindergarten programs. But every engine sputter had her looking out the window, hoping against hope to see Nolan's truck pulling in. Every time her phone buzzed, her heart raced, only to crash when it was just a spam call or a text from Izzy.

By late afternoon, when she went to pick up Emmie from Izzy's, her emotions were frayed. She forced herself to focus on Emmie's excited chatter about finger painting and story time, and thankfully her murmured sounds of appreciation satisfied her. Until they arrived home.

"Where's Nolan's truck, Mommy?" Emmie asked as Maya helped her out of the car.

"She's working on another project this week." Not quite a lie, but the truth burned.

"When will she be back? We still have to put the sparkly paint on my closet doors. Nolan said she would show me how."

Maya's throat closed. She'd forgotten that conversation, made one afternoon over hamburgers at Scoops. "I'm sure she'll be back soon, baby."

"When?"

"I don't know exactly."

Emmie's face fell. "Did I do something wrong? Is she mad at me?"

"Oh, sweetie, no." Maya pulled Emmie close, inhaling the scent of strawberry shampoo and playground dust. "Nolan isn't mad at you. You're her favorite little unicorn expert, remember?"

"Then why isn't she here?"

How could she explain the adult complications that had torn apart something so simple and good? How could she tell her five-year-old daughter that sometimes people made mistakes that couldn't be forgiven, that sometimes loving someone wasn't enough?

"Nolan has other jobs and other places she needs to be sometimes," Maya said finally. "But that has nothing to do with you. Nolan cares about you."

Emmie's gaze seemed far too searching for a five-year-old, but then Emmie had been through more than most her age. "Okay."

When Emmie seemed to believe her, the tension twisting in Maya's middle unwound a little. Still, she couldn't just pretend Nolan didn't exist. Couldn't cut her out of their lives like a malignant tumor. The connections were already too deep, too complex.

She'd have to find a way to coexist with Nolan, because exiling her completely wasn't an option, not when Emmie adored her. Not when her own heart might shatter if Nolan truly disappeared from their lives.

❖

Wednesday morning, Nolan parked at the end of Sycamore Drive and sat in her truck for a full five minutes, staring at the closed front door until her eyes ached. The week had been a blur of meetings and sleepless nights. Two meetings a day since Saturday had left her steady but raw, like a burn patient with fresh skin—healed enough to function, sensitive to the smallest touch.

Tim's words from their Monday session echoed constantly. "You can't hide from the work that needs doing. The house or your heart."

She'd chosen the house. It was safer. Or so she told herself.

Late Saturday night, she'd driven past the Roadrunner twice and sat in the parking lot for twenty minutes as muscle memory warred with eighteen months of hard-won wisdom. The neon signs beckoned, the burn of whiskey tingled in the back of her throat—gone but not forgotten, like the memory of how alcohol silenced the chaos in her head. But Tim's voice sounded louder, as did the quiet, steady voices of those in the meetings she'd chosen over the raucous revelry of the Roadrunner.

Sunday she'd worked in the shop, finally putting the finishing touches on Maya's clock. After that, she'd driven into the hills and hiked, trying to exhaust herself enough to sleep without dreams of Maya. Ten miles through pine forests and rock scrambles, and still she'd lain awake until three a.m., replaying every moment of that kiss, every word that had followed.

She'd started three different texts to Maya and deleted them all. What was there to say?

Sorry I'm the kind of person who might have killed your wife?

Thanks for the reminder of why I keep people at arm's length?

I understand why you can't look at me without seeing evil?

None of it would change anything. Some things, once broken, couldn't be fixed.

Gruff met her at the truck, his expression carefully neutral. "Glad to have you back, boss. Maya's been asking after you."

The words hit her like a physical blow. "Has she?"

He nodded. "Little Emmie, too. Every day. Wants to know when you're coming back, how you're doing." Gruff studied her face. "Maya seems worried about you."

Nolan climbed out, checking her tool belt with unnecessary attention to detail. "Just want to check the progress. Make sure everything's up to standard."

"'Course you do." Gruff's tone suggested he didn't believe that for a second. "Though I'll tell you, the backsplash looks pretty damn good without micromanaging."

Nolan pushed through the front door, welcomed by the familiar scent of sawdust and paint. Three days felt like three years. Every detail looked different, or maybe she was seeing it differently, knowing it wasn't really hers anymore. Knowing she was just the hired help again, nothing more. When had this become more than just a job? She already knew the answer. That first night when she'd sat at the table with Maya, legs just touching, poring over details of a dream, Maya's dream had become hers. And Maya...Maya had become more than a client.

Nolan checked the kitchen first. Finishing details told the difference between slap-'em-up amateurs and professionals. Each small white rectangle in the backsplash had been placed with mathematical precision. "Looks good, Gruff."

Gruff grunted.

She grinned at the unspoken *'course*. The grin felt foreign, a forgotten expression.

Maya walked into the kitchen, her curls escaping from a messy ponytail, a pale-blue paint smudge on her cheek. She wore an old T-shirt and jeans with holes in the knees. Beautiful and fragile, and so far beyond Nolan's reach it hurt to breathe.

"Oh," Maya said, her cheeks coloring. "I didn't hear your truck."

"Gotta check that last delivery," Gruff said and backed out in a hurry.

"I parked up the road a bit," Nolan said.

"Oh."

The silence stretched.

"Backsplash looks good," Nolan finally said.

"Mmm," Maya replied, studying her face with the intensity of a medical exam, searching for signs of...what? Breakdown? Relapse? "How have you been?"

Nolan stiffened, shields snapping into place with practiced ease. "I'm fine."

"Gruff said…"

"What?" Nolan asked. "What did he say?"

"Just that you hadn't been around. I just…" Maya glanced around as if checking for eavesdroppers. "Are you taking care of yourself?"

The concern in Maya's voice was almost worse than anger would have been. At least anger would have been honest and uncomplicated. This careful worry felt like pity, and pity was the one thing Nolan couldn't stomach.

"If you're asking whether I'm drinking, the answer is no." The words came out sharper than she intended, cutting through the careful politeness she'd been trying to maintain. But she couldn't take them back, and part of her didn't want to.

Maya flinched but held her ground. "I wasn't—"

"Yes, you were." Nolan forced herself to step back, to breathe like Tim had once suggested. Count to ten. Don't make it worse. Don't let the anger, or the voice inside telling you just one drink won't matter, win. After a minute, she answered. "I'm sober, Maya. Still counting days. Still going to meetings. Still here. Whatever that's worth."

The relief that flashed across Maya's face was quickly hidden, but Nolan caught it anyway. The fact that Maya had been genuinely worried about her drinking should have felt good, should have meant something. Instead, it just highlighted the impossible gulf between them. Maya could worry about her from a distance, but she could never trust her, never let her close enough to hurt Emmie or her.

"I should check the trim work." Nolan turned away before she could say something they'd both regret. She made it halfway down the hall before the doorbell rang. Outside the window, Aisley's maroon SUV pulled into the driveway, its clean lines and pristine paint job looking like something from another world compared to her mud-spattered pickup.

Perfect. Just what this moment needed.

Nolan continued down the hall, checking the crown molding and striving for as much distance from the front door as she could get. The trim needed another coat of primer, and fuck, Maya's voice carried clearly from the front door, bright with cheer.

"Aisley, hi! Come in."

"Hey, you." Aisley's voice was warm and easy. *Aisley* was uncomplicated. Everything Nolan wasn't. "How's the renovation going?"

"Great, actually. We're making real progress."

Someone walked past the living room from the entryway. Nolan focused on the window trim, measuring what didn't need it, adjusting what was already perfect. Their conversation carried as clearly as if she was standing in the room with them.

"The kitchen looks amazing," Aisley was saying. "That backsplash is perfect. Must be nice to have a space that works again."

"It is. I kind of miss the chaos, though. Having Nolan and the others here every day—it made the house feel so alive."

Nolan stilled. It made the house feel alive. Past tense.

"Listen," Aisley said, and something in her tone made Nolan strain to hear better. "I know this is short notice, but there's this new pizza place that just opened in Riverside Park. Great food, outdoor seating, and they have this amazing playground area. I was thinking maybe Friday night? You and Emmie?"

Nolan tensed, the silence stretching longer than it should have.

"I don't know," Maya said slowly. "I could ask Izzy to watch Em—"

"No need," Aisley interrupted, voice bright and eager. "The whole point is that it's family-friendly. Kids eat free on Friday nights. There's live music and face painting, besides the play area. Emmie would love it. What do you say?"

More silence. Nolan set down her measuring tape, her whole body coiled tight. This was what she expected, maybe even wanted, wasn't it? What Tim had said she needed to put first? What was best for Maya.

Maya moving on, choosing someone steady. Someone who didn't come with warning signs or the baggage of addiction and self-destruction.

"That sounds really nice," Maya said finally. "Emmie would love the playground."

"Great! I'll pick you up at six?"

"Perfect."

"Oh," Aisley added, "I checked the forecast, and we might get a thunderstorm or two. In case you'd rather not risk it."

Maya laughed, sounding genuinely happy. "That's why we have rain slickers. Plus, Emmie is half duck. She loves the rain."

"Great, then…"

Nolan stopped listening, the rushing noise in her head a comforting shield. She should feel nothing. Hadn't she sworn on day one of her sobriety to stop telling herself lies? She *knew* this was best.

So why did it feel like someone had reached into her chest and squeezed her heart until it stopped beating?

CHAPTER SEVENTEEN

Nolan spent the rest of the week avoiding Maya and hoping she wouldn't notice. She met on-site with Gruff to check on the work progress in the mornings and checked in by text in the afternoon. She kept busy driving from site to site, walking the jobs, and in the evenings, meetings. But when she slowed down, even for a few minutes, she'd imagine Maya and Aisley at some trendy brewpub, Emmie playing on swings while they shared a meal and conversation that didn't carry the weight of secrets and trauma.

She didn't resent Maya the chance to laugh again, to enjoy time with someone who didn't come with the kind of baggage she did. And Emmie deserved to see her mother happy. She missed Emmie almost as much as Maya, but they'd both forget her soon enough when the job was done. That was the way this all would have ended anyhow. Her moving on when the house was done, a shadow passing through their lives and soon forgotten.

Friday afternoon, Gruff hunted her down at the office building site.

"Gonna need you to talk to Maya," Gruff said.

"What? Why?" For just a second she heard Tim's voice echoing the same words.

You need to talk to Maya.

As if she needed reminding of the importance of taking personal inventory and admitting when she was wrong.

"The roof is looking like it'll need more work than what we expected. Some of the sub-structure is rotted out."

"And we're just now finding this out?" Nolan snapped.

Gruff held up both hands. "The flashing around the chimney wasn't high enough, but we couldn't see the water damage until we pulled the old shingles off. I didn't think I ought to be the one to tell her."

"You're right." Nolan rubbed her eyes. "I'll take a look tomorrow and talk to her. Thanks for the heads-up."

"Got plans tonight?" Gruff asked as the crew started loading their trucks.

"Haven't decided." Nolan packed up her tools with mechanical precision, each item returned to its designated place in her toolbox. Order and control. The illusion that she had some say in how her life unfolded. Gruff tagged along as she carried the gear to her truck.

"Decided about what?" Gruff asked in his innocent and annoyingly insistent way.

Nolan sighed, not about to tell him she didn't want to go home to an empty house where she would fill the silence by telling herself she should just let Maya go. That she never should have imagined a future with her.

"I've got paperwork."

"That'll be there next week." Gruff frowned. "It's Friday night, and if I'm not mistaken, you haven't been out with us for weeks. Frannie's birthday was last week, but we never got around to celebrating. We're heading over to the RR now. Stop in and be sociable for a bit."

The last place Nolan wanted to be was the Roadrunner, but sitting alone in her house while Maya was out with Aisley would be infinitely worse. At least at the bar, she could pretend she was choosing to be around people instead of hiding from the truth of her isolation.

"Yeah. All right."

Even happy hour at the Roadrunner was exactly as depressing as Nolan had expected. The same faces telling the same stories, the same careful dance of pretending everything was fine while drowning sorrows in whatever anesthetic was available. She'd forgotten how loud it was, how the conversation and music and clinking glasses created a wall of noise that somehow made the silence inside her head even more deafening.

She made the rounds, congratulated the birthday girl, and escaped to the back corner booth she'd occupied for years before getting sober. Gruff played pool with some of the younger guys from the crew and tried to pretend he wasn't watching her, worry written on his craggy face. Everything looked exactly the same—the cracked vinyl seats, the neon beer signs, the jukebox that still played the same mix of country classics and 80s rock. She still felt like an alien, observing a life she'd once thought was normal, but at least the urge to a have a drink and return to that place had dulled. That was new.

She was nursing her second Coke when Janet appeared, carrying a drink. "Mind if I sit?"

"Hi, Janet." Nolan tried to summon some enthusiasm. Failed. She gestured to the empty seat across from her. "Sure. Go ahead."

Janet slid in next to Nolan in the cramped booth instead, close enough for her perfume, a sharp, tangy scent that smelled nothing like Maya's, to settle on Nolan's skin.

"I was hoping I'd see you again." Janet laughed lightly. "You look better than last time. Not as strung out."

Strung out? No, that wasn't what she'd been. What she'd been, what she *was*, was torn up over losing a woman she'd never had. "I'm fine."

"Well, it's good to see you looking like yourself," Janet said. "Not that you don't always look good."

Like herself? Who was that, anyway? Nolan wasn't sure anymore. When she said nothing, Janet went on in a rush.

"Look, I know things were weird last time. And I get that you're not looking for anything serious. But if you ever want some friendly company—dinner, a movie, whatever—I'm still interested. No pressure, no expectations. Just…company."

Nolan looked at Janet, really looked at her. Pretty in an understated way, kind brown eyes, laugh lines that spoke of someone who enjoyed life. Available and interested. Uncomplicated. Everything that should appeal to her. Everything that had appealed to her before Maya turned her world upside down.

"That's generous of you," Nolan said finally. "But I'm in a complicated place right now."

"Because of someone else?"

The question hung between them. Nolan could have lied, deflected, or changed the subject. Any of the dozen conversational escape routes she'd perfected over the years. Instead, she nodded.

"Ah." Janet's smile turned knowing, tinged with sympathy. "The complicated ones are always the hardest to get over."

"Not sure I want to get over her." As soon as she said it, a weight lifted from her chest. From her heart. Was that why speaking the truth mattered so much?

"Then maybe you should tell her that."

"I'm not sure that's a good idea."

"If I was her, I'd want to know." Janet squeezed Nolan's shoulder and returned to her friends at the bar, leaving behind a faint trace of perfume and a message that cut straight to the bone. Nolan stared into her Coke, wondering when her life had become so tangled. When had she gone from avoiding connections altogether to aching for one that seemed impossible?

Her phone buzzed. Tim.

How'd the week go?

Fine, she texted back.

Her phone rang immediately.

"Is that why you've been running out of the meetings like your ass was on fire?" Tim said. "'Cause I sort of thought it was so you wouldn't have to talk about what was really going on."

Nolan looked around the bar, suddenly desperate for air that didn't taste of beer and desperation. She stood, phone pressed to her ear, and pushed through the crowd toward the exit.

"Maya has a date tonight," she said once she was outside, the cool air hitting her face like a benediction.

"And?"

"And nothing. She's moving on. Which is what she should do."

"Is it?"

"Of course it is. She deserves better, and she knows it. She deserves someone who doesn't come with eighteen months of baggage and a list of amends longer than a CVS receipt."

"Maybe. But that's not your call to make." Tim, as usual, sounded patient but firm. "Have you talked to her yet? Really talked?"

"What's the point?"

"The point is that you're probably both miserable, there's a kid involved who doesn't understand what's happening, and you're trying to solve this by running away. Which is exactly what you used to do when you were drinking."

That hit home extra hard, driving the air from her lungs. "That's not—"

"Isn't it? You told me you care about this woman. You told me she matters. Hell, you told me she's different from anyone you've ever known. But when things got complicated, you disappeared. How's that different from climbing into a bottle?"

Nolan wanted to argue, to defend herself, to point out all the reasons why this situation was different. But the words wouldn't come. Because Tim was right. She'd run. Just like always. The only difference was that this time, she'd done it sober.

"She wanted me to go," Nolan said finally, the words scraping her throat raw. "When she found out what I was."

"Did she? Or did she react to finding out you'd been hiding something that scared the hell out of her?"

In the background, the bar's music pounded on. That world, where people didn't carry the weight of past mistakes like stones in their pockets, wasn't hers anymore.

"Part of me is angry that she's holding me responsible for what some other drunk did," she said. "Then there's this voice in my head that says maybe I deserve it. Maybe anyone who's ever driven drunk deserves to carry that guilt forever, even if we didn't hurt anyone. I can't fix what I am, Tim."

"You're not supposed to fix what you are. You're supposed to be honest about it. And give her a chance to decide what she can handle."

"And if she can't?"

"Then at least you'll know. But right now? You're making decisions for her based on fear. And that's not fair to either of you."

"Damn it, Tim, I know that."

"Where are you right now?"

Nolan sighed. "In the parking lot outside the Roadrunner."

"That's not where you need to be. You need to be working your program. Especially during a time like this."

"I've been going to meetings. But—I don't know. It's hard to pay attention."

"Because you're thinking about her?"

"Yeah. And before you say anything, I want to make things right with her again."

"Okay. So do it."

"I'm not sure how."

"What do we say in the program? When you do wrong, you own it right away and apologize. You don't run from it. That leads back to the bottle."

"But she won't even talk to me."

"Be an adult and figure it out. You have to apologize to her. In person. And you need to do it as soon as possible."

"I hear you," Nolan said. "I'll work it out."

"Good. In the meantime, go home and read your literature. Journal your thoughts and feelings. Then do something productive. Get out in the workshop."

"I should."

"Yes, you should. And you should call me. Every day for the next two weeks. I want to know how you're doing, okay?"

"I will."

After Tim hung up, Nolan sat in the parking lot for a long time, watching people come and go from the various bars and restaurants that lined the streets in that part of town. Friday-night revelers living their regular lives. Dating. Laughing. Making mistakes and trying again.

Maybe Tim was right. Hell, even Gruff was making excuses for her to talk to Maya. Maybe she was running. Maybe she owed it to herself—to Maya and to Emmie—to try once more. To be brave enough to stay and fight for what mattered.

But first, she had to figure out what to say. And whether it was already too late to say it.

❖

The string lights overhead cast a warm glow across the restaurant's outdoor patio as dusk settled over the town. Emmie had been shy at first about joining the other children in the small playground area, but now she eagerly clambered over the jungle gym and swing set. Her laughter floated on the night breeze, lifting Maya's spirits as nothing else could.

"She might be half duck," Aisley remarked, "but the other half is monkey."

Maya laughed, touched that Aisley remembered what she'd said about Emmie loving the rain. Touched also that Aisley had even thought to suggest a place for dinner where Emmie could play.

"This was a great idea," Maya said. "Thank you for thinking of it."

"I'm glad you're enjoying it." Aisley sat beside her on the picnic table bench, her bare, deeply tanned leg inches from Maya's. Her short-sleeved checked shirt and khaki shorts displayed her toned muscles as the breeze rustled her dark hair.

"It's been a while since I've done anything so easy and fun," Maya said, wanting Aisley to know she appreciated her thoughtfulness. She *should* be enjoying this—the crisp evening air, the excellent pizza, and certainly the company. Aisley was everything a woman could want in a friend, or maybe more. Intelligent, kind, and stable. No unexplained absences or uncomfortable silences. No secrets. Maybe it was just too soon to take pleasure in a woman's company, but she had a hard time staying in the moment. And a harder time not wondering where Nolan was or if she was all right.

"I don't imagine you've had much of a chance to relax with the major overhaul on the house," Aisley said. "What's the timetable to finish?"

"Getting closer," Maya nodded, taking a sip of her IPA. "There's apparently some issue with the roof they just discovered. I don't know the details yet."

"Roof issues can be tricky," Aisley remarked, stretching her legs out, comfortable in her body. "I'm glad you've got Nolan on it, though. She seems to really know her stuff."

Maya's heart squeezed. "The best. Nolan and her crew have been—" She stopped herself. Had been what? Amazing? Reliable? Until they weren't? Until Nolan started disappearing every afternoon, sending terse text updates instead of stopping by as she once had? "They've been very professional."

Where was she these past few days? The question had circled in her mind all week. After their confrontation, Nolan had practically vanished, appearing only when necessary, their interactions reduced to construction updates and polite nods. Maya caught herself looking for Nolan's truck in the driveway each morning, listening for her footsteps on the porch and the vibration of her laugh resonating through the house. How was she doing? Was she struggling the way Maya was? Did she miss them—not just her, but Emmie, too?

"Earth to Maya," Aisley teased gently, eyes curious. "You drifted away there for a moment. Everything okay?"

"Sorry." Maya smiled, embarrassed. "Just mentally cataloging all the things still left to do on the house."

"Is that all?" Aisley's expression turned serious. "Because I'm a pretty good listener if you need a friendly ear."

Maya looked away, focusing on Emmie, who was now carefully building the Great Wall of China out of big plastic blocks. Even from a distance, her focus was clear in the determined set of her jaw. Her confidence and sense of adventure were finally starting to shine through again. The move *had* been good for her. Now if she would only stop fretting over Nolan's absence.

"I'm sorry," Maya said again. "I'm not being very good company."

"No apology needed." Aisley squeezed Maya's hand briefly. "I hope we can be friends."

Maya considered telling Aisley everything. About the soul-crushing loss of Dantas, about the exhaustive task of trying to rebuild her and Emmie's lives, about how important Nolan had become to both of them. And about the betrayal she'd felt when she'd learned Nolan had kept such a critical part of her life from her.

But she couldn't.

Aisley was becoming a friend, possibly one day more than that. But she didn't know Aisley well enough to reveal how she'd pushed away someone who made her feel alive for the first time in years because she was scared. Or to confess that she couldn't stop thinking about Nolan despite her best efforts.

Instead, she said, "It's complicated."

"Well, like I said," Aisley replied, "anytime you want to vent, I'm happy to help, even if it's just listening."

"You're already helping." Maya forced a smile. "Good company, no drama. Exactly what I need right now."

Uncomplicated. Easy. Safe. This was the kind of friendship—maybe one-day relationship—she should be cultivating. No surprises lurking beneath the surface. No connections so intense they scared her. Nothing that could shatter her carefully reconstructed life.

"I hope," Aisley said softly, "when you're ready for something more, you'll let me know. Because I'd like that."

Maya nodded. She heard what Aisley wasn't saying, and a small part of her whispered, *Why not? You like her. She's kind and smart and very good-looking.* She searched for a flare of interest, for the surge of attraction, for that unidentifiable *something* that grew out of a unique connection, and failed. Maybe she'd never find that again.

But she had, hadn't she. Just with a woman who was wrong for her.

"Mommy, watch this," Emmie called, hanging upside down from the monkey bars, her face flushed with pride and exertion.

"I see you, sweetheart," Maya called back. "Don't climb any higher, okay?"

"Okay."

"She's pretty athletic for her age," Aisley said.

"She is." Maya laughed. "Sometimes I'm amazed that I had a part in creating someone that amazing."

"I'd say she's lucky to have such a great mom."

The compliment should have warmed her. Instead, it made her think of Nolan, how she'd once said almost the same thing, but with a look in her eyes that went beyond admiration. A look that said she saw all of Maya—her strengths and weaknesses, her hopes and fears—and found her beautiful.

"She loves to dance," Maya said, wanting to chase away thoughts of Nolan, and just like that, the night of the Christmas pageant came back to her. The waiting for Dantas. The phone call. The rending of her soul.

She stood abruptly. "I should probably get her home, or I'll never get her to sleep."

Aisley stood, frowning. "You okay?"

"Yes, of course." Maya walked toward Emmie, needing the space. She couldn't risk caring, not again. She couldn't put herself or Emmie through that again. "Come on, honey. Time to go home."

Emmie came running and took Maya's hand, warm and trusting. When Maya turned back to Aisley, she had her smile back in place. "This has been great."

"It has," Aisley said, falling into step with her. "I was hoping I could call you. That we could do something else again soon."

"I can't promise. I've got so much going on," Maya hedged. She liked Aisley, enjoyed her company. Would that be enough? "But yes, of course."

Aisley smiled, easy and relaxed. "Perfect."

As Aisley pulled out of the parking area, Maya's phone beeped. She got so few texts, she assumed it was important.

"Sorry," she said, "I should check this."

"Of course," Aisley said.

Can we meet tomorrow morning at your place? Need to discuss the roof. And a few other things.

Those last five words made her heart race in a way nothing about this pleasant evening had managed to do. She stared at the screen longer than necessary, her thumbs hovering uncertainly.

"Bad news?" Aisley asked.

"No," Maya said quickly. "Just the contractor. There's an issue with the roof that needs addressing."

"On a Friday night? That's dedication."

"That's Nolan," Maya said softly, then caught herself. "I should probably respond."

She typed and deleted three different replies before settling on: *OK. 9 am works.*

Simple and practical. No hint of the way her pulse had quickened at the thought of seeing Nolan again—really seeing her, not just the brief, passing encounters of earlier in the week.

Her phone buzzed again almost immediately. *9 am it is. Thank you.*

Two words that shouldn't mean anything. And yet.

"Everything alright?" Aisley asked, concern evident in her voice.

"Yes," Maya said, pocketing her phone. She smiled at the woman who represented everything she should want. "Everything's fine."

But she couldn't help wondering what *other things* Nolan wanted to discuss. Despite her best efforts to move on, she had things to settle with Nolan before she could.

Chapter Eighteen

Maya's stomach fluttered as Nolan turned into the driveway at exactly nine o'clock. Nolan parked the truck carefully, the way she did everything. She hesitated after climbing out, folder and clipboard under one arm, and stared at the house, her expression guarded and, uncharacteristically for her, unsure. Everything about her movements spoke of caution, of a woman who had been wounded and wasn't sure of her welcome.

Maya's heart hurt to see her looking almost afraid to approach her. The guilt spurred her out the door. "You're right on time! How unusual."

Nolan blinked, and for an instant, a smile blossomed, the sight so beautiful Maya's spirits lifted. Was that what she'd been missing all week? That look of pleasure on Nolan's face whenever they met?

Maya smoothed her palms over her jeans. Why hadn't she chosen something nicer than one of her oldest pair of jeans and the sweater with the hole in the hem she'd thrown on that morning? Not that this was anything more than a business meeting about roof repairs. Not that it mattered what she looked like. But the flutter in her chest when she opened the front door contradicted every rational thought she'd been trying to convince herself of since the last time they'd spoken.

"Morning," Nolan said in a tone that lacked any hint of the personal.

She'd worn the familiar canvas pants and steel-toed boots along with a navy T-shirt, but for some reason the way the faded cotton hugged her shoulders and stretched over the curve of her upper arms made Maya's mouth go dry. And were there even more gold highlights in her wheat-blond hair, or was that just the sunlight shimmering off the tousled strands?

Had she ever truly *looked* at Nolan before? Because God, she was gorgeous.

"Good morning." Maya stepped back, catching the faint scent of sawdust and cedar as Nolan joined her. Something else she recognized and had probably just gotten used to. But today? Every sense tingled. "Um…coffee? I made a fresh pot."

"That'd be great, thanks."

Inside, Nolan scanned the living room, drumming her fingers against her thigh. "Fireplace surround looks good. Gruff's been keeping things moving."

"He has." Maya hesitated. "Emmie asks for you every day."

The words spilled out before she could stop them, more honest than she'd intended.

A flash of vulnerability flickered in Nolan's eyes, quickly shuttered behind her professional mask. "How's she doing? Still okay at school, I mean?"

"Better every day." Maya led the way to the kitchen, grateful to have something to do with her hands as she poured coffee into two mugs. "She misses you. Wants to know when you'll be back."

The confession hung between them, as tangible as the steam rising from the coffee. Maya handed Nolan her mug, their fingers brushing. The brief contact sent a jolt along her skin, and she pulled back too quickly, nearly spilling her coffee.

"I miss her, too," Nolan said quietly. "Both of you."

Maya's heart stumbled in her chest. "I…" The sound of racing feet in the hall caught her attention. "Brace yourself."

Emmie flew into the kitchen, her light-up sneakers slapping the floor, and launched herself at Nolan. "You're here!"

The transformation in Nolan's face stole Maya's breath. The careful reserve vanished, replaced by unguarded joy.

"Hey there, sport. How's my favorite unicorn expert?" Nolan bent and swept her up in one arm, balancing her on a hip. The motion was so natural, so much like what Dantas might have done, Maya's eyes filled.

"Can we paint the stars on my closets today?" Emmie flung her arms around Nolan's neck. "Can we go get ice cream?"

"Slow down, Em." Maya couldn't stop herself from smiling at the pure happiness on both their faces. "Nolan and I have some house stuff to talk about this morning."

"Okay. After that?"

Nolan glanced over Emmie's head at Maya, her gaze questioning. Hope and uncertainty warring in their depths.

"We'll see, baby," Maya murmured. "First, Nolan and I have to talk."

About a lot of things, someday.

Nolan set Emmie down. "Got any new drawings to show me?"

"Yes. I'll get them." Emmie raced off.

"So. The roof." Nolan's tone shifted to brisk and businesslike. "Let me show you the photos of what Gruff found when they pulled back the shingles around the chimney. It won't take long, and then I'll get out of your hair."

"You don't have to run off." Maya carried the mugs to the table where they'd sat that first night creating a plan for the work that was now almost finished. "Emmie will want you to see her latest creations."

"Sure." Nolan sat beside her at the table, seeming to keep a careful distance between them.

Maya caught her scent again and remembered the way their legs had so innocently and easily touched. The few inches between them now seemed like a mile, and the separation ached. "Thank you. For being so good to Emmie."

Nolan regarded her in that intense way she had. "You don't have to thank me. I care about her."

Such simple words that struck so deep. Maya bit her lower lip, struggling to make sense of her wildly shifting emotions. She drew a breath. "So, the bad news?"

"Not a disaster," Nolan said quickly, sliding several printouts from her folder, "but more than I originally thought."

Maya leaned closer, following Nolan's pencil as she tapped the image of the roof. Her shoulder touched Nolan's, and when she didn't pull away, neither did Nolan.

"Right here." Nolan, her voice oddly rough, pointed to the base of the chimney. "The flashing pulled away here and here."

Nolan had a scar on the top of her right hand, pale and thin. Had she gotten that at work? In the Army? Her hands were work-hardened and strong, but gentle when she'd lifted Emmie, when she'd touched Maya's face as they'd kissed.

"Maya? See what I mean?"

Maya jerked to attention. "Right, sorry, yes."

"There's some water damage to the underlayment. The roof is probably the original, and they used roofing felt back then. We'd recommend a synthetic material now—more durable."

"So you have to replace more than you anticipated."

"Yes. I'm sorry. I checked that area, but this wasn't obvious until we started pulling the old shingles."

"How much longer will this add to the timeline?" Maya forced herself to concentrate on the details and not the way Nolan's bare forearm skated against hers when she reached for her mug.

"Depends on the extent of the underlying damage." Nolan made notes on her clipboard. "I'll need to get up there with Gruff to assess the full scope."

"What about the cost?"

"Depends again."

Nolan quoted a figure that made Maya wince internally. The settlement money from Dantas's death had left her financially secure, but every unexpected expense still increased her urgency to start working at a paying job soon.

"I know it's more than we planned," Nolan said, misinterpreting her silence. "I can work with you on a payment schedule if—"

"No, it's fine." Maya shook her head. "I want it done right."

They sat close in the silence with Nolan's scent enveloping her. Memories flooded back of Nolan's arms around her, the taste of her lips, and the complete safety she'd felt in that moment before everything had shattered. Maya shivered.

"Maya," Nolan said, her voice dropping to something barely above a whisper. When Maya turned, the careful professionalism had cracked, revealing a raw longing that stole Maya's breath. She leaned closer, drawn as if by a tether slowly tightening. Nolan's eyes darkened, and Maya was falling.

Emmie ran in, waving a slightly crinkled drawing. "Here's my favorite painting. Look, Nolan."

Nolan jerked back. "Let's see. Oh, hey, that's an amazing horse. Look at those wings."

Maya's head spun. What was she doing? Besides almost making another mistake.

As if she'd done it a thousand times, Emmie, jabbering about the details of her flying horse, clambered up onto Nolan's lap at the same time Maya's phone rang.

"I should take this," Maya said. "It's Izzy."

"Maya," Izzy said excitedly. "You'll never guess what just happened."

"What?"

"Remember my friend Sarah who has the ranch up north? Her golden just had puppies. They're eight weeks old and ready for homes. The boys have been begging for a dog forever, and I'm thinking this might be the perfect time. But here's the thing—there are four left, and I was wondering…"

"Wondering what?" Maya asked, though her stomach tightened with the certainty that she knew exactly where this was headed.

"Would you consider getting one for Emmie? I know it's sudden, but they're absolutely adorable, and Em could use something to love that's just hers, and—"

"Izzy, slow down." Maya glanced at Nolan, who pretended to study her clipboard while obviously listening.

Emmie tugged her sleeve. "Can I say hi to Izzy?"

"What?" Maya said, pulled between the two conversations. "Yes, hold on, Iz. I'm putting you on speaker. Nolan's here, too."

"Hi, Izzy," Emmie called.

"Hi, sunshine."

"I don't know anything about puppies," Maya said, already sensing a losing battle, "and with the house still torn up—"

"Puppies?" Emmie's eyes went wide. "We're getting a puppy?"

"We're not getting anything," Maya said quickly. "Aunt Izzy was just—"

Izzy would not be stopped. "We could go look today. Just to see them. No commitment. What do you say?"

Maya glanced at Nolan, hoping for some kind of solidarity… rescue…anything. Nolan grinned. Maya narrowed her eyes.

You're not helping, she mouthed.

Nolan pressed her lips together, obviously trying not to laugh.

Izzy barreled on. "Nolan, hi. I was just telling Maya about these puppies. What's your vote? The house is mostly done, right?"

Nolan suddenly looked ready to flee. "I don't think—"

"You'll come, too, right, Nolan?" Emmie jumped down and spun in a circle, purple and yellow flashing from the soles of her shoes. "You can help me pick one. Please, Nolan?"

"Em, we're not picking any—" Maya started.

"Looking doesn't hurt anything," Izzy interrupted cheerfully. "We'll swing by and get you in an hour. Nolan, you'd be doing us a favor. Sarah said the puppies are rambunctious, and an extra pair of hands would be helpful."

Nolan glanced at Maya, uncertainty written across her face. "I don't want to intrude."

Maya took in Emmie's hopeful face, then Nolan's careful expression. The smart thing would be to say no, to maintain the distance they'd been trying so hard to establish. But something in the air felt hopeful, full of possibilities, and she couldn't fight everyone.

"All right. We'll come look. But just to look, Emmie. No promises."

Emmie pressed against Maya's side and looked at Nolan. "You and me and Mommy can pick one together, right?"

Nolan's smile softened, the guardedness dropping away completely. "*If* your mom says it's okay, sure, I'll help."

An hour later, Maya sat wedged into Izzy's SUV with Emmie, chattering excitedly, between her and Nolan. Manny and Luis provided running commentary with soccer updates, possible dog names, and whose bed the dog would sleep in.

"No one's," Izzy advised them. "Your puppy will have their own bed, but you can keep it in your room if you want."

"Okay." Manny's grin said he might have secret plans.

"Can my puppy sleep in *my* bed?" Emmie asked.

"We haven't decided about a puppy," Maya said.

"But if we do?"

"*If* you do," Nolan said, "I could make you a special indoor house where your puppy could be safe and comfy. Dogs like their own beds sometimes."

Emmie's gasp was filled with wonder. "You could?"

Nolan glanced at Maya. "If you get one."

Maya's heart skipped at the warmth and humor skating across Nolan's face. What she couldn't understand was how the moment could feel so right with so much left unsaid.

❖

Sarah's ranch sprawled twenty minutes outside town, weathered outbuildings scattered across the property and horses grazing in distant pastures. Sarah, in her fifties with laugh lines etched around her eyes, met them by the barn. "Welcome. Come on in."

She led them to a large pen where four golden balls of fluff scrambled in the sun, yipping and tumbling over each other. Maya's resistance crumbled the moment she saw them.

"Two of them have already gone to new homes," Sarah said.

"Look, Mommy." Emmie pressed her face close to the wire enclosure. "They're so little."

Sarah opened the gate, and the kids raced into the enclosure. Puppies swarmed them, licking any available skin.

Maya laughed as a particularly bold one attempted to climb up her leg. "They're adorable, but—"

"Look at this one." Manny held up a roly-poly puppy with enormous paws. "He came right over to us!"

Manny passed him to Luis, and when the puppy licked his face, Luis announced, "He's ours."

Emmie sat cross-legged on the ground with the puppies climbing all over her. One in particular seemed drawn to her—a female with intelligent eyes and a white patch above her eyes who kept returning to Emmie's lap even when distracted by her siblings.

"That one's got good instincts," Sarah commented. "She's been the calmest of the litter. Very intuitive about people."

Nolan crouched beside Emmie. "What do you think, Em? Do you like her?"

"She's perfect," Emmie whispered, stroking the puppy's soft fur. "Look, Mommy, she likes me."

Maya's heart ached as she watched them together, her doubts evaporating. Emmie hadn't looked this happy since before the accident, without the shadow of loss that had haunted her for so long. And Nolan was so patient with her. So caring.

"Puppies need lots of love and lots of care," she said weakly.

"I'll help," Emmie promised, eyes huge with hope. "I'll feed her and walk her and teach her tricks and everything." Her face clouded. "Except, what about when I'm in school?"

"I'll help you, honey," Maya said gently.

"Hey," Nolan said. "The crew loves puppies. We'll help, too." She glanced at Maya. "I mean, until we finish up."

Maya met Nolan's gaze, and that electric charge sparked between them again. The offer was so typically Nolan. Generous and thoughtful, with no expectation of anything in return.

"What would we name her?" Maya asked, and Emmie's face brightened again, if that was even possible.

"Star," Emmie declared immediately. "Because she has a white star on her forehead, see?"

"Star," Maya repeated, testing the name. "I like it."

Three hours later, they were headed back to Maya's house with two new puppies—Star for Emmie, and the rambunctious male Manny and Luis had decided should be called King.

"Emmie," Izzy said, "what do you think about bringing Star to our house tonight. The puppies will be a little lonely at first, so maybe a puppy sleepover will be a good thing. Then tomorrow we can go shopping for all the rest of the supplies they need."

She looked at Maya in the rearview mirror as she spoke, and Maya wanted to hug her. Did Izzy know she wanted time alone with Nolan?

"You can if you want to, Emmie," Maya said.

"Yes," Emmie said, carefully cradling the puppy in her lap. "I don't want her to be lonely. Lonely is scary."

A piece of Maya's heart broke all over again, and she said yet another silent thanks for Izzy being right again. Emmie did need something of her own to love. She hugged Emmie and kissed the top of her head. "You'll make sure she's never scared, then."

❖

"Well," Maya said, standing in the foyer with Nolan as Izzy drove off with the kids and puppies, "that was unexpected."

"Good unexpected?" Nolan asked.

"Mmm. Jury's still out on that, but this will be good for Emmie." Maya faced Nolan. Without the children's chatter filling the air, the space between them vibrated, the tension of the long day when they could barely speak to each other building inside. "Thank you. For coming today, for helping with everything. Emmie was so happy to have you there."

"What about you?" The question slipped out quietly, almost warily.

Maya hesitated. Wasn't it time to stop hiding what she felt from Nolan? And from herself? "I was happy, too."

Nolan let out a breath, as if she'd been expecting a blow that hadn't come. "I should probably go. Let you have some peace and quiet."

"You don't have to." The words tumbled out before Maya could stop them. "I mean, if you wanted to stay for dinner."

"Maya." Nolan's voice tightened. "I'm not sure that's a good idea."

"Why not?"

"Because of this." Nolan gestured between them. "Because every time we're in the same room, I want things I shouldn't want." She pushed a hand through her hair. "Because I'm not the person who killed Dantas, but I still scare you. And you deserve better than that."

Anger flashed through Maya, hot and unexpected. "Don't I get to decide what I deserve?"

"You don't understand—"

"Then explain it to me." Maya stepped closer, close enough to see the flecks of gold in Nolan's blue eyes. "Stop deciding what's best for me and just tell me the truth."

"You know," Nolan said wearily, "that's what my sponsor said."

Maya grasped Nolan's hand and squeezed gently. Nolan had never once mentioned anything about how she dealt with her recovery, and Maya was afraid she might bolt before she said more. "What's his name?"

"Tim." Nolan stood frozen for a long moment, conflict warring across her face. "He said I didn't have the right to decide anything for you."

"He sounds smart."

Nolan grimaced. "Smart, for sure. And he probably has had easier sponsees than me."

Maya laughed, relieved and touched that Nolan was trying to open up. "You're awfully hard on yourself. What else did he say?"

"That I should tell you everything. Just be honest."

"I think that's exactly what I need right now." Maya waited. The next step was Nolan's.

"I'm sorry I didn't tell you earlier that I'm in recovery. I have no excuse." Nolan jammed her hands in her pockets.

Maya tried to imagine being in Nolan's place. When would the right time have been? If she looked beyond the hurt and anger, she wasn't sure she could name the perfect time.

"I accept your apology," Maya said softly. "I wish you had said something earlier, but I can understand why you didn't."

"Thank you," Nolan said. "I should go."

"You already said that. Is that all?"

"Yes. There's more." Nolan took a long breath and looked into her eyes. "The truth is that I think about you constantly. That when I'm not here, I'm counting the hours until I can see you again. That watching you with Emmie today, seeing how happy you both were…" She drew a shaky breath. "The truth is that I'm falling in love with you, and it terrifies me because I don't know how to do this without screwing it up. I don't even know if you'd consider…" She shook her head. "I can't see why you'd even want me."

Maya's heart pounded so hard her chest ached with each beat. Nolan might be in love with her? "Oh, Nolan. You have no idea what a special woman you are."

"But?"

Maya bit her lip. "I don't even know if I've got that kind of love left inside me. When Dantas died, I believed that part of me died with her."

"I understand," Nolan said with quiet resignation.

"I don't think you do."

Before Nolan could retreat further, Maya gripped her shoulders and kissed her. Nolan's arms immediately came around her waist, and Nolan kissed her back, a fierce kiss that stole Maya's breath. She shivered, clinging to the heat and strength of her. When she pulled away, she was breathing hard. So was Nolan. "I want you."

"Even knowing I've got issues? Baggage I'm still working through?"

The vulnerability in Nolan's voice cracked open another layer of the ice she'd layered around her heart. Maya cupped Nolan's face in her hands, her pulse racing at the way Nolan's breath hitched.

"I spent last evening with someone who's everything I should want," Maya said softly. "And all I could think about was you."

"Maya—"

"I'm tired of fighting this," Maya whispered. "Tired of pretending I don't want you. But I can't make promises."

"I don't want promises. Just honesty." Nolan studied her for a long moment, her thumbs tracing gentle circles on Maya's waist. "If you're sure."

"I'm sure," Maya said, and kissed her again.

CHAPTER NINETEEN

The instant Maya kissed her, Nolan pulled her into her arms, deepening the kiss, as if she'd been starving for only that. The softness was gone. Urgent hunger took its place. Maya slid her hands up Nolan's back, pressing ever closer, tilting her hips into Nolan, wanting, needing the hard heat of her everywhere. Her breasts ached, and her core pulsed in time with her pounding heartbeat. So fast, so good. So terrifyingly good. Maya angled her head to take Nolan deeper, the taste of her, the softness of her lips, intoxicating.

"Nolan," Maya whispered, "you feel so good."

"I've been wanting this for weeks," Nolan murmured against her neck. "Are you okay?"

"A little scared."

Nolan tensed and eased away just enough to meet Maya's gaze, her arms still encircling her. "Of me?"

Maya shook her head. "Of me…of how much I want this. I don't even know…it's been so long. So long. I'm not sure of anything."

"We don't have to hurry," Nolan said. "We don't even have to do anything more than this."

Maya raked her hands down Nolan's back, cleaving to her again. "Yes, we do. We damn well do."

Nolan grinned, fire leaping in her eyes. "Can we do what we're gonna do in the bedroom?"

"Yes." Maya grabbed her hand and dragged her down the hall. When she pulled Nolan into the bedroom, she stopped short and stared at the bed. A new bed. One she'd never slept in with anyone else. One where she'd never made love.

"Oh," she murmured.

"Maya…" Nolan clasped her nape gently, her grip tender as she rubbed her thumb along the tight muscle in Maya's neck. A soothing touch that eased her nerves. "Tell me."

"So much is running through my head right now, and I don't want to get lost, not now."

"I'm willing to wait as long as it takes." Nolan ran a finger along the edge of Maya's jaw.

Maya gripped her shirt and yanked her closer, sealing her mouth to Nolan's. She kissed her with all the pent-up urgency she'd been denying for weeks, skating her teeth along the edge of Nolan's jaw and nipping lightly until Nolan groaned. The sound sent an arrow piercing through her, a drumbeat of need pounding in her depths so unexpectedly she moaned. A rush of freedom followed. Touching Nolan awakened a place that had been locked away behind sorrow, grief, and guilt.

The awakening hit like lightning, brilliant and transformative. Every nerve ending came alive under Nolan's hands, every shared breath electric with possibility. She'd forgotten her body could sing like this, could demand and receive and give with such fierce intensity. The realization made her bold, hungry for more of whatever this was between them.

Nolan framed her face, held her into the kiss, and Maya dove deeper. Tasting her, nibbling and teasing until Nolan, strong, tough, controlled Nolan, shuddered.

Nolan's need nearly undid her. The power of it, the trust, made Maya's knees weak. *She* had done this—reduced this incredible woman to tremors and gasps and desperate need.

Maya leaned back and searched Nolan's face. Her eyes were hazy, unfocused, and Maya laughed. "Does that feel like I want to wait?"

Nolan pressed her forehead to Maya's. "It feels like heaven."

The simple words hit deeper than any elaborate declaration. Heaven, as if Maya's touch could offer salvation, as if this moment between them transcended the ordinary world they'd been navigating so carefully for weeks.

"I need you to know something," Maya murmured. "Before we go any further."

"Anything," Nolan said. "Whatever you need, whatever you want."

"There are no ghosts in this room."

Voicing the truth struck Maya harder than she had expected. This moment and what they shared belonged entirely to the present, to her and Nolan and the choices they made together. The past existed, would always exist, but it had no claim on what happened next.

Nolan smoothed her hands over Maya's shoulders and down her arms until she linked her fingers with Maya's. She never broke their gaze. "I've seen you with Emmie all these weeks. I know how big your heart is and how much room there is in it. And I know that Dantas will always be there." Nolan kissed her, a gentle touch of lips that did more to ease Maya's sorrow than a thousand condolences ever had.

Nolan's kiss held permission and understanding, acknowledgment and acceptance. Nolan's words set another piece of Maya free. Free to love the woman she had loved her whole life and would always love. But giving her permission, too, perhaps, to love again. Maya's heart filled with the love she had carried and the connection that might be growing. The guilt she had wrestled with for months loosened its grip, replaced by something that tasted remarkably like grace.

For now, the connection, the closeness, and promise of passion was enough. "Then come to bed with me."

Maya slipped her hands under Nolan's T-shirt and pressed her palms to Nolan's stomach. Muscles tensed beneath her fingers, and, laughing, she ran her hand down the center of Nolan's belly until she hooked her fingers beneath the edge of her pants. "I think I would like to undress you."

Nolan's eyes widened.

Maya laughed again. "First time for you?"

"Yeah."

"Good."

Maya grabbed Nolan's T-shirt in both hands and lifted it over her head, then the tank top underneath. Her breath caught. She'd known about the muscles, had watched Nolan work for weeks, but she hadn't expected the softness beneath the gentle curves or the elegant flow of her breasts. She traced the curve of Nolan's collarbones, skimmed down the center of her chest, and cupped her breasts in both hands.

"Your hands feel so good on me," Nolan said, eyes closing for an instant.

"I plan to touch you everywhere before I'm done." Maya knelt slowly and kissed her way down the center of Nolan's body. She undid her pants very slowly, watching Nolan's face, and slid down the zipper. The sound, loud as a rifle shot, stirred her until the quivering in her depths threatened to drive her mad. She pressed her cheek to Nolan's belly. "I'm not sure I can keep doing this without losing my mind."

"That's good," Nolan said breathlessly, "because if something doesn't happen soon, I'm going to go mad."

"Really? And what exactly would you like?"

"To be naked with you. To touch you, to lie with you, to make you come."

"I like the sound of that." Maya gripped Nolan's pants and pulled them down. "Really, Nolan? These boots are sexy, but not right now."

Nolan laughed. "I can help you with that. You know, if you let me."

"As long as you hurry." Maya unlaced them, and Nolan kicked them free, stepping out of her pants next.

"God," Maya said, "I love the way you look."

"Now you."

Heady with the newfound sense of power, Maya tugged Nolan to the bed. "Sit."

Nolan, naked except for her briefs, sat, her gaze riveted to Maya. Maya undressed, loving the way Nolan's chest heaved with each breath. Loving her for letting her explore a part of herself she never knew was there. Who knew removing her clothes could be so incredibly exciting?

"Like?" she asked as she dropped the last garment on the floor.

"More than that," Nolan said, her voice a husky groan. "I've never seen anyone so beautiful."

Then Nolan, quicker than Maya anticipated, grabbed her around the waist and pulled her down onto her lap. Maya threaded her arms around Nolan's neck and kissed her again, part of her content to never stop, part of her needing so much more, and quickly.

Maya pulled away. "My head says slow, but my body says fast. God, I'm a little undone here."

"I can get behind fast." Nolan turned Maya onto her back and, after shedding her briefs, stretched out over her, angling one thigh between Maya's. The sudden pressure against Maya's center brought her arching off the bed.

"Oh, you feel good." Maya wrapped her legs around Nolan's, pressing closer, wanting her touch everywhere. "Touch me. Hurry."

Nolan kissed her throat and slipped one hand down to the delta between her thighs.

Maya cried out again, the merest caress bringing her so close to the edge. "God, you're going to make me come right away."

"I am," Nolan whispered against her ear. "I love how hot you are right now, how wet. How fucking beautiful."

The words, Nolan's fingers stroking in just the right way and just the right place, pushed her higher and higher. She dug her fingers into Nolan's shoulders, and Nolan glided inside her. Her breath fled. Her heart trip-hammered, and her brain blanked. All she knew was need.

"More," she cried. "God, Nolan, more."

Her entire being hummed, saturated with pleasure, heating her body from her head down to her toes. So incredibly good. And then Nolan was filling her, deeper and deeper, and she was erupting.

"Don't stop," Maya gasped. "Don't stop."

"Never." Nolan kissed her, deep and possessive, stroking her again and again. Maya lifted her hips, took her deeper still, and climbed again.

"I'm close. I'm coming again."

Nolan thrust against her thigh, hot and wild.

"Fuck," Nolan shouted, exploding with her.

Maya held her, reveling as Nolan clung to her, her strength gone, vulnerable and spent. *This* was what she had been missing—not just the physical release, but this profound intimacy. The way Nolan's guard completely dropped in the aftermath, leaving her open and undefended. The way their breathing synchronized as they descended together, hearts still racing but beginning to slow.

"That's about the sexiest thing I've ever experienced," Maya finally whispered. "You are so hot."

"First time. Like I said," Nolan said, her voice thick and drowsy, "not my usual style."

Maya laughed. "Oh? Used to being in charge, are you?"

"Not used to losing it like that."

Oh, she liked the sound of that. She liked knowing that her urgency, her need, was echoed. Sex had never been about feeling powerful before. Not like this. Nolan had trusted her enough to surrender control, to be vulnerable in the most intimate way possible.

"I want to make you come again," Maya said abruptly.

Nolan raised her head an inch or so, her brows raised. "Really?"

Maya grinned. "Really. Right now."

"I don't know if I can." Nolan kissed her. "You sort of destroyed me."

"Well, let's find out." Maya pushed her over onto her back and straddled her. "First, I want to explore."

She took her time, watching Nolan's face as she stroked her chest, her breasts, her nipples. Touching Nolan made her wet all over again, and she rocked against Nolan's middle, driving herself nearly out of her mind.

"Touch me right now," she said.

Nolan slid a hand between them, found her clit, and massaged her. The orgasm blew through her, and she flung her head back, buffeted by the storm. At the peak, she fell forward, bracing her hands on Nolan's shoulders, her hair draping her face.

Nolan ran her thumb along her cheek. "You're gorgeous, Maya. And so unbelievably sexy."

"Hold that thought," Maya gasped and pushed lower on the bed until she was between Nolan's thighs. She reached up, found Nolan's hand, and interlaced their fingers again. She needed the connection, and as Nolan gripped her fingers tighter, she took her into her mouth.

Nolan groaned. "Fuck, Maya. I can't take that for long."

Maya didn't tease, but found the spot that made her hips lift and stroked, following Nolan's silent signals. When Nolan tensed and shuddered, a groan wrenched from her chest, Maya's spirit soared.

Contentment settled into her bones like warmth returning to a frozen limb. Maya crawled back up to lie beside Nolan, pulling the sheet over them both. The urgency had passed, leaving behind something quieter but no less profound. She traced lazy patterns on Nolan's chest, marveling at how natural this intimacy had become in the space of a few hours.

For the first time in so long, she was whole again.

Nolan's arm tightened around her, drawing her closer. "That was…"

"I know." Maya pressed a kiss to the hollow of Nolan's throat, tasting salt and satisfaction. "We're good at this."

"Surprisingly good." Nolan's laugh rumbled through her chest. "I wasn't sure we would be."

The admission made Maya lift her head to meet Nolan's eyes. "Were you nervous?"

"More like terrified." Nolan's hand traced along Maya's spine, sending pleasant shivers across her skin. "Not about the sex part. About the after part."

Maya understood. The after was where things got complicated, where hearts had to be navigated alongside bodies, where the future became something that required decisions rather than just desire. But lying here now, skin to skin, the after didn't seem terrifying at all. It seemed like possibility.

"How do you feel about the after now?" Maya asked.

Nolan's smile was soft in the dim light. "Like maybe I've been worrying about the wrong things."

Nolan awakened in the darkened room, Maya curled against her side, her arm around Maya's waist. She hadn't awakened with a woman since before she got sober. Even then she rarely stayed after an encounter. She slowly, carefully stroked Maya's shoulder, not wanting to wake her.

"Mmm." Maya turned, snuggled closer, and rested her hand between Nolan's breasts. "Hey."

"Hi."

"It's late, isn't it," Maya said.

Nolan turned her wrist and checked her watch. "Midnight. Do you want me to go?"

Maya rose on an elbow. The unicorn night-light by the door cast enough glow to show her frown. "Why would I?"

"I'm not sure what comes next," Nolan admitted. Shouldn't she be the one running away right now? That was what she usually did, although she'd never called it that. Being independent, avoiding complications, that's what she'd told herself. *Staying safe* was more like it. She was already long past that with Maya. Since the first time they'd kissed, she'd been standing on the edge of a cliff, waiting to jump with no idea where she'd land. Now her heart had made the choice for her.

"Neither am I," Maya said.

"Are you sorry?"

"No," Maya said instantly, and the certainty in her voice settled some of Nolan's fears. "How could I be? I feel wonderful. And I don't know if I should feel guilty or not, but I don't."

"Why do you think you should feel guilty?"

Maya was quiet for a long time. Nolan stroked her hair. "Maya?"

"For living when Dantas didn't," she finally said.

"You weren't there, were you?"

"No," Maya said. "I was with Emmie at a holiday preschool performance. I was mildly annoyed at Dantas for being late." She laughed, a laugh filled with tears. "But she usually was, so not very."

"So," Nolan said, feeling her way along like a blind person in new surroundings. "You couldn't have taken her place, and that's what you wish, isn't it?"

Maya caught her breath.

"I'm sorry," Nolan said quickly. "I don't know anything about it. I shouldn't have said—"

"No." Maya caught her hand and kissed her knuckles. "You're right. I *do* wish sometimes Dantas was here and not me. So she could be the one to grieve, to have to figure out how to start over again, to keep living."

"I didn't know her," Nolan said, "and I'm sorry you lost her. But I'm very glad you're here."

"I'm not sorry I had a chance to meet you," Maya said. "And I know it's selfish, but I'm glad I'll have the chance to see Emmie grow up."

"It's not selfish to love," Nolan said.

Maya sighed. "You know, you're very good for me."

Nolan's heart soared. No one had ever said that to her before. "Thank you."

"Should I also mention that the sex was fantastic?" Maya said.

"Don't mind hearing it." Nolan kissed her. "And I agree."

Maya laughed. "Can I ask you something else?"

"You can ask me anything."

"Is it hard for you, not drinking?"

Nolan blinked. Not a question she'd expected, but not a surprising one. Maya was direct. No games, no manipulation. So…like they'd agreed, truth. "Not always, but there are moments when I struggle still."

"I don't want to do anything to make your life harder," Maya said quietly.

Nolan *should* have expected this. Maya's default was to take on the responsibility for most everything in her life. "It's not the people in my life that are the problem. It's what I do about what's inside me—what I feel and fear or I don't want to face. Those are the parts of me I have to work on."

"Is there anything that I can do that will help you?" Maya inched closer, wrapping an arm tightly around Nolan's waist.

Nolan tilted Maya's chin up until their eyes met. "Maybe the best thing we can do for each other is what we've already agreed on. No lies, no secrets."

"Can we add that I'd like to see you again, like this?" Maya murmured, nipping lightly at Nolan's chin. "Alone, naked, in bed?"

"That's a good place to start." Nolan kissed her again, softly and carefully, letting Maya know that she was the only one she wanted.

CHAPTER TWENTY

Maya woke to the buzzing of her vibrating phone on the bedside table. For an instant, confusion reigned. Where was she? Who was beside her in the bed? And then, as she grappled for her phone, a flood of images and sensations snapped into focus. Nolan's body pressed against hers, Nolan's mouth hot and urgent on her neck, her breasts, her center. The sharp cry torn from her own throat. The muffled curse wrenched from Nolan's as she climaxed. Wondrous and terrifying.

"Hello," she said hoarsely, finally getting the phone to her ear.

"You're not answering your texts," Izzy said.

Maya rubbed her face. "Um, what time is it?"

"Oh my God, don't tell me you're still asleep. I hate you."

Squinting, Maya checked the time. Seven thirty. In the morning? Of course it was morning. Sunlight bathed the room. Beside her, Nolan stirred, and she automatically reached for her hand. Nolan's fingers, warm and firm, enclosed hers.

"Sorry," Maya said. "Is something wrong?"

"It depends," Izzy said with a tiny hint of snark coming through. "If you consider three children who didn't sleep all night, two puppies who have to pee every hour, and no sleep a problem."

Maya laughed. "Oh, I remember now. Someone thought it would be a good idea to buy three children under ten a pair of puppies."

"I love you, but right now you need to be very, very careful," Izzy said.

Still smiling, Maya inched closer to Nolan, sliding one leg over hers. She didn't think about it until she'd already done it, and then wondered if it was okay. But then Nolan's hand skated down her naked back and rested on her hip. Okay then. That must be all right.

"I'm sorry," Maya said. "Well, not exactly, but I'll come and get her. Can you give me an hour?"

"Why does it take you an hour to drive fifteen minutes?"

"I'm still in bed, and I need to shower and have some coffee and—"

"What aren't you telling me? Because this is not normal. You're the early morning riser. Aren't you the one who always said you can get half the day's work done by nine in the morning?"

"So once in a while I break my habits," Maya said.

Nolan chuckled softly, and Maya flushed. Last night she'd not just broken old habits, she'd broken new ground. Unknown territory on every front.

"All right," Izzy said. "But I can't promise there won't be bodies floating in the pool when you get here."

"You don't have a pool."

"I'll find one."

Laughing, Maya said, "I'll be there soon, I promise. Love you."

"Yeah, yeah," Izzy said and hung up.

"Uh-oh," Nolan said. "Are you in trouble?"

Maya rolled onto her side, pressed closer until she was completely engulfed in Nolan's embrace, and kissed her. "Not so much."

"Does that hour include a shower, coffee, and sex?" Nolan murmured, kissing her throat.

Instantly aroused, Maya guided Nolan's hand between her legs. "What do you think?"

Nolan groaned, rolling Maya onto her back. "I think if you told me no right now, I might cry."

Maya wrapped her arms around Nolan's shoulders. "We can't have that, can we?"

Nolan kissed her again, urgent and fierce, before rising on one arm to meet Maya's gaze. "I want to watch you come."

Maya drew a sharp breath. "Then don't blink."

Nolan laughed and stroked her teasingly. "I happen to know you're very patient. I've seen you with a five-year-old, remember?"

Maya tilted her hips and covered Nolan's hand with hers, pushing her lower. "You're not five, and I'm not patient. I want you inside."

Nolan's eyes darkened, a muscle jumping in her jaw. "Hold on."

She came fast and hard, matching Nolan's intensity. Muscles limp and breath short, she gasped, "I have no idea what you do to me, but I really like it."

Nolan grinned. "Like we said, we're good at this."

Maya clasped Nolan's nape and drew her down to nibble on her lip. "I'd like to try something different this time."

"Anything, any time," Nolan said.

Maya pushed her over. "I want you this time. But it won't be quick."

"Why do you like to torture me?" Nolan said.

"Truth?" Maya reached between Nolan's thighs and stroked her.

"Fuck," Nolan groaned. "Yes, that's what we agreed, right?"

"Patience, remember?"

"Go easy then if you don't want me to come."

"Truth," Maya repeated, not sure she *could* go slowly now. Nolan was so sexy when she was turned on, so open to anything she wanted, so trusting. All she wanted to do was take her. Please her. "I like the way it feels when you want me to do whatever I want."

Nolan cupped her cheek, her fingers trembling. "Why wouldn't I? When what pleases you makes me feel amazing?"

"How lucky am I, then?" Maya kissed her and picked up the tempo. When Nolan came, groaning against her throat, a wave of tenderness swept through her, the beauty leaving her reverent.

She pressed her face to Nolan's neck and closed her eyes. So good just to float in the sea of contentment.

Maya jerked awake. "Oh my God, what time is it now?"

"Is it still Sunday?" Nolan muttered.

"I think so, but my mind is a little hazy."

"If you don't show up, Izzy's going to come and get you," Nolan said.

"I know. But God, I could spend all day here with you like this."

"We should try that sometime."

Sometime. Another time. Would there be more? Maya wanted another time.

But not today. She sat up.

"You want to come with me? I'm sure Emmie would love to see you."

"If I do, Izzy's going to know that I stayed here last night."

"Do you mind that?"

"I don't care," Nolan said, "but I thought you might."

"Izzy is my sister. She loves me the way no one else ever has or ever will. She's known all my sins, all my sorrows, and there's no reason she shouldn't know my happiness, too."

Nolan's eyes widened. "Maya, when you say that, I can't tell you what it means to me."

"I'm glad."

"Do you think you'll be there for a while?"

"Undoubtedly. It's Sunday. It's a great time for the kids to be together, and there are the puppies."

"How about I come over around lunchtime? I have an idea for something for the kids."

"All right." Maya hesitated. "Are you going to go to a meeting?"

"As a matter of fact, yes. After I get a shower and a cup of coffee."

"Is it all right that I asked?"

"Of course. And just so you know, I don't go every day, but a few times a week or whenever I think I need it."

"Then let me put the coffee on, and we'll shower."

Nolan grinned. "A shower sounds like a good idea."

Maya kissed her. "Some other time, cowboy. We're on the clock here."

"Some other time," Nolan murmured. "Yeah, that works for me."

"For me, too," Maya said, and vowed not to question what she couldn't answer yet.

Forty-five minutes later she pulled into Izzy's and followed the sounds of barking puppies and shouting children around the house to the fenced backyard. Izzy sat on the rear deck in a flannel shirt and cut-off denim shorts, pink bunny slippers, and a mildly frazzled expression.

"Seventy-two minutes," Izzy said without looking up from her coffee mug.

"Sorry, sorry." Maya climbed the steps beside her, pulled one of the deck chairs closer, and sat. All three kids ran around in the backyard with two ecstatic puppies. "I am so glad you decided to keep them all last night. Because honestly, that looks nuts out there."

"This is nothing. It's been going on all night." Izzy didn't really sound like she minded.

"Well, at least Emmie's going to sleep well tonight."

"Don't be so sure. That puppy can keep you awake."

"That's okay," Maya murmured. "Seeing her happy like this, I'd buy ten puppies if I had to."

Izzy squeezed her hand. "How are *you*?"

Maya glanced at her. "I'm good. Why?"

"Because when you're off your schedule, that usually means something's going on."

Maya considered for ten seconds. "Nolan stayed the night."

Izzy drew a sharp breath. "I'm assuming she didn't sleep on the sofa."

"She didn't sleep a lot at all," Maya said.

"Okay. Give me a minute." A few seconds later Izzy said, "Are you okay?"

"I had no idea how I would feel, but I feel wonderful. Tired," she said with a smile, "but wonderful."

"Oh boy," Izzy said. "I'm glad you're good."

"But?"

"I just don't want you to get hurt."

Maya turned in her chair to face her. "What do you mean?"

Izzy set down her coffee mug and rubbed her temples. "I care about Nolan. I do. She's been wonderful with Emmie, and she seems like a good person who's trying to do right by everyone. But she's in recovery."

"I know that."

"Do you? Do you really understand what that means?"

Maya bristled slightly. "She doesn't drink anymore. She goes to meetings. She has a sponsor. She's been sober for—"

"Less than two years," Izzy finished quietly. "Which is great. Really. But addiction is forever. It's not something that gets fixed and then you move on. It's something she'll be managing for the rest of her life."

The words hit harder than Maya expected. She'd known, intellectually, that Nolan's sobriety was ongoing work, but hearing it laid out so starkly made something twist in her chest. "What are you saying?"

"I'm saying that loving someone in recovery means you're signing up for that, too. The meetings, the sponsors, the constant vigilance. The knowledge that relapse is always a possibility, no matter how strong their recovery is."

Maya stared out at the children playing, watching Emmie chase Star around the yard with pure joy on her face. "Are you telling me not to see her?"

"No," Izzy said firmly. "That's not my decision to make. But I am telling you to think about whether you're ready for all of it. Because if you're not, if you get scared and bail when things get complicated, that could destroy both of you."

The weight of responsibility settled on Maya's shoulders. She hadn't thought about it that way—about how her own fears or doubts could impact Nolan's recovery. "I would never—"

"You wouldn't mean to," Izzy said gently. "But you've been through hell. You lost Dantas. You're still figuring out how to be a single mom. Are you sure you're ready to take on someone else's recovery, too?"

Maya wanted to protest, wanted to say she was sure, but she'd promised Nolan truth, and that meant facing her own. And the truth was, she didn't know. She'd been so caught up in the way Nolan made her feel, in the connection between them, that she hadn't fully considered the long-term implications.

"Al-Anon is a support for families and friends of people with addiction," Izzy said softly. "Maybe you should consider going."

"I know what it is, but not much else about it," Maya said. "It's like AA, but for the people who love someone with addiction, right?"

Izzy nodded. "I looked into it when Johnny first started at AA. He didn't have much support back then. The focus is helping you understand what you're dealing with, how to support without enabling, and how to take care of yourself in the process."

Maya nodded slowly. Needing support to love someone felt overwhelming, but maybe that was exactly why she should do it. "Do you think I'm making a mistake?"

Izzy took her hand. "I think you're falling in love, and that's never a mistake. But I also think you need to go into this with your eyes wide open. Nolan deserves that, and so do you and Emmie."

The mention of Emmie made Maya's breath catch. Would Nolan's recovery affect her somehow? What if Nolan relapsed? She had to think about more than just herself.

"Hey," Izzy said, squeezing her hand. "Don't spiral. I'm not trying to scare you off. I'm trying to make sure you're prepared."

"I care about her, Iz. More than I ever expected to care about anyone again."

"If you slept with her, I know how much you already care. That's why you've got to be smart about this."

Maya nodded, watching as Emmie took off across the yard, Star tumbling behind her.

"Mommy, look how fast she is," Emmie called.

"I see, baby. She's amazing."

Emmie grinned and ran back to the boys, the puppy yapping at her heels.

"She's already attached to Nolan," Maya said quietly.

"I know. Which is another reason to make sure you're both ready for whatever comes next."

Maya leaned back in her chair, the weight of all the decisions pulling at her. Last night had seemed so simple, so right. But maybe simple wasn't realistic when it came to building a life with someone.

"I'll investigate Al-Anon," Maya said. "Information never hurts, and after this last year, I'm no stranger to accepting help from others."

Izzy smiled. "As a matter of fact, there's a meeting Tuesday night at the community center. I'll go with you, if you want."

"You looked it up?"

"I had a feeling we'd need to have this conversation eventually. I've been watching you two dance around each other for weeks."

Maya laughed despite her concerns. "Was I that obvious?"

"Honey, you've been obvious since the day she walked into your house. I was just waiting for you to figure it out."

While the kids played, Maya churned through all the conflicting emotions: worry that she wasn't ready to make decisions that would affect not just her but Nolan and Emmie, too; worry that she was letting loneliness or plain old lust cloud her judgment, worry that heartbreak was as much a possibility as joy. But underneath the worry was the memory of how right it had felt to wake up in Nolan's arms, how easily they agreed on what mattered to them, how unequivocally Nolan had accepted her asking about her meetings. Openness and truth.

Wasn't that what mattered?

Maybe love was always complicated. Maybe there were no

guarantees with anyone. But maybe the important thing was being willing to learn, to grow, and to face the complications together.

"Izzy?"

"Yeah?"

"Thank you. For looking out for me."

"Always. That's what sisters are for."

❖

Nolan pulled into Izzy's a little after noon. She turned off the ignition and sat in the truck for a few minutes, hoping she hadn't made a mistake coming over. Maybe she should have texted Maya to find out if Izzy was upset. Maybe Izzy didn't even know what had happened between them. Maybe she was rushing things too much. Maybe by now Maya had changed her mind. Maybe, maybe—a million maybes that she couldn't answer.

One day at a time was how she lived her life, managing her sobriety, and she needed to manage the rest of her life that way, too. One thing was certain: She wasn't going to lie to herself about how she felt about Maya. She wasn't just falling for her, she was over the moon in love with her. She'd never felt anything like it before. When she was away from her, all she could do was think about her, about when she'd be able to see her again. And now that they'd made love, she wanted to touch her every second.

She needed to go slow. She knew that. But every fiber of her being longed for Maya, lusted for her. She'd said as much, used those exact words at the meeting just an hour before.

"My name is Nolan, and I'm an alcoholic," she'd said, looking out over the faces of people who understood, people who'd been where she was. "I feel pretty amazing today, but pretty scared, too. I've met someone I really care about, someone I want to have a life with." She'd paused, gathering courage. "I don't want to make mistakes, but I can't turn away either. I've never been very good at relationships, and I need to figure out how to love someone and keep steady on my recovery course at the same time."

The responses had been encouraging—reminders to take it slow, to keep coming to meetings, and to remember that her sobriety had to come first because without it, she had nothing to offer anyone. Tim had pulled her aside afterward to remind her that honesty was still the most important thing, both with herself and with the woman she loved.

Now she climbed out of her truck just as Maya walked around the side of the house. Nolan paused, the door still open, and stared. Maya was so beautiful. And now she knew how beautiful she was in so many other ways.

"Hi," Maya said softly, glancing behind her. She kissed Nolan quickly. "I missed you."

"Hi." Nolan's heart did some complicated dance in her chest. "Missed you, too."

Maya peeked into the back of her truck. "What's all this?"

"I thought I'd build something for the kids. They seem to like it when we put things together."

"You have to be one of the most thoughtful people I've ever met," Maya murmured.

"Just something simple that I know how to do."

"You have a lot to learn about yourself, Nolan Wright," Maya said. "Because *simple* you are not."

"Funny," Nolan said, "that doesn't sound as scary as it used to."

Maya took her hand. "Come on. Let's go join the party."

"Best invitation I've ever had," Nolan said.

Truth.

CHAPTER TWENTY-ONE

July

Maya finished piling sandwiches onto a platter in the spanking new kitchen and checked on Emmie in the backyard. She and Star were busy rolling a ball inside the fenced area, the puppy's yaps of excitement mixing with Emmie's delighted giggles. Impossible now to imagine their little family without Star's boundless energy and unconditional love.

She hurried out front, where Nolan, Erica, and Gruff were finishing the last section of roof. The entire week had been a whirlwind—puppies, adjusting to preschool being closed for a few weeks until the summer session started, and balancing her new online editorial course with everything else. The course was harder than anticipated, but expanding her skills mattered, and building something sustainable for herself and Emmie gave her purpose and a sense of control.

At that particular moment, though, Nolan was the only thing on her mind. Nolan had taken off her shirt and wore only a sports bra and shorts, her tanned shoulders glistening with sweat in the afternoon sunlight. The muscles in her legs stood out as she braced herself against the roof's slope, a drill in one hand, setting one of the shingles in place with careful precision.

Maya laughed at herself. Probably not a good idea standing out here all day watching the confident way Nolan moved, the easy competence in everything she did. Someone might notice the staring. When the sound of the drill quieted, she yelled up, "There are sandwiches and lemonade down here if anybody wants some."

Nolan turned and looked down, a slow grin spreading across her face. "Best invitation I've had in a week."

The last time Nolan had mentioned invitations—and what had followed—brought heat rushing into Maya's cheeks. Even thinking about that night made her pulse quicken.

As Nolan came down the ladder, followed by the others, the play of muscles in her arms as she descended, those same arms that had held Maya, those hands that had touched her with such exquisite care, were impossible to ignore. So she indulged for a moment. Who could blame her, really.

"Everything's in the kitchen," Maya said, trying to keep her voice steady. "Emmie's in the backyard with the puppy, and I don't want to leave her out there too long."

"Don't worry, we've got it." Nolan ran a finger down the back of Maya's bare arm as she passed. The touch was light, casual to anyone watching, but electricity shot straight through Maya's system.

"Gruff," Nolan called, "check on Emmie out back, will you?"

"On it, boss," Gruff yelled back with a knowing grin.

Maya's pulse jumped about fifty points. That tiny touch shouldn't have sent heat skimming through her, not in the middle of a workday surrounded by crew, but it did. Nolan knocked her off balance with the slightest touch every time.

"We have a nice new sink in the bathroom if you and your crew want to wash up," Maya managed.

Nolan stepped closer, close enough that the clean scent of her skin mixed with honest sweat filled Maya's senses.

"Any chance we'll be alone this week?" she murmured, too low for anyone else to hear.

The question sent heat spiraling through Maya's core. "I wish. But Emmie is spending the night with Izzy's boys on Saturday night. It's Johnny's birthday party, remember?"

"Ah, right." Nolan frowned. "Where is Emmie going to sleep?"

"At the boys' father's house. Brian's taking them for the weekend."

Nolan's eyes narrowed. "This guy—you know him well? He's a good guy?"

The worry in Nolan's voice, the protective set of her face, made Maya's heart leap. "Brian? I've known him since he was a kid. He made mistakes, and their marriage didn't work, but he's a good dad. He loves those boys, and he's good with Emmie."

Nolan shook her head. "Cheating on Izzy doesn't make him sound like such a good guy."

"A human one, I guess." Maya sighed. "But I trust him with Emmie."

"Okay, if you trust him, that's what matters. And she'd speak up if something felt wrong."

Maya paused. Nolan's concern ran deeper than casual worry. "You're speaking from experience, aren't you?"

Nolan glanced away, then sighed. "Not what you're thinking. Nothing physical ever happened to me. But my father? He used words like he used a hammer—made me feel like I was always walking on eggshells, never knowing what would set him off."

Maya's heart clenched. "I'm so sorry."

Nolan shrugged. "Taught me that adults don't always have kids' best interests at heart, even when they should."

Before Maya could respond, Gruff yelled from the doorway. "Hey, boss, you coming? There won't be any food left if you don't hurry. Fran's already on her second sandwich."

"In a minute," Nolan called back, never taking her eyes off Maya. "Tell her to save me something or she's fired."

Gruff laughed. "I don't think that will scare her."

Gruff disappeared, and Maya squeezed Nolan's hand. "Emmie is my heart. I will never let anything happen to her. But that protective instinct of yours, it means everything to me."

"I know you'd protect her. I didn't mean to imply—"

"I love that you care about her," Maya said. "That you think about her safety. It tells me exactly the kind of person you are."

Some of the tension left Nolan's shoulders. "I'm new at this, you know. This whole thing…caring about someone else's kid isn't something I ever expected. If I overstep or do something wrong, you can tell me."

Nolan's expression, so uncharacteristically vulnerable, made Maya want to pull her close. "Caring about Emmie is never going to be wrong. And you're not overstepping. You're already part of our lives, and her well-being matters to you. That's exactly how it should be."

"I care about both of you," Nolan said quietly.

The admission hung in the air. Maya fought the urge to say something even more revealing, something too soon to say, too frightening, maybe, for both of them.

Gruff saved her from the decision. "Boss, I'm not kidding. Fran's eyeing your sandwich now."

"You'd better go," Maya said, though everything in her wished they could be magically transported somewhere else for just an hour. God, she wanted to touch her. Really touch her. "Before there's a mutiny."

The worry flew from Nolan's face, replaced by a decidedly self-satisfied smirk. "You know what you do to me when you look at me like that?"

"Like what?" Maya asked innocently.

"Like you want to do something out here in public that you probably shouldn't."

Maya laughed, delighting in the way Nolan's eyes darkened. "Oh, you like that, do you?"

"I like it plenty. When you want me like that, I feel like I could conquer the world."

"You already have," Maya said softly, the words slipping out before she could stop them.

Nolan's expression grew serious, intense. "Maya—"

"Go eat," Maya said, suddenly feeling too exposed. "Before your crew finishes everything."

Nolan hesitated for a moment, clearly wanting to pursue what Maya had just said, but finally nodded. "This conversation isn't over."

"I hope not."

Nolan walked into the house, and the confident set of her shoulders, the easy grace in her movement, captivated Maya's attention again. Everything about Nolan attracted her—her competence, her kindness, and the way she genuinely cared about Emmie's well-being. It was becoming harder and harder to imagine life without Nolan in it.

A spiffy red convertible pulled over to the curb and Aisley climbed out, looking like she'd stepped out of a magazine in white shorts and a turquoise top that matched her eyes perfectly.

"Nice ride," Nolan said neutrally as she walked back outside, sandwich in hand. Her tone was carefully casual, but tension showed in the way she strode straight down to Maya's side.

"Thanks. I confess it's an indulgence, but it's fun to drive," Aisley said with an easy smile. "Great for summer road trips."

"I'll bet," Nolan said, taking a bite of her sandwich.

"Hi, Maya," Aisley said, her attention shifting to Maya. "No training camp today, so I thought I'd stop by and see how the house is coming. It looks like you're almost done."

"We are," Maya said, glancing at Nolan. "Another week or so, right?"

"Just about. Always got finishing details left," Nolan said, her tone professional now. "Got the roof almost done. One more day and the major structural work is over. Then it's trim, paint touchups, final inspections."

"That's wonderful. Congratulations." Aisley's smile was warm and genuine. "It must feel good to see it all coming together."

"Yeah, it does." Nolan glanced at Maya. "I'm gonna go grab some more lemonade. Good to see you again, Aisley."

"You too, Nolan." Aisley turned back to Maya. "Izzy mentioned there's a big celebration at Johnny's tomorrow night and invited me along. I was wondering if you were planning to be there."

"I am. He's my cousin, so I wouldn't miss it. The whole extended family will be there. It should be fun."

"Sounds like it. I could swing by and give you a ride if you want. Save you the hassle of driving."

Aware of the subtext beneath the offer, Maya said, "I appreciate it, but I'm good."

"Okay. Maybe some other time? There's a great picnic spot out on Goldwater Lake. Canoeing and such, too, that Emme might like."

Maya took a breath, needing to be clear. "Aisley, I had a great time when we went out for dinner, and I hope we'll be friends. You're smart and funny, and any woman would be lucky to have your attention. But, well, just so there's no misunderstanding between us, friendship is all I can offer. I hope you understand."

Aisley's smile never faltered, though Maya caught a flicker of disappointment in her eyes. "Hey, thanks for being direct. I appreciate honesty. Saves everyone a lot of confusion." A glance toward the house where voices and laughter drifted from the kitchen. "And since I'm a frequent visitor to Izzy's, and I think I might be coaching your daughter in another year or two, we'll be seeing each other plenty. Friendship sounds perfect."

"I'm glad you feel that way. Really."

"Me too." Aisley glanced at the house again, her expression thoughtful. "Life's too short to waste time on people who aren't completely crazy about you. Though I have to say, if things don't work out, you know where to find me."

Maya laughed despite herself. "I'll keep that in mind."

"Good luck with the rest of the construction," Aisley said.

"Thanks," Maya called as Aisley headed for her car. "See you Saturday."

In the kitchen, Nolan leaned against the counter, the rest of the crew having moved back outside to the deck with Emmie and the puppy.

"Everything okay?" Nolan asked, her expression carefully neutral.

"Everything is fine. She offered me a ride to the party tomorrow night, but I told her that wouldn't be necessary. Not now, and not in the future."

Nolan's posture relaxed slightly. "She's the one you had dinner with. The one who was all the right things for you."

"*Almost* all the right things," Maya said, moving closer. "She's beautiful, successful, and steady. She makes me laugh. On paper, she's exactly what I should want."

"But?" Nolan asked, voice still carefully controlled.

"But she doesn't move me the way you do. She doesn't make me feel like I'm coming alive when I never thought I would again. She doesn't make my heart race when she walks into a room, or make me lose my train of thought when she touches me." Maya reached up to cup Nolan's face. "She doesn't keep me awake at night thinking about her the way I think about you."

"Jesus, Maya." Nolan's voice was rough. "Come on, it's the middle of the day. You say things like that, and I can't even think straight, let alone keep my hands to myself."

Maya laughed, delighting in the way Nolan's careful control was fraying. "Would some lemonade help cool you down?"

"You're kidding me, right? Lemonade," Nolan said, smiling now, "would not help."

Maya wrapped her arms around Nolan's waist and stole a quick hug. Unable to resist, she kissed her quickly, stepping back before either of them could deepen it. "Let's go join the others before people start to talk."

"Start?" Nolan shook her head, grabbed a glass of lemonade, and followed Maya outside. "That ship is long gone."

❖

The minute Nolan walked out onto the back deck, Emmie raced across the yard like a small hurricane and threw her arms around Nolan's legs, her face beaming with pure joy.

"Nolan, are you going to make me a treehouse like the one you made for Manny and Luis?"

Nolan glanced at Maya, seeking guidance. Maya just smiled and remained silent, clearly enjoying watching Nolan navigate Emmie's enthusiasm.

"Only if you help me build it," Nolan said.

Emmie bounced on her light-up sneakers, which immediately caused Star to bark and try to bite her glowing toes. Emmie dissolved into giggles, making Nolan grin. Emmie's uninhibited delight was absolutely contagious. Such a simple thing, a child's laughter, but knowing she had even a small hand in creating that happiness satisfied her in a way nothing else ever had.

When the puppy started attacking Emmie's shoelaces, Nolan bent down and scooped up the wiggling bundle of fur, holding her at eye level. "You need to learn some manners, Ms. Star."

"She's a free spirit," Emmie announced solemnly, as if this explained everything about the puppy's behavior.

Nolan laughed, looking down at the serious expression on Emmie's face. "Oh really? And who told you that?"

"Izzy did. She said that's okay because the world needs free spirits."

"Well, then that must be true," Nolan said, setting the puppy down gently, "because Izzy is one of the smartest people I know."

"When are we going to build the treehouse?" Emmie asked, not to be deterred from her mission. "Can we start tomorrow? Can it have a rope ladder? And maybe a telescope?"

Maya laughed from her spot on the deck. “Slow down, baby. Let Nolan finish our house first.”

“What do you say,” Nolan said, crouching down to Emmie’s level, “when we finish working on the house, the very next project we tackle is your special treehouse?”

“Yes,” Emmie shouted and threw her arms around Nolan’s neck.

“What else do you say, Em,” Maya said gently.

“Thank you,” Emmie said seriously.

“You’re very welcome,” Nolan said, her throat tight. When was the last time she’d felt like she deserved such uncomplicated affection? She squeezed Emmie gently and set her down. “Go play with Star, but try not to let her eat your shoes.”

Emmie bounded back down the steps into the backyard, Star tumbling after her like a golden shadow. Nolan settled into a deck chair with her lemonade next to Maya, where she could watch both child and puppy play.

“How does she do that?” Nolan sipped her drink. “Talk me into doing just about anything with one smile?”

“Family skill,” Maya said with obvious pride.

“Ain’t that the truth,” Gruff said with a hearty laugh. “I’ve seen how fast Maya gets you moving when she asks for something, boss.”

Heat rose in Nolan’s cheeks. “Shut up, Gruff.”

“Just saying,” he continued, clearly enjoying himself as he rose. “Well, kiddos, rest break is over. Let’s get back to work and finish this roof before the weather turns.”

The crew filed out, leaving Nolan and Maya alone on the deck. The afternoon had grown warm, and a light breeze carried the scent of the wild roses that grew along the back fence. Peaceful, domestic in a way that was new, a contentment Nolan had never expected.

“Is it really okay with you?” Nolan asked. “About the treehouse?”

“You won’t make it too high, will you? She’s still so small.”

“No, I was thinking more like a platform, maybe four feet off the ground, with a railing and a couple of wide steps instead of a ladder. Something safe but still fun.” A pause, suddenly uncertain. “When she’s bigger, maybe we could add to it…”

Too fast again, making plans for the future. Assumptions about being around as Emmie grew up. Plans Maya might not want.

Maya gently stroked her arm. "When she's bigger, she can have a proper treehouse with a rope ladder and maybe even a pulley system for hauling up the puppy. Maybe when she's eight or nine."

"Right." Nolan's stomach twisted. Three or four years in the future. Not something she'd ever done, planning that far ahead, not even when she was in the Army. "We could do that."

"If you've got time," Maya said carefully, "I wanted to tell you about something."

Maya's tone put Nolan on guard. Had she screwed up somehow? If she had, she'd have to fix it. Her running days were over. "Okay."

"I went to a meeting Tuesday night." Maya turned to face her. "An Al-Anon meeting."

Of all the things she'd expected Maya to say, that wasn't even on the list. "You did? Why?"

Maya glanced down at where Emmie and the puppy were racing around unsuccessfully trying to catch butterflies. "I wanted to learn a little about what your world is like, what you deal with every day." Maya paused, seeming to choose her words carefully. "What I should know if we're going to keep seeing each other."

Nolan set down her glass, her hands not quite steady. None of the women she'd dated had shown the slightest interest in understanding her sobriety beyond accepting that she didn't drink. Most had treated her recovery meetings like a minor inconvenience to be scheduled around. "You didn't have to do that, but it means a lot to me. I don't want my recovery to become your problem."

"That's just it. I care about you. I care about us, whatever this is becoming." Maya's voice was soft but firm. "I did it for me, too. I realized I was asking you to let me into your life without understanding a huge part of what your life actually looks like."

"What was it like? The meeting?" The unease in Nolan's middle settled. Maya was taking their relationship, what it meant to be with someone in recovery like her, seriously. Honestly and openly, just like they'd agreed.

"Eye-opening. And empowering, too. People talked about recovery not happening outside a relationship. That it's woven into everything, but there's a difference between being supportive and being enabling. I will always have choices." Maya paused for a moment. "I also realized how hypocritical I'd been—judging you for something someone else did. I was holding you responsible for every drunk driver, and that wasn't fair."

Maya's words struck Nolan deep. "Thank you. It matters that you don't see me like the person who killed Dantas."

"I know, and I'm sorry that it took me so long to see the difference."

Nolan reached for Maya's hand, amazed by how natural the gesture had become. Maya wasn't just accepting her recovery, she was actively working to understand it. An enormous and humbling difference. "Are you going to keep going? To the meetings?"

"I think so. At least for a while." Maya intertwined their fingers. "I want to do this right."

"I never expected this. I mean, no one's ever cared enough to even *think* about doing what you've done."

"Well, *I* care. I want to do us right."

Maya's openness again. Not just honest. Vulnerable and brave. Nolan's heart played a complicated riff in her chest. A flutter of hope mixed with terror. This was the point where things usually got complicated, where the reality of her recovery started to feel like too much work for someone else to take on.

But Maya wasn't running. Maya was learning.

"Tim always says that recovery is about showing up honestly, every day. Not just to meetings, but to life." Nolan met Maya's eyes. "I want to show up honestly with you. All of me, including the parts that are still figuring things out."

"I want that, too. That's why I went to the meeting. I want to know how to show up for you." Maya's expression looked a lot like the future Nolan had never dared to imagine for herself.

Recovery had taught her to take things one day at a time—every day, and then the next day, and then the next day. But when she put a lifetime of one day at a time together, she could build something lasting.

She could build a future.

CHAPTER TWENTY-TWO

Late Saturday afternoon, Maya dropped Emmie and Star off at Brian's, who deserved to be sainted despite his past sins, and hurried home to shower and change. The hot water sluiced over her shoulders, washing away the tension she'd been carrying all week. Tonight mattered. Their first public outing as whatever they were becoming.

Standing in front of the full-length mirror afterward, she smoothed down her snug-fitting lavender sweater and took in her tapered black jeans. The sweater brought out the green in her eyes, or so Izzy claimed. The jeans hugged her curves without being obvious about it. The new, ankle-high black boots with the skinny heels she'd purchased with Izzy during the shopping expedition they'd squeezed in Tuesday added just enough edge to keep the outfit from being too sweet. Along with the black leather bracelet Emmie had picked out, the outfit seemed to strike the right balance. Casual but a little sexy, too. This was her first real date with Nolan, after all.

After a quick stop at her dresser to spray on some perfume—the same jasmine scent she'd worn the night they first kissed—she ran her fingers through her hair and hurried toward the front door, second-guessing her choices with every step. Too dressy? Not dressy enough? Did the boots make her look like she was trying too hard?

Waiting on the front porch, she mentally shook her head, still not quite believing the turn her life had taken. She and Nolan had become lovers almost without her conscious choice, unlike every carefully planned decision she'd made in her adult life, before the shape of that life had simply ended. Then along had come Nolan, and she'd followed her impulses and her heart while her logical mind went on vacation.

Nolan's truck turned into the driveway. The familiar set of Nolan's shoulders, visible through the windshield, sent butterflies dancing in her stomach. She hadn't been looking for love again, hadn't believed it possible. She would always love Dantas, would miss her forever, but love had found her again, and she didn't regret it.

Not for a second.

❖

Nolan cut the engine and checked her watch. Fifteen minutes early, but Maya was already waiting. And looking amazing. She swallowed, her throat suddenly dry. Every time she saw Maya after they'd been apart, or she just happened to glance up from some bit of work and caught sight of her, her heart shot into overdrive. Along with her hormones. Instant heat check.

She needed to back-burner those thoughts right now. She was about to meet a whole bunch of Maya's friends and family. Their first time out together publicly as…what? A couple? Were they a couple? They'd slept together, and Maya had made it clear to Aisley that she wasn't available, but they hadn't really talked about what they *were* to each other.

The uncertainty made her stomach churn. Going on two years of sobriety, and she still felt like she was fumbling through relationships like a sixteen-year-old. At least teenagers had the excuse of inexperience. She was a grown woman who should know how to handle this stuff by now.

Maya started down the walk to meet her, and Nolan grabbed the box on the seat beside her and jumped out of the car, every anxious thought evaporating. Maya looked more than beautiful. She glowed. She looked happy.

"Hi," Maya said as she approached the truck, a slight breathlessness in her voice that Nolan had rarely heard.

"Hi yourself. You look incredible." The words came out rougher than intended, weighted with everything she couldn't quite say yet.

"I'm so glad you're early," Maya said. "I don't know why I'm nervous, but if I had to wait another minute, I'd be back inside changing again."

Nolan laughed. "I changed my clothes three times. I never do that.

First I tried khakis and a button-down shirt. I looked like I was going to a business meeting. Next, jeans and a T-shirt. Too casual." She gestured to the ribbed, navy blue V-necked polo and dark denim jeans. "I quit after this."

"I like it," Maya murmured. "The shirt matches your eyes."

Nolan smiled despite her nerves, some of the tension easing from her shoulders. Maya was nervous, too. That was oddly comforting. Uncharted territory for both of them, maybe. She held out the box. "I wanted to get this back to you."

Maya's brows rose as she took the box. "What…oh! Oh, look at it. It's perfect."

Nolan grinned. "It works."

Maya hugged the box with her grandmother's clock inside to her chest. "You've truly fixed all the broken parts now."

Maya stepped closer, close enough that Nolan could smell her perfume—jasmine and a darker, seductive scent underneath—and rose on her toes. Maya kissed her, soft and swift, with an undercurrent of promise that made Nolan's knees weak. "Thank you for this."

"I couldn't wait to get here this afternoon," Nolan muttered. "And you smell…great."

"I couldn't wait to see you alone," Maya murmured against her lips, "but we should probably go before I change my mind about leaving the house."

"Would that be such a bad thing?" Nolan slid her arms around Maya's waist, feeling the warmth of her through the soft fabric.

"Terrible thing," Maya said, but the husky note in her voice betrayed her completely. "Izzy would never forgive me if I missed Johnny's party. She's been planning this for weeks."

"Right. Priorities." Nolan reluctantly stepped back. "I'm glad you like the clock. Working on it helped me through some hard times."

"Then I'm doubly thankful," Maya said. "Let me put it inside where it will be safe."

On the way to Izzy's, Maya related Emmie's excitement over Star, asked about the final details left on the house, and described the latest assignment for her editorial course. Underneath the casual conversation, Nolan sensed a current of anticipation that crackled in the air. Every time Maya laughed, every casual brush of Maya's hand against her arm sent sparks through her.

Nolan parked out front behind a line of pickups and family-sized SUVs. Maya surprised her by taking her hand as they walked around to Izzy's backyard, which had been transformed with strings of white lights that twinkled like stars in the gathering dusk. People clustered in groups with drinks in hand or sat at long tables with plates of food. Johnny held court at the grill, surrounded by some of the crew Nolan knew and strangers who bore a striking resemblance to Izzy and Maya.

Maya's extended family.

Nolan's jitters returned full force.

"There you are!" Izzy appeared at their side as if she'd been watching for them, pulling Maya into a fierce hug before turning to Nolan with a grin. "And don't you two look good together."

Heat rose in Nolan's cheeks, but Maya just laughed, completely unself-conscious. "Subtle as always, Iz."

"Life's too short for subtle." Izzy glanced pointedly at their joined hands. "Come on, Nolan, let me introduce you to the relatives properly. Fair warning. They're going to ask a million questions about the house renovation. They've been following the progress like it's a soap opera."

Nolan shot Maya a *save me* glance. Maya just smiled and shrugged. No rescue in sight.

"Uh, okay," Nolan said as Izzy grabbed her arm and dragged her away.

The next hour passed in a whirlwind of introductions and conversations. Maya's extended family was warm and welcoming, the kind of people who made her feel as if she belonged before she'd even learned their names. They asked about the house, about her business, about her plans for the future, and seemed genuinely interested, not just making polite talk.

Maya had brought her, and that seemed to be enough of an introduction.

Nolan relaxed despite her nerves, drawn into discussions about everything from the best local tile suppliers to Maya's uncle's theories about sustainable building materials. She finally managed to slip away to find Johnny.

"Happy birthday," she said, slapping him on the back. "Great party."

Johnny smirked. "Welcome to the family, man. Make sure you treat my cousin right."

Nolan met his gaze straight on. "I plan on it. And you don't have to tell me I'm lucky. I know it."

"Aw," Johnny said. "You spoiled my fun."

"Sorry, guy," Nolan muttered, catching sight of Maya and Izzy near the back fence, their heads bent together in the intimate way of sisters sharing secrets. The stiff set of Izzy's shoulders and the way Maya kept glancing toward the house set off her trouble radar. Was Izzy warning Maya that their relationship was a bad idea? Had one of the relatives said something to one of them about her?

Nolan mentally pulled up short. This was her old pattern—finding reasons to panic, ways to sabotage good things before they could fall apart on their own. That was then, before Maya. This was now, and Maya mattered too much to give in to the voice inside her head telling her she didn't deserve Maya, didn't deserve to be loved.

When Maya headed inside to the kitchen, Nolan said a quick goodbye to Johnny and followed. Izzy's kitchen was quiet compared to the party outside, lit only by the soft glow from the string lights filtering through the windows.

"Hey." Maya stood at the counter filling a pitcher of lemonade. Even in the dim light, her eyes were warm, but worried.

"You okay?" Nolan asked.

"I'm fine," Maya said. Too quickly.

"Maya," Nolan murmured. "Truth, remember?"

Maya sighed. "It's nothing important. Really."

"It is if something's bothering you." Nolan looked around. Still alone. She stroked Maya's arm. "What's going on?"

"Oh, just Pris being Pris." Maya hesitated and seemed to make a decision as her eyes sparked the way they did when she was irritated. "She caught me out by the refreshment table and tried giving me some advice."

"What happened?" Nolan tamped down her temper. Whatever it was, Maya could handle it. But damn it, why couldn't Pris take no for no? "Did she insult you again?"

"No, actually, she insulted you."

Nolan clenched her jaw. "What did she say?"

"Besides not so subtly reminding me that the two of you go way back?" Flames leapt in Maya's eyes. "Like I didn't know that?"

"Damn it. We haven't been—"

Maya cut her off with a hand wave. “I *know* that. Which is exactly what I told her. Along with the fact that her jealousy was a waste of energy, because you were with me now.”

Nolan gaped. “You told Pris that?”

“I did.” Maya tilted her head. “Do you mind?”

“Hell, no.” Nolan had never been claimed by anyone before, and she liked the feeling. Liked belonging. “I’m all yours.”

Maya studied her for a long moment. “Good.”

“What else did she say?”

“She asked me if I knew you had a drinking problem.”

Nolan stiffened. Better Maya found out now how other people viewed her, before they went any further. “I see.”

Maya took her hand, never looking away for a second. “I told her you had explained all that, and that I couldn’t be prouder of how hard you worked on your sobriety.”

Nolan closed her eyes and rested her forehead on Maya’s. “You’re amazing. No one has ever stood up for me the way you do. Or believed in me.”

Maya wrapped her arms around Nolan’s waist, and hope returned to Nolan’s soul.

“You might be surprised,” Maya said. “I didn’t tell you this the other night, but Izzy came with me to the Al-Anon meeting Tuesday night.”

“Izzy went with you?”

“Izzy loves me and wants what’s best for me.” Maya moved closer, close enough that Nolan could see the flecks of gold in her eyes. “And since I chose you, and everything that means, she wanted to understand, too. To support me in supporting you.”

“Support you.” The words tasted bitter. “My life is making yours complicated. I’m sorry.”

“No,” Maya said sharply, framing Nolan’s face. “*Life* is complicated—everyone’s life. It’s what we do about it that matters.” Her touch was warm, grounding. “I love you. I choose you. And I want all of it—the meetings, the sponsor calls, the good days and the difficult ones. All of you. Whatever comes, we face together.”

Together. The word unlocked a place that Nolan hadn’t even realized was shut tight. For the first time since she’d gotten sober, someone was choosing her along with her recovery—not in spite of it, not around it, but as part of the whole package of loving her.

"I love you." The words tumbling out, rough and honest. She pulled Maya close, burying her face in the curve of her neck, breathing in jasmine and the scent of home. "I love you so much I probably should be scared, but I'm not."

"What are you?" Maya said.

"Happy." Nolan leaned back and stroked her face. "So damn happy."

"I love you, and I'm looking forward to every day with you." Maya kissed her, a kiss that spoke of tomorrow. Finally, she whispered, "We should probably get back."

"Another minute," Nolan said, holding her close. "I just need a minute to believe this is real."

"It's real," Maya said, her voice soft but certain. "*We're* real. And we're going to make this work, one day at a time."

"Okay." Nolan finally pulled back to meet Maya's eyes. "One day at a time."

"Starting with today," Maya said with a smile that lit up the dim kitchen. "And today, you're going to let me introduce you to everyone as my girlfriend, and we're going to dance badly to whatever music Izzy's inevitably going to start playing."

"Girlfriend?" Nolan tested the word and found it fit better than she'd expected.

"If that's okay with you. We can negotiate the terminology later."

Nolan laughed, the sound surprising her with its lightness. "Girlfriend works for me. The dancing? Maybe not so much."

"Good to both," Maya said, and kissed her again, soft and sweet and full of promise. When they broke apart, her eyes were bright. "Why don't we skip the dancing and you come back to my place. If you want."

"I want very much." Heat shot up Nolan's spine. "What about the party?"

Maya glanced toward the door, where the sounds of celebration continued unabated. "Johnny's got plenty of people to help him celebrate. And besides," she stepped closer, her voice dropping to that husky register that made Nolan's knees weak, "I've been thinking about having you all to myself for days."

"Now you tell me," Nolan muttered, already reaching for Maya's hand.

One day at a time.

The words that had sustained her through the hardest moments of her recovery now held the promise of a future she'd never dared to imagine—a future where she didn't have to choose between sobriety and love, where someone would walk beside her through both.

❖

The minute the door closed behind them, Maya wrapped her arms around Nolan's neck and kissed her. The house felt different with Emmie gone—quieter and charged with possibility. And she didn't want to waste a single minute. She pushed her leg between Nolan's, pressing her center to Nolan's hard thigh. Heat bloomed in her depths, immediate and electric.

"We have the house to ourselves," Maya whispered.

"We do." Nolan gripped Maya's hips, her fingers spreading wide. "Something you had in mind?"

Maya's breath caught. The words had been building inside her all evening, through Johnny's party, through the drive home, both pretending they weren't thinking about this moment.

"I love you. That's for always. And I want you—right now." She kissed Nolan again, skimming the tip of her tongue over the silky surface of Nolan's lips. "And that's for always, too."

"You have no idea how that makes me feel." Nolan's grip on Maya's hips tightened, pulling her even harder against her thigh.

Maya whimpered, the pressure delicious and maddening. Breathless with need, she managed, "I have a pretty good idea." She skated her mouth over Nolan's jaw. "But I'd really like you to show me, and soon. You make me so hot so fast."

Nolan's eyes darkened. "I want to take you to the bedroom. I want to please you properly." Her voice roughened. "Does that work for you?"

Pressure spiraled through Maya's core. "Yes. God, yes."

Nolan lifted her in one fluid motion, and Maya instinctively wrapped her legs around Nolan's waist. Nolan chuckled, the sound a little smug.

Maya bit her ear. "You can congratulate yourself when the job is done."

Nolan laughed, bumping gently against the wall as she navigated the hallway. "This is one project I intend to take a long time finishing."

"Take as long as you want," Maya said as Nolan carried her to the bed, "as long as you get started soon."

Standing by the bed in the dim light cast by the unicorn night-light, Nolan stripped, her gaze never leaving Maya's. Entranced by Nolan's body, enchanted by the desire written so clearly on her face, Maya pulled her clothes off. Nolan's breath came faster with each inch she bared.

"I love that you want me," Maya murmured.

"I love you." Nolan covered her, skin against skin, heart to racing heart. "I want you so damn bad I might just explode."

Maya edged her leg between Nolan's, groaning at the slick heat that greeted her. "Go ahead. I love when you lose it all over me."

Nolan buried her face in Maya's neck, one hand tangling in her hair. "Give me a minute. I want this to last."

Maya thrust her leg harder. "Why? We have all night. We'll just start again."

"Fuck," Nolan muttered, her hips pumping in time to Maya's. "You feel so good. Maya…"

Maya cradled Nolan's hips, urging her on. Nolan's harsh breathing and her deep groans ignited Maya's need. She gasped, a quick spike of pleasure her undoing. "Oh, no. I'm going to come."

Nolan shuddered. "Me too."

Maya cried out, the searing release too much to bear. Nolan's hoarse shout echoed hers in the still room. Maya held on tight, wanting the moment never to end.

"It won't," Nolan whispered.

"What?" Maya asked drowsily. God, she was wasted.

"It won't end. *We* won't end." Nolan rose up on an elbow and kissed her with the sweetness of a promise that ended in the fierceness of a vow. "I swear."

"Did I say that out loud?" Maya kissed the hollow of Nolan's throat. "I don't know how you do that to me."

"You do things to me I never expected," Nolan said, her voice thick. "You have from the beginning."

Maya raked her fingers through Nolan's hair, holding her close, the touch of her body everywhere stirring sweet, aching need. "I want to touch you, everywhere. All the time."

Nolan moaned. "Anything you want."

Maya took her time exploring—the sensitive spot behind Nolan's ear that made her gasp, the way her breath hitched when she kissed her collarbone, the tremor that ran through her when she gently bit her shoulder.

"Maya." Nolan's voice was strained, her body restless. "I need to touch you."

Maya shivered. "Yes."

She rolled onto her side, facing Nolan. "I'm yours."

The first touch of Nolan's fingers between her thighs ripped a cry from her throat. She'd been too ready for too long, but oh, she wanted to savor. "Don't make me come yet."

Nolan groaned. "You're so amazing, so hot and ready."

"Inside," Maya whispered, lifting her hips. "Slow. I want you deep when I come."

Nolan filled her, and Maya bit her lip, trying not to come right away. She clasped Nolan's neck, pulling her close, kissing her as the explosion gathered. Nolan stroked, long and slow, and she was lost. Her breath caught in her chest, her heart fluttered, and her mind blanked. Pleasure swamped her, flung her into the whirlwind, and left her weak and trembling.

"I love the way you touch me," she said when she caught her breath.

"I don't plan on ever stopping," Nolan whispered, pulling her close.

"I love you," Maya murmured. "In case I didn't mention that."

Nolan laughed. "Can't ever say it enough. I love you."

"I didn't expect you, didn't think I could feel this way again." Maya cupped Nolan's face. "Now I can dream again."

"I didn't imagine this, didn't know I could feel this much." Nolan brushed a strand of hair from Maya's face and kissed her, a soft, sweet kiss full of promise. "I'm exactly where I want to be."

"Good. Because I'm not letting you go anywhere." Maya smiled. "Ever."

Chapter Twenty-three

August

"Mommy, stop. I wanna go inside already." Emmie batted Maya's hand away from her hair with the impatience of someone who had important business to attend to.

Maya paused in the act of smoothing down a cowlick that had defied all attempts at taming. Around them, other children bounced and chattered with first-day excitement while parents lingered, many of them like her, reluctant to let go. The early August morning was cool with the promise of warmth, the kind of weather that whispered of new beginnings.

"Sorry, baby. I was just trying to fix—"

"Nolan says I look super." Emmie adjusted her new Bluey backpack with the serious air of someone preparing for a great adventure. The matching lunch bag clutched in her small hand contained her carefully chosen favorites: a peanut butter and honey sandwich cut into triangles, apple slices, and the homemade cookies they'd baked together yesterday.

Maya glanced at Nolan, brows raised. "Well, then of course you do."

Nolan—who Emmie believed hung the moon and stars, just like the stars Nolan had helped her paint in her bedroom what seemed like a century ago. In only a couple of months of sharing a home with Nolan, Emmie had effortlessly accepted her as family. Nolan and Emmie were just fine about the first day of school, but she was a mess. Somewhere behind the suddenly imposing double doors of Lincoln Elementary awaited Ms. Patterson's kindergarten classroom, with its reading corner and art supplies and the promise of a world expanding beyond their small family unit. What if Emmie got anxious, or scared, or—

Nolan's hand settled on her shoulder, warm and reassuring. Her smile was soft, her gaze understanding. She'd been watching Maya fret over this day for weeks.

"Ready to walk our girl to the door?" Nolan asked, her use of *our* sending warmth flooding through Maya's chest.

"Come on, Mommy." Emmie bounced on her toes, face alight. The transformation from the anxious little girl who'd first arrived in Prescott was remarkable. Gone were the nightmares and the clinging, replaced by this confident child who tackled new experiences with enthusiasm.

Maya took Emmie's offered hand, her heart swelling when Emmie immediately reached for Nolan's as well. They followed the crowd up the concrete path. Inside, the hallway buzzed with chatter and the squeak of new sneakers on polished floors.

Maya knelt in front of Emmie and rested her hands on Emmie's shoulders. "You're going to have the best day, okay?"

"I know." Emmie grinned. "And tonight you have to call Grandma and Grandpa so I can tell them everything."

Maya's smile felt wobbly around the edges. Her parents had been back home for a month now, and watching them fall in love with Emmie all over again had been one of the unexpected gifts of this new chapter. That and their instant acceptance of Nolan had healed the last cracks in her heart. "They can't wait to hear all about it."

Emmie's face grew serious. "Do you think Mommy D can see me?"

Maya's throat closed, and words wouldn't come.

"I'm sure of it, sport," Nolan said, crouching beside them. "She'll always know all the amazing things you'll do as you grow up."

Emmie's smile blazed like the sun emerging from the clouds. "Okay. I'll go now."

Nolan took her hand, and Maya grasped the other. When they reached the classroom door, Maya kissed her cheek.

"Have fun, sweetie."

"Don't forget to play with Star."

"First thing," Nolan said.

"Okay, bye." Emmie peered into the classroom filled with kids. "I see Wally!"

And as quick as that, she was gone.

Maya swiped at the tears threatening to fall, her legs strangely unsteady. "Do you think we should wait, just to make sure she's all right?"

Nolan slipped an arm around her waist, pulling her close against her side. "I think she's doing great. I know you'll worry, but you've done an amazing job giving her all the confidence and security she'll need. She's going to be incredible. Look how far she's come already."

Maya leaned into Nolan's warmth, drawing comfort from her steady presence as they walked outside. "I know she'll be fine. It's just...she's growing up so fast. Soon there'll be homework and field trips and...and, oh God, dating."

Nolan laughed. "There'll be a whole lot of time before that, and we'll be there for all of it."

Maya turned to Nolan, the certainty in her voice making her pulse quicken. "We will, won't we."

"Yep." Nolan opened the SUV door for her. "Every day."

"You know what this means," Maya said as Nolan pulled out into the line of departing minivans and SUVs.

"What?"

"We have six hours until pickup. Six whole hours with the house to ourselves." Maya reached across the console to take Nolan's hand.

Nolan glanced her way, her eyes sparkling. "Six hours, huh? However will we fill the time?"

"I have a few ideas." Maya lifted their joined hands to press a kiss to Nolan's knuckles. "Starting with breakfast someplace fancy, where we can sit like grown-ups and drink coffee that's actually hot."

"And after breakfast?"

"After breakfast," Maya said, her pulse jumping at the husky note in Nolan's voice, "we go home to our beautiful house and spend the afternoon making love."

Nolan squeezed Maya's hand. "I like this plan."

"Oh good," Maya said. "Wait till you find out what else I have in mind."

Nolan laughed. "Whatever it is, I'm in."

One day at a time, as Nolan always said.

Maya leaned her head on Nolan's shoulder. Living life one day at a time was just fine when you could count on love.

About the Authors

In addition to editing over twenty LGBTQIA+ anthologies, **Radclyffe** has written over seventy romance and romantic intrigue novels, including a paranormal romance series, The Midnight Hunters, as L.L. Raand.

She is a three-time Lambda Literary Award winner in romance and erotica and received the Dr. James Duggins Outstanding Mid-Career Novelist Award from the Lambda Literary Foundation. A member of the Saints and Sinners Literary Hall of Fame, she is also an RWA/FF&P Prism Award winner for *Secrets in the Stone*, an RWA FTHRW Lories and RWA HODRW winner for *Firestorm*, an RWA Bean Pot winner for *Crossroads*, an RWA Laurel Wreath winner for *Blood Hunt*, a Book Buyers Best award winner for *Price of Honor* and *Secret Hearts*, and a 2023 Golden Crown Literary Award winner for *Perfect Rivalry*. The first book in the Red Sky Ranch romance series, *Fire in the Sky*, was a 2024 GCLS romance award winner. She is also a featured author in the 2015 documentary film *Love Between the Covers*, from Blueberry Hill Productions. In 2019 she was recognized as a "Trailblazer of Romance" by the Romance Writers of America. She was named a Woman of the Year by *The Advocate* (2021), included in the Out100 (2022), and was selected for *Curve*'s Power List (2025).

In 2004 she founded Bold Strokes Books, one of the world's largest independent LGBTQ publishing companies, and is the current president and publisher.

Find her at facebook.com/Radclyffe.BSB and follow her on Twitter @RadclyffeBSB.

Ronica Black lives in the greater Phoenix area where she enjoys doing anything creative, exploring the great state of Arizona, and spending time with family and friends. She does it all with her little rescue pup, Frankie, by her side.

Books Available From Bold Strokes Books

Feeling Lucky by Krystina Rivers. What happens when, despite suddenly having enough money to buy almost anything, Lucy and Tanner start to discover that maybe all they need is each other? (978-1-63679-876-9)

Iceberg by Gun Brooke. When Lady Arabella hires Zandra, she never expects to find love, especially not as a disaster looms on the horizon. (978-1-63679-908-7)

It Happened One Semester by Aurora Rey. After a Pride night hookup, can eager new Assistant Professor Hudson Greene and Dean of Advising Callie Shaw overcome the odds and ace falling in love? (978-1-63679-814-1)

It's Kind of a Bad Idea by Sarah G. Levine. What happens when an emotionally unavailable serial dater meets the one woman she can't help but fall for—who happens to be the one woman who told her not to? (978-1-63679-920-9)

Thankful for You by Tagan Shepard. Everyone deserves to find their person. Maybe Karen has finally found hers? (978-1-63679-884-4)

What Happens On Location by Nan Campbell. How can Helen produce a successful movie when its director is the woman responsible for the demise of her marriage? (978-1-63679-904-9)

When Love Comes Around by Radclyffe and Ronica Black. Can Maya Sanchez and Nolan Wright trust each other enough to build something real, or will the past tear them apart? (978-1-63679-930-8)

Anywhere with You by Margo Glynn. On a road trip through the Great American Southwest, two friends discover nature, hope, and each other. (978-1-63679-907-0)

Burning Bridges by Lesley Davis. Can Clancy and Jude crack the case of eight missing women—and the secrets of their own hearts? (978-1-63679-872-1)

Dreams Entangled by Sophia Kell Hagin. Amid self-doubt, secrets, a pandemic, fear of attack and attempted murder, Pirin and Gracie's attraction turns to love, and their lives will never be the same. (978-1-63679-892-9)

Echoes of Love by Catherine Lane. As Hazel's and Jo's paths intertwine, they're swept up in a whirlwind of long-buried secrets, sizzling chemistry, and memories that won't be denied. (978-1-63679-835-6)

The Fame Game by Ronica Black. Wild child Hollywood actress Luna Kirkman begins dating Hollywood's leading man, only to fall for his straitlaced sister instead. (978-1-63679-858-5)

Moonlight Obsession by Sheri Lewis Wohl. All it takes to stop a clever killer is moonlight, love, and a silver bullet. (978-1-63679-831-8)

My Boyfriend's Wife by Joy Argento. Amid betrayal and heartbreak, can two women discover a love that could heal their pasts and rewrite their futures? (978-1-63679-866-0)

Tapout by Nicole Disney. A struggling MMA fighter finds her edge in an underground ring, but as she falls for the magnetic and ambitious promoter behind the matches, their dangerous world threatens to destroy everything they've fought to rebuild. (978-1-63679-924-7)

An Extraordinary Passion by Kit Meredith. An autistic podcaster must decide whether to take a chance on her polyamorous guest and indulge their shared passion, despite her history. (978-1-63679-679-6)

Heart's Appraisal by Jo Hemmingwood. Andy and Hazel can't deny their attraction, but they'll never agree on the place they call home. (978-1-63679-856-1)

That's Amore by Georgia Beers. The romantic city of Rome should inspire Lily's passion for writing, if she can look away from Marina Troiani, her witty, smart, and unassumingly beautiful Italian tour guide. (978-1-63679-841-7)

Through Sky and Stars by Tessa Croft. Can Val and Nicole's love cross space and time to change the fate of humanity? (978-1-63679-862-2)

BOLDSTROKESBOOKS.COM

Looking for your next great read?

Visit BOLDSTROKESBOOKS.COM
to browse our entire catalog of paperbacks, ebooks,
and audiobooks.

Want the first word on what's new?
Visit our website for event info,
author interviews, and blogs.

Subscribe to our free newsletter for sneak peeks,
new releases, plus first notice of promos
and daily bargains.

SIGN UP AT
BOLDSTROKESBOOKS.COM/signup

Bold Strokes Books is an award-winning publisher committed to quality and diversity in LGBTQ fiction.